the

NANTUCKET
RESTAURANT

A NOVEL

PAMELA KELLEY

sourcebooks
landmark

Published by Sourcebooks Landmark, an imprint of Sourcebooks
P.O. Box 4410, Naperville, Illinois 60567-4410
(630) 961-3900
sourcebooks.com

Previously self-published as *The Restaurant* in 2020.

Cataloging-in-Publication Data is on file with the Library of Congress.

Printed and bound in the United States of America.
VP 10 9 8 7 6 5 4 3 2 1

A very special thanks to my early readers, Cindy Tahse, Jane Barbagallo, Taylor Barbagallo, and Amy Petrowich. I appreciate you all so much.

1

Jill O'Toole wasn't supposed to be surfing the net on a busy Thursday afternoon. Her to-do list was a mile long, and the most pressing item was front and center on her desk. A crisp, three-page Excel spreadsheet of candidate research that her assistant had printed out, highlighted, paper-clipped, and delivered to her an hour ago. Names and numbers of people she needed to call ASAP.

Instead, she was mesmerized by a food blog, which was one of her guilty pleasures. It featured mouthwatering photos, recipes, and related stories that made her long to be home puttering around her own kitchen, slicing and dicing, stirring and tasting. No time to browse today however, for she was on a mission to find a foolproof recipe for the kind of rich, dense, fudgy chocolate cake that would inspire moans at first bite.

Jill could almost always tell just by reading the recipe what a dish would taste like, and she knew that the one she'd just found was as close to the signature dessert at Mimi's Place as she was going to get. Hopefully, Grams would agree.

For as long as she could remember, they'd always gone to Mimi's Place for Grams's birthday. An elegant, two-storied restaurant that was walking distance from Grams's Nantucket home, Mimi's Place served Italian-influenced meals that were simple yet exquisite comfort food. Certain dishes, such as their wafer-thin eggplant parmesan, were so amazing that Jill finally gave up ordering them anywhere else.

Usually, these birthdays consisted of just the immediate family—Jill and her sisters, Emma and Mandy. Mandy's husband, Cory, and their two young children, Blake and Brooke, were always there too, since they lived on Nantucket. But Emma's husband, Peter, usually stayed home in Phoenix. He barely knew Grams, and it was just so far to come. Emma and Peter had separated two months ago. And Emma hadn't said why, only that she'd fill Jill and Mandy in when she saw them.

Jill and her sisters had always been close to Grams, but even more so since their mother passed away almost twelve years ago after an unexpected and short battle with pancreatic cancer. Their father had followed six months later. The doctors called it a massive coronary; Grams said it was simply a broken heart.

Last year, when Grams turned ninety, they threw a real party at Mimi's Place. Grams had always been a social butterfly, eating out once, if not twice a day, because she couldn't justify cooking for one. All her friends who were still living and able to make it came, along with what seemed like most of Nantucket. Everyone knew and loved Grams and wanted to celebrate her. They filled the entire restaurant, and it was quite a party. This year, however, would be different. Grams had decided about nine months ago that it was time to downsize. Her house, just off Nantucket's Main Street, where she'd lived for over fifty years, was too big.

"As much as I hate to admit it, the stairs are killing me, and I don't have the energy to start renovating now. I'm going to move into the assisted living at Dover Falls."

Still determined and feisty at barely five feet tall and maybe ninety-five pounds, Grams had smiled brightly and added, "Connie Boyle is there. She goes to Foxwoods casino once a quarter. There's a whole busload that goes. Doesn't that sound fun?"

A month after making her announcement, it was a done deal. Grams sold two other properties that she'd owned for many years and rented out to summer tourists. She wasn't ready to part with her main residence though, or even to rent it out just yet.

Grams settled in quickly at Dover Falls and always sounded happy whenever Jill or one of her sisters called, but recently she'd admitted to feeling a bit under the weather. A nasty bout of bronchitis had turned into pneumonia and left her so weak that she didn't have the strength to venture out at all, let alone make the traditional trip to Mimi's Place. Grams's suite at Dover Falls had a small kitchen they could use, so the new plan was for Jill to make the cake ahead of time and then just see what everyone was in the mood for when they all arrived.

Jill was mentally making a shopping list of the ingredients she'd need when an instant message from her assistant flashed on the computer screen.

> Billy's on his way in. I told him you were busy, but he wouldn't listen. Just wanted to give you a heads-up.

Thank God for Jenna. She was the best assistant Jill had ever had, and she couldn't imagine working without her.

"I knew you weren't on the phone," Billy said, barging into the office and sitting on the edge of her desk. He picked up the spreadsheet of names. "Have you even called any of these candidates yet? You know how important this search is?"

Jill sighed. Her partner, Billy Carmenetti, was prone to drama. He wore expensive suits, drove a shiny new BMW, and had house accounts at several of the hottest restaurants. If you didn't know him better, you'd think Billy wanted people to think he was someone important. But Jill did know better. She knew that he just liked nice things because he'd grown up without them. At six foot two, with thick, almost black hair, dark brown eyes that perpetually danced with mischief, and a long, lean body, toned from daily gym workouts, Billy was hard to miss.

He was also one of the most generous people she knew and one of the nicest, even if he did drive her crazy on a daily basis. They'd been best friends and business partners for well over a decade, and it was only a month ago Jill realized that she might be in love with him. The idea had slammed into her, fully formed and obvious, and she was struggling with what to do about it.

"I know, I know. I'm about to dive into it. I just had something important I had to handle first."

Billy turned as the printer whirred and groaned. Curious, he leaned over and plucked the freshly printed page from the tray. He glanced at it, then raised his eyebrows at Jill. "Chocolate cake? Are you kidding me?"

"Oh, relax. It's for Grams's birthday. I'm on this search. Don't worry. We'll fill it."

"We have to. If we don't, we won't get the rest of their business. I heard from their CFO that they are using this search as a test to see how we do and what caliber of candidates we can produce. If we get into this company, it could launch us to the next level. Continued business for years to come."

"Don't you have somewhere you need to be, other searches of your own to worry about?" Jill teased.

"I'm going, I'm going." He swung his legs off her desk

and headed toward the door. He turned back and smiled, his voice softer this time. "Tell Grams I said happy birthday."

And that was one of the many reasons why she loved Billy. He adored her grandmother. More importantly though, he was just a good person, through and through. And they were as close if not closer than most married couples. Everyone said so and constantly asked why they weren't a couple. They'd always laughed it off and said it was impossible as they'd been friends forever. They were like brother and sister as well as business partners. So the realization that she might be in love with him was troubling. Especially when she considered that Billy had never given the slightest inkling that he was even remotely attracted to her.

2

Mandy Lawson was running late, and that was unacceptable. She was never late. She had called ahead, told the women at the club she'd be there at a quarter past ten, and they told her not to worry. But she couldn't help it. Mandy was a worrier. It was her Virgo nature; she craved organization and made to-do lists for everything. And things generally went smoothly—except for today, when everything seemed to be out of sync.

They'd spent almost thirty minutes searching the entire house for her eleven-year-old daughter Brooke's homework assignment, which was highly unusual, because Brooke never lost things. She was a bit like her mother that way, conscientious and orderly—unlike her younger brother, Blake, who was more of a dreamer and prone to forgetfulness. They found the assignment finally. It was already in Brooke's backpack, neatly folded and tucked away deep in a side pocket.

"Oops, I forgot that I put it there as soon as I finished."

"So you wouldn't forget it," Blake teased.

Mandy glanced at the clock, which seemed to be on fast-forward. "We have to go now. Grab your bags, and get in the car."

It was a gorgeous sunny day on Nantucket. As they walked to the car, she could see an incoming ferry in the distance. Their home was right on the water, just a few minutes away from downtown Nantucket. Mandy waved at a neighbor walking by with her dog, a golden retriever who kept stopping to sniff at the grass and sand at the side of the road. That was one thing that was so Nantucket to her, the sand along the side of all the roads, reminding her that they were living on an island.

Twenty minutes later, Mandy pulled into the busy parking lot at the Nantucket New School. The kids jumped out of the SUV, gave Mandy a quick kiss goodbye, and ran to join their friends who were already in line. Mandy watched until they were all inside the building. Both children loved it there, and Mandy liked everything about it, especially the fact that as a private school, the classes were smaller and they encouraged children to explore individual interests.

Before she drove off, Mandy checked her makeup in the mirror and added a swipe of pink lipstick. She wanted to make sure she looked polished for the event. She was in one of her favorite outfits—tailored, caramel-colored pants and a pale pink cashmere sweater that looked gorgeous with her vintage pearls. She'd just had her hair touched up yesterday, so the bits of gray along her hairline were gone, and Tony had added deep golden highlights to her dark blond hair that made it shimmer. It just touched her shoulders and gave the illusion of being all one length, but a few clever long layers gave it some shape and movement. Her usual style was just tucked behind her ears, and on her, it worked beautifully, giving her a crisp, somewhat preppy look. Or as her husband, Cory, teased her, it was "old money hair," which he appreciated.

Mandy and Cory had started dating their sophomore year at Boston College, and except for one two-week period during senior year when Mandy was feeling ignored and broke up with him, they'd been together ever since. They'd both been business majors, and immediately after graduation, each started working in Boston's financial district. Cory joined Brown Brothers Harriman as a junior investment analyst, and Mandy went to Fidelity Investments as a market research coordinator.

Mandy quickly fell in love with the marketing aspect of her job and moved into the communications group where she handled events and wrote copy for marketing materials. After working for two years, Cory went back to school, to Harvard for his MBA. Upon graduation, he had his pick of offers and decided to return to Brown Brothers Harriman, this time as a senior investment strategist, advising high-net-worth clients on where to put their money.

Cory had a plan. From the time he'd left to get his MBA, he knew he'd be heading back to BBH. They knew him there, and he was getting to know many of their top clients, building relationships that would one day pay off.

That day came five years later, when Cory and his college buddy, Patrick Harris, left to start their own hedge fund, as interest in alternative investments was skyrocketing. Word quickly spread throughout the community about the hot new hedge fund led by two young financial wunderkinder. Many of Cory's former clients at BBH wanted to invest, and by offering access to Cory and Patrick's hedge fund, BBH was able to satisfy their clients, make an additional profit, and allow Cory to quickly establish a solid customer base. Which was exactly what he was counting on.

Patrick's company did the same, and within a year, Cory and Patrick had over two billion dollars under management with year-end growth of thirty-three percent, which drastically increased demand and made them both millionaires many times over. Running a hedge fund was a high risk, high reward business, and when things went well, it was one of the most lucrative niches in the world of finance.

After that first crazy year, Cory and Mandy built a gorgeous custom home on Nantucket. It was originally just going to be a summer home, but Cory fell in love with the island, and Mandy was happy to be back in her hometown. After one summer, Cory decided he could work just as easily from

Nantucket, and they could serve their client base well by having an office downtown, as many of their clients also had second homes on the island. Patrick ran the Boston office, and Cory had a small team on Nantucket and occasionally went to Boston for meetings.

Mandy became pregnant for the second time when the Nantucket house was finished, and they decided that it made sense for her to stop working and stay home. They didn't need the money, and Mandy wanted to be there for her kids.

Besides, Cory thought it was better for his business if she wasn't working. Their image of the perfect family, with two beautiful blond children and a sunny, stay-at-home wife, was a great marketing tool. Not that he needed it though. His business had exploded as everyone wanted a piece of the next big thing, and their hedge fund was consistently delivering huge returns.

For something to do, Mandy got involved with some local women's groups and found a way to put her business skills to good use, organizing various charity events. Today's event was for the town library and was being held at the newer country club, the one that had a seven-figure initiation fee. Cory and Patrick were among the charter members, as Patrick and his wife, Daisy, were on Nantucket often. Daisy especially loved it on the island and often stayed for weeks at a time.

Though Mandy adored Patrick and had known him since their college days, she had never really warmed up to Daisy. Patrick had met her at a party his friends had thrown to celebrate their first year in business, when the buzz about them was turning into a roar. Daisy was from Charleston and was a true Southern belle, always perfectly made up and accessorized. When she poured on the charm, men were dazzled. Patrick proposed just a few months after they started dating, and they married less than a year later.

Mandy had tried countless times to reach out to Daisy, but for some reason, she always held her at arm's length. Daisy was always sweetly pleasant to her in public, but there was an underlying note of dislike that surfaced now and then. Cory said that Mandy was being paranoid, that of course Daisy adored her. He couldn't imagine that she wouldn't feel that way, but Mandy knew better.

Daisy was on this charity committee too and was the first person Mandy saw as she ran through the door.

"Nice of you to join us," Daisy said sweetly, then turned back to continue tacking swirls of pink crepe paper to the wall.

"I called. Didn't they tell you?" Mandy said, scanning the room. It looked like they were almost done decorating. The room looked wonderful and bright, with streamers of pink and white cascading in waves from the ceiling and along the walls.

"Did you? Maybe they did mention something. I've just been so busy that I must have missed it." Daisy looked up at Mandy, waiting for a reaction to the dig. When she didn't get one, she sighed and added, "They're out back."

Mandy hurried to the back of the restaurant where the other women on the committee were addressing place cards and looking over table settings. Her close friend Barbara looked up and smiled.

"See, no worries. We're just about done here."

"Thanks, you all did a great job with the decorating. I'm sorry I wasn't here to help."

"Don't be ridiculous. You did everything else. This event is going to be great."

Mandy relaxed a bit and poured herself a cup of coffee, then sat down to review the agenda. As the committee chair for this event, she really had done just about every-thing except the decorating. She'd negotiated the contract with the club, chosen a caterer, ordered the food and the entertainment, and carefully chosen the guest list, creating a buzz that made this a must-attend event in their social set. Hopefully the end result would be a cascade of gener-ous checks. To help loosen the purse strings, Mandy also came up with the idea of having an informal wine tasting, with several wines available on each table so people could taste them all and relax and enjoy.

The event went off beautifully. Everyone commented on how great the food was and what a clever idea to do the wine tasting. And it did seem to put everyone into a good and generous mood. The silent auction raised a record amount, and Mandy expected that for the next few weeks, large checks would be trickling in. Everyone was thrilled with the results, except perhaps Daisy, who had hoped to chair the event and was clearly miffed that the committee had overwhelmingly wanted Mandy to run it.

"I still think it would have been better if we'd had this at that new restaurant downtown, Basil's. The food there is top notch."

Barbara shot a knowing glance at Mandy and then said, "Well, I haven't heard any complaints. In fact, I've heard nothing but compliments, especially for the great job that Mandy did in putting this altogether."

"Right. Well, I'm ready for a glass of wine." Daisy made a beeline for the bar, which was nearly empty now that all the party attendees had finally left.

"Has she always been such a bitch?" Barbara asked Mandy once the rest of the group had followed Daisy to the bar. They were all ready to relax now that the event was over and everything had gone off smoothly.

"Pretty much. You'd think we'd be somewhat close, given that our husbands are always together. Sometimes I almost sense a bit of competitiveness there or envy, but then I just shake it off because there's no reason for it. Cory's right. I'm a little paranoid when it comes to Daisy. I just can't figure her out."

"I wouldn't waste your energy trying. She's not worth it. Come on. Let's make our way to the bar. I've heard raves about one of the chardonnays we were serving, Cakebread. Sounds like my kind of dessert!"

Mandy's cell phone rang as they reached the bar. She told Barbara to order her a glass of whatever she was having.

She saw her caller ID on her phone flash and realized she had several missed calls, one of them a Nantucket number that she didn't recognize. She'd turned the ringer off so she wouldn't be disturbed. It was Jill calling, and that was odd, because she never called during the day.

"Hey, Jill, what's up? Is everything all right?"

"It's Grams. Nantucket Hospital just called to let me know she came into the ER from Dover Falls and is being sent to Boston, to Mass General. They suggested the family come as soon as possible."

Mandy had never heard her older sister sound so scared and realized the hospital must have tried to reach her too.

"Are you flying in tonight? I can grab a flight and meet you at Logan." Then they could grab a cab together to Mass General.

"I'm on my way now, flight leaves in an hour. Can you call Emma?"

"I will. I'll ask her to meet us at Mass General."

3

"Emma, I'll always love you, but I'm in love with Tom." The surreal words kept replaying over and over again in Emma's mind while she sipped her Absolut and tonic and stared out the tiny airplane window. "…can't help it…in love with Tom. Never meant to hurt you…" She knew that part of it was true. Peter didn't have a mean bone in his body. They'd been married almost fifteen years, and everyone, including Emma, thought they were a perfect couple.

Peter was a popular English professor at Arizona State, where they'd both graduated and met as juniors. He was also a budding author, and they'd just recently celebrated the launch of his second book, a sequel to the first in a mystery series about an English professor who moonlights as an amateur detective. Emma's photography career was

going well too. She'd recently had several national assign-
ments that seemed to be generating some positive buzz,
and her first gallery show just a few weeks ago had exceeded
everyone's expectations by completely selling out.

Everything had seemed almost perfect in their lives,
until a month ago when her husband told her he was in
love with another man. He was in love with another man!
How could she not have known? She'd asked herself that
question a million times it seemed, and in retrospect, she
supposed there were signs. She just didn't see them for
what they were.

She'd thought it was a good thing when Tom, Peter's
best friend from college, was transferred to Phoenix. She
was happy that Peter had someone to go fishing with and
to play racquetball with. Since he was more active and
going to the gym more often, she didn't think anything of
it when he lost weight and started dressing better.

Because she knew how much Peter loved fishing, she
still didn't think anything of it when he and Tom started
going away for a night or even the whole weekend. After
all, it was a long drive to the mountains, and since Tom
had a cabin there, it made perfect sense for them to stay
over instead of making the long drive back, didn't it? She
felt foolish now, but the truth just never crossed her mind,
not even once.

It was also true that their sex life had been virtually
nonexistent for the past few years. Now that she did think
about it, they'd never really had the kind of crazy chemistry

where you want to have sex all the time. They both had busy schedules and were exhausted at the end of the day, and Emma realized that sex really hadn't been a priority for either of them for a very long time.

She'd just gotten used to it because they had such a comfortable relationship, friendly and easy, and they really enjoyed spending time together. They liked the same restaurants, shared similar tastes in books and movies, and overall were content relaxing together at home, watching TV and catching up on each other's day. Sadly, she realized that they were best friends, not lovers.

Emma wondered if she would feel better or worse if it had been another woman instead of a man. She supposed it might be worse, but she wasn't sure. She felt like a complete and total failure, like maybe she had somehow caused the end of her marriage, though intellectually she knew that was ridiculous. The thing was, she felt like she just didn't know anything anymore. And she hadn't told her sisters yet.

All that Jill and Mandy knew was that she and Peter were having some issues and had separated. She'd told them she'd fill them in when she saw them; it would only be a few weeks. She just wasn't ready to talk about it yet, not even to them. She knew she'd just break down and cry if she did. The hurt was too fresh and too confusing. She needed these few weeks to gather her strength and wrap her mind around what had happened and to somehow begin to process it.

She was worried about Grams now too. Jill had sounded so anxious when she'd called earlier to see if she could change her flight to today instead of tomorrow. Grams had always been so feisty and full of health that it was hard to imagine her being sick at all.

Wispy snowflakes started to fall as the airplane taxied across the runway to the gate. It was almost five, the very heart of rush hour in Boston.

Emma stepped off the plane and made her way through the security exit, beyond which people were lined up waiting for their loved ones to arrive. Normally Emma flew into Nantucket and would be on the lookout for a familiar face. Either Mandy or Jill, sometimes both, would be there waiting for her. But not this time. Grams was at Mass General, one of the top hospitals in Boston. Mandy and Jill were with her, and Emma had told them she'd just jump in a cab and meet them at the hospital. Without traffic, she'd be there in less than fifteen minutes, though with rush hour, it would likely take a bit longer. She didn't have any luggage though, just a carry-on bag, so she quickly made her way outside where a line of cabs waited and got in the first one.

"Mass General please," she said to the driver and then settled back into her seat, trying to calm her nerves. She hoped she wouldn't be too late.

Room 215 at Mass General was small but comfortable, and Mandy had worked her magic to give it a homey touch. Rosy candles lined the counter, and a gorgeous arrangement of Winston's finest flowers, in pretty shades of pink and peach and cream, looked elegant in a thick, square, cut-glass vase. A powder-blue blanket made of the softest fleece imaginable was carefully tucked around Grams to make her as comfy as possible. Grams was actually sitting up in bed now, surprisingly energetic given her condition and prognosis. Her voice was raspy and her color was pale, but she spoke clearly and with determination.

"Your sister is on her way? She'll be here soon?"

"Emma called from the airport a little while ago. She should be here any minute," Mandy assured her. She and Jill were sitting in chairs pulled up close to Grams's bed. Grams had been dozing off and on since they'd arrived and had woken from her latest nap about fifteen minutes ago. She seemed to be gathering her strength, as if she had something important to say. Jill held her hand and smiled, trying not to let her worry show. She wondered if her grandmother was fully aware of how sick she was.

Jill and Mandy had been at the hospital since eight a.m. They'd flown in the night before and saw Grams once she was settled into her room. She'd mostly been sleeping, but they stayed by her side for several hours before staying the night at the Wyndham, which was a short walk to the hospital. The doctor had stopped by and told them that Grams's lungs were failing due to complications from pneumonia, and he admitted her age was a factor. He thought that she might have a day or two at best.

"I know that I'm dying." Grams's tone was matter-of-fact, serene even. "It's fine. Really," Grams insisted as Jill opened her mouth to protest. She looked at both girls, and Jill saw a hint of a smile in the eyes that seemed both tired and wise. "I've had a wonderful life and a long one, and it's my time. I'm tired, but I have a few things to say."

"Grams, are you thirsty? Do you want some water…or some wine?" Mandy teased gently. Grams had always loved her wine, white especially.

"A bit of water would be nice. Thanks, honey."

Mandy handed her a cup of ice water with a straw bent at an angle so it would be easier for her to reach. Grams took a sip as Emma peeked her head in the door.

Hugs and hellos were exchanged, and then Emma pulled up a chair between the others.

"Grams has something to tell us," Jill said. Her grandmother's eyes were strangely bright, and Emma sensed that she'd arrived with little time to spare.

"I am so proud of you girls. My three bright lights. You've brought me so much joy. I know your mother would be just as proud. Your father too, of course," Grams added hastily.

"Grams, we love you so much!" Jill's voice was thick with emotion, and Mandy and Emma chimed in together, "We all love you, Grams."

"My three beautiful girls. I want so much for all of you. Happiness and love. I believe in you, and I have a gift for you, and a bit of a secret too." There was a faint hint of mischief in her voice and a flit of a smile across her face. But she was clearly starting to tire again and took a moment to collect her thoughts and to summon enough energy to continue.

"So I've done something... Left you a gift that means the world to me. You have no idea. But you will, someday." She paused and looked intently at each woman in turn, and none of them had any idea what she was talking about. But they all smiled back, and she continued.

"You girls used to be so close. I know you think you still are. You talk on the phone, and you do the email thing." She made a face that showed what she thought about email.

"But you don't spend enough time together. It's important to be near family, to be close to them, always." She closed her eyes and snuggled into her pillow. It was several long moments before she opened them again and spoke, her voice wobbly and weak but still determined. "I want you to go to Mimi's Place and be together. That is my gift to you. That, and my love for you always."

Grams closed her eyes again and let out the most peaceful sigh. She drifted off to sleep and didn't wake again. An hour later, she inhaled deeply and exhaled slowly and didn't take another breath. Mandy nudged her arm, but she didn't move. Emma reached out and felt for a pulse, and there was nothing.

Jill was still holding her hand, and tears ran down her face.

"I think she's gone."

To Jill, the next five days were a blur. She felt numb as they went through the motions and did the things one did at a time like this. They met with the funeral director, a cheery woman named Charlotte, who had clearly adored Grams. "She was so full of life, that one. She came in twice over the past year to update the music. Said she wanted to make sure there was no 'cry music' at her service. Nothing but upbeat and happy."

That made Jill smile. It was so like Grams. She had told all three of them often that she didn't want her funeral to be a morbid thing with music that made people sad. She wanted them to dance and have a party to celebrate her life. Grams was so determined. She had already planned it all down to the very last detail. She'd booked the funeral service, made all the arrangements, right down to picking out the coffin and music.

"I don't want you girls to have to worry about all that. Just remember that it's at Cleary and Arlidge. Call and ask for Charlotte." Grams was certainly right about that. It did make things easier. So much easier than it had been when Grampy died ten years ago, and they went along with Grams to get everything sorted out. She was so sad and detached back then that it was difficult for her to focus on anything, especially the details for her husband's funeral.

Grams had also left instructions for her mercy meal to be at Mimi's Place, of course. She wanted everyone to enjoy themselves and to remember all the good times. Grams always did love a party.

———————

"Eat, drink, and be merry," Jill said, forcing a smile and lifting her glass to clink it against Mandy's and Emma's. They were sitting at a big round table at Mimi's Place. Just being there was a comfort. It was Grams's favorite restaurant on Nantucket by far, and it always reminded them of her. The room was cozy and plush with dark cherrywood and soft burgundy velvet seat cushions. What saved the room from being too dark was plenty of windows that allowed soft natural light to brighten the room.

Jill felt her muscles finally relax as she leaned back in her chair. Everything was done now—well, almost. They still had to clear out Grams's house, but there was no rush on that, and none of them had the energy to tackle it just yet. Plus, they'd talked about it a bit and decided that at least for the next year or so, they'd keep it rather than selling it. That way, they'd always have a place to call home on Nantucket.

"It would be perfect for either of you if you wanted to stay for longer than a day or two," Mandy said. "Of course, you know you're both always welcome to stay with me as long as you like, but this would give you your own space and peace and quiet."

At that moment, Ray Bartlesby, who was in his late seventies and had been managing Mimi's Place for longer than Jill had been alive, stopped by their table. Emma pulled out a chair, and he sat down.

"Your grandmother would be so pleased to see you three laughing together. She was such a special lady."

"Ray, thank you so much for everything. As usual, the food was amazing," Mandy said.

"Rose was like family." Ray's voice cracked, and his demeanor, so polished and professional at all times, slipped for just an instant, revealing a glimpse of genuine sadness. Jill and her sisters had been a little overwhelmed and so grateful for the outpouring of sympathy and support they'd received. So many people who had known Grams in some way over the years had come to pay their respects.

"How is your family, Ray?" Jill asked. She'd talked to his wife, Cindy, earlier, and she had mentioned that they'd just become great-grandparents for the first time and were absolutely thrilled.

"Everyone's great, just great, thanks." He glanced around the bustling room, full of people mingling, drinking, and eating, filling their plates at the buffet table, while servers in elegant black-and-white uniforms stocked whatever was running low and efficiently cleared empty dishes and glasses away. "I suppose it finally is time to retire. I'll really miss this place though."

Emma patted his arm. "I can't imagine how they'll run it without you," she said.

Ray chuckled. "Oh, they'll be fine. It's just time. Long overdue if you ask my wife. She's ready to retire to Florida yesterday." He stood up as one of the servers caught his eye. "Please excuse me. Duty calls." Some kind of crisis in the kitchen, from the looks of it. Jill suspected that he would miss this job quite a bit. Retirement wouldn't be nearly as exciting.

"This place without Ray will just seem so odd," Mandy said.

"I used to think that too," Emma agreed. "After all, he's been here as long as any of us can remember."

They were silent for a moment, and then Jill reached for the half-full bottle of Chianti in the middle of the table and refilled each of their glasses.

"Okay, so let's talk about you now." She focused her attention on Emma. "What are you going to do about Peter? Can you work things out, do you think?"

Emma still hadn't shared the details with them yet. The timing hadn't felt right. It didn't seem appropriate to whine about her marriage woes when they were writing Grams's obituary and making arrangements to bury her. But now—well, she supposed Grams would have quite a lively opinion about the matter.

"Grams never really got to know Peter. I wish she was here to give me her wisdom. I can almost hear what she'd say," she mused.

"Was he unfaithful?" Mandy asked, and Emma just nodded. It was still too hard to say the words.

"No kidding? Who was she?" Jill exclaimed, clearly surprised by this revelation.

Emma smiled wryly. "He," she corrected. After allowing a moment for that to register, she added, "It's his friend Tom."

"The one who recently moved to Phoenix?" Mandy asked.

"The very same. They evidently had a short fling when they were in college. Peter said it didn't happen again until just recently, when Tom was transferred to Phoenix and looked him up."

"That's such a surprise. How do you deal with that kind of news?" Jill asked.

"Not very well," Emma admitted with a nervous laugh. "If you're me, you run away and hide, and you question it from every possible angle. But there are no good answers."

"Well, you need to take a vacation and figure out what you're going to do next." Mandy reached over and grabbed her hand. "Stay with me, as long as you like. We have plenty of room."

"Or come to Manhattan. We can have a blast, go shopping and out to eat, whatever you feel like doing," Jill offered.

"Thanks, both of you. I've been thinking a lot about this though, and what I've decided is what I really need to do is focus on work and keep busy. I'm flying home tomorrow night and moving out. I have a room already booked at a spa in Scottsdale, and I'm going to go apartment hunting. I can't stay in our house anymore. There are too many memories there."

She saw the sympathy in their eyes and anger at Peter on her behalf, which was understandable, and she loved them for it.

"I don't hate Peter. He is who he is, and I know he never meant to hurt me, but I just think I need some distance from him now. It's too hard."

Mandy wasn't ready to give up though. "Think about staying here a few more days at least. You can easily reschedule your flight. Let us take care of you for a bit, and let yourself relax and recharge."

Emma was too exhausted to protest. It was easier to put the decision off. "I'll think about it and will let you know tomorrow." They were meeting at the attorney's office at eleven to go over the will. Emma didn't expect that to take long. Grams had a modest savings account and the house and had always told the girls that whatever she had would go to the three of them equally. She figured she could probably suggest a nice lunch with Mandy and Jill, and then she'd be ready to head to the airport. She was anxious to get on with her life.

4

Alvin Eldridge had been Grams's attorney for over thirty years. He was nearly seventy, with plenty of snow-white hair and a neatly trimmed beard. His eyes were cheery as he welcomed the women into his small office on Main Street. It was an elegant old building with a distant view of the harbor.

"Come in, come in." He ushered them into a conference room and offered water or coffee, which they all declined. Once they were settled comfortably around the table, he opened a thick manila folder, handed a copy of the will to each of them, and started reading through it. Everything was pretty much as expected right up until the end. He paused, and they thought he was finished, but then he leaned forward and said with much drama, "There is an addendum to the will, which your grandmother instructed me to save until the very end." He handed a single sheet of paper to each of them.

"She has a bit of a surprise for the three of you. I understand that you are not aware that she is—or rather was— the sole owner of Mimi's Place, one of Nantucket's finest restaurants?"

"Grams owned Mimi's Place!" Jill exclaimed, looking up from the sheet of paper she was holding.

"How could that be?" Mandy asked.

"How come she never told us?" Emma looked at Mr. Eldridge for an explanation.

"I was sworn to secrecy. I don't think many at the restaurant, except for a select few, knew either. Your grandmother wanted it that way. She never actively managed the place. It was always handled through a trust."

"So what do we do with it? We sell it, right? None of us knows how to run a restaurant," Jill stated.

Mr. Eldridge cleared his throat. "Well, this is where it gets a bit more interesting. Your grandmother seems to have a plan in place. You can certainly sell the restaurant if you choose."

"Good, so you can handle that for us? Or put us in touch with people who can arrange for a sale?" Jill sounded relieved and ready to be finished with everything. Emma was also hoping they could wrap this up today and she could be on her way.

"Yes, of course. But there is a catch. You can sell the

restaurant, but not just yet. Please see the last paragraph. Your grandmother spells it out in her own words."

Mandy started reading aloud. "'My girls, I know this will come as somewhat of a shock, but I am the sole owner of Mimi's Place and have been for forty-three years, since I won the restaurant in a bet. A game of poker actually, but that's too long a story to go into here. As you know, Mimi's Place is special to me and always has been. We've shared many wonderful times there, and I hope that the three of you will learn to love the place as much as I do. The restaurant is yours to do with what you will, but before you can sell Mimi's Place, if that is what you choose to do, all three of you must first work there in any capacity you choose for exactly one year.

"'I also left a quarter of it to Paul Taylor, my executive chef for the last twelve years. You must all work with him, running the restaurant together. After a year, you can choose to sell if that is your wish. If you decide not to work together for one full year, then your shares will automatically go to Paul, as I know he loves the restaurant as much as I do. I trust that soon, the three of you will too.'"

Mandy and Jill both glanced at Emma. They all knew Paul Taylor but didn't realize he was the chef at Mimi's Place. Emma was shocked and a bit discombobulated to learn this, but she quickly regained her composure and smiled.

"Well, isn't that a surprise? How nice for all of us and for Paul too."

An hour later, Jill, Mandy, and Emma settled around a table at Brant Point Grill in the White Elephant Hotel. It was one of the most elegant hotels on the island with an air of quiet luxury. It was directly on the waterfront with a lovely view of the harbor, but all three stared at their menus, unable to make a decision.

"Everything looks good." Jill flipped a page of her menu as her cell phone buzzed again. The ringer was off, but every few minutes, it buzzed. This time, she didn't get to it quickly enough, and it vibrated wildly, slithering across the glass tabletop until it collided with her water glass. As soon as she saw the number on the caller ID, she stood.

"Oops...sorry, I have to take this one. It'll just be a second."

Mandy raised her eyebrows at Emma as Jill started talking.

"Hi, Billy. No, he's not closed. I can't close him on a number until we know what the company is able to do." She glanced at her watch. "I should be back by four. I'll see you then." She ended the call, and as soon as she set the phone down, it started buzzing again. She ignored it and turned her attention back to the menu, but less than a minute later, she picked up the phone, checked email, and began furiously typing a response. When she finished, Mandy reached over, grabbed the offensive phone, and dropped it into her over-size tote bag where the constant buzzing would be muzzled.

Jill opened her mouth to protest, but Mandy cut her off. "You'll get it back as soon as we're done here. An hour off won't kill you, my dear."

"You're right. I'm sorry." Jill picked up a crusty dinner roll from the basket that had just landed on the table. She ripped off a chunk of bread, smeared a bit of butter on it, and popped it in her mouth.

"Is it always like that?" Emma asked. She couldn't imagine having a job where the phone rang off the hook. It was unsettling. She preferred peace and quiet and in fact did her best work in complete silence, which allowed her to concentrate so fully that she entered an almost trance-like "zone" that was so familiar to writers and other artists.

Jill laughed. "That's nothing. You should see what it's like in the office. It's crazy, but I do love it."

She really seemed to, Emma realized, seeing the glimmer of excitement in her sister's eyes. Jill was so successful and amazing at what she did and was clearly anxious to get back to it. Emma shuddered at the very thought of what her sister did for work though. Not in a million years could she call absolute strangers on the phone and persuade them to consider changing jobs. Emma had phone phobia. She dreaded calling anyone that she didn't know very well, for even something as simple as scheduling a doctor's visit.

Not for the first time, Emma marveled at how very different the three of them were. She knew that she was the quiet, creative one. Jill was the aggressive businesswoman, and Mandy was just so polished and organized that she made everything look easy. Even now, as she took charge to get the three of them focused.

"Here comes the waiter," Mandy said as he approached their table. "We need to make some decisions. What does everyone want?"

"I have no idea." Emma was having a hard time deciding until another server walked by carrying two gorgeous leafy salads topped with grilled scallops. "That looks delicious."

"It is," the waiter assured them. "The scallops are local, from Nantucket Bay. The chef brushes them with an orange butter sauce before they go on the grill. There's also sliced avocado, pecans, and crumbled goat cheese with an orange, sesame, and ginger vinaigrette."

Emma closed her menu. "I'll have that."

"Me too," Jill and Mandy both said at the same time.

"Can you tell we're related?" Jill asked with a grin.

"It's an excellent choice." He smiled and gathered up their menus.

"Okay," Mandy began. "Seriously, what are we going to do? None of us has ever run a restaurant. And both of you are scheduled to be on a plane home this afternoon."

"I have quite a bit of restaurant experience actually," Emma said. She'd been thinking about nothing else since they'd left the attorney's office, and for the first time in weeks, she felt a bit of excitement building. Maybe Grams was onto something with this strange bequest.

"You worked as a server. You've never managed a restaurant," Mandy corrected.

"True, but I worked as a server for several years. At the Barnacle, some of the waitstaff had been there for over twenty or thirty years. When it was slow, we used to sit out back and discuss how we'd do things differently. This might not be such a crazy idea after all. A year goes by quickly, and it's not like we really have a choice." Emma looked around the table, then added, "Unless we're willing to just walk away and let Paul have Mimi's Place."

"Well, that's another factor—Paul. How do you feel about working with him?" Mandy asked.

Emma sighed. She'd been shocked at the news initially, but she didn't see why it needed to change anything.

"That was another lifetime. I'm sure Paul and I could find a way to work together. We both moved on years ago."

"I don't see how it's possible though." Mandy was always the voice of reason. "Jill runs a multimillion-dollar business in Manhattan, and you live clear across the country, and I'm just a stay-at-home wife and mother. I really don't see how this could work."

"First of all, you're not 'just' a stay-at-home mother. Look at all those incredible charity events you're always pulling together. Not everyone can do that. And I don't have to live in Phoenix, especially now that I'm getting divorced." Emma turned her attention to her other sister. "And, Jill, you've said many times that you could work from anywhere, that all you need is a laptop and a phone."

"Well, yes, but…"

"So theoretically, you could work from here?" Emma pressed.

"Theoretically, I could," Jill conceded. "But it would be difficult."

They were all silent for a moment, and then Mandy leaned forward in her chair. "But not impossible." She was obviously warming to the idea.

"Besides, New York isn't far at all. You could probably get back there once or twice a month if you wanted to," Emma added.

"There's three of us," Mandy began. "We can split our time up, so we won't have to always be there together."

———

Jill was surprised that Emma and Mandy seemed to have done a complete turnaround on Grams's crazy idea. Her ears picked up a faint buzzing sound, and she realized that somewhere deep inside Mandy's purse, her cell phone was ringing again. She sighed. It might be nice to have a break from the constant grind, and it would only be for a year.

"So, Mandy, are you saying you want to do this too?" Jill asked when the waiter arrived with their salads.

Mandy took a bite of a scallop before answering. "Oh, these scallops are amazing." She paused for a moment, savoring the flavor. Then she put her fork down and spoke, her tone serious. "Yes, I want to do this. Grams wanted it for us, and I can't help but think that the timing is a good thing, sort of meant to be. I've been thinking for a while now that I wanted to do something, maybe find a part-time job now that the kids are a bit older."

"Okay, so what do we do now then?" Jill asked.

"I think you and I should still fly home as planned," Emma began. "I only need a few days to get things settled, pack, and fly back. I can go back in a few months to take care of anything I missed. How much time do you think you'll need?"

"Well, Mandy's right. Manhattan really isn't that far, so I should only need a few days too. Especially since I'll be going back more often."

"Where do you think you want to stay?" Mandy asked. "There's plenty of room with me, or of course there's Grams's house. It has four bedrooms, and you'd be just a short walk from Mimi's Place."

"I'd love to stay at Grams's place I think," Emma decided. "With that many bedrooms, we could each use one as an office too, if we like."

"Works for me," Jill agreed.

"I'll call to schedule a meeting next week with Ray and Paul to go over everything."

"Okay, then it's settled." Jill lifted her water glass. "To Mimi's Place."

Emma and Mandy clinked their glasses together.

"To Mimi's Place."

Jill strode into her office at a quarter to four.

"I'm so sorry about your grandmother. How are you doing?" Mary's face reflected concern and care. She was a stellar receptionist and was so naturally kind and caring that she had a calming effect on everyone from nervous candidates to Jill and Billy and the rest of the staff.

"Thank you, I'm doing okay. Is Billy in?"

"He's in his office with Tony and Nicole. They seem excited about something."

Jill headed back to her office, which was down the hall from Billy's. As co-owners, they each had a corner office with floor-to-ceiling windows overlooking the city.

As she walked through the office, various employees offered their condolences. The energy level was high as usual. Everyone was either on the phone or tapping away on their keyboards. Jill caught a glimpse of the "board," where everyone tracked their placements for the month, and saw that the overall number was up considerably. They must have closed several deals in the last few days. She dropped her bag and coat in her office before going to see Billy.

Tony and Nicole, two of their recruiters, were still in his office, the three of them gabbing away when she walked in.

"Hey! How are you?" Billy got up from his desk and walked over to give Jill a big hug.

"I'm fine. So what are you all celebrating?"

Billy's eyes lit up as he glanced at Tony and Nicole before answering. "These two just set a record for the biggest placement in our company's history."

"They filled the MacGregor search?" It had to be. Typical fees were in the twenty-five to thirty percent range of the candidate's starting salary, but this client had offered to pay forty percent to ensure that they were given the highest possible priority, given that this was also an extremely difficult search and they wanted an added incentive to stay focused and not give up.

"That's right. A four-hundred-and-twenty-thousand-dollar fee!"

"Congratulations, you two! That's quite an accomplishment."

Tony and Nicole were two of their top performers. Tony, the seasoned recruiter, was grinning like a little kid, and Nicole, who was still considered a rookie with less than two years of experience, was beaming.

"On days like this, I really love this job!" Nicole exclaimed, then added, "And it still amazes me sometimes how much we're paid to just find people. I know there's way more to it, but still, it's a lot of money."

Jill was thrilled for all of them, and even after her many years in this business, it still amazed her too at times how they were able to command the fees that they did.

"Billy, when you have a minute, could you swing by my office? I need to talk to you about something."

He immediately looked alarmed. "Is everything okay?" And then, "Am I in trouble?"

Jill chuckled. "Of course not. Nothing's wrong. I just want to bounce an idea off you."

Twenty minutes later, she finished telling Billy about Mimi's Place and Grams's request and that she wanted to work from Nantucket for the next year. It didn't go over very well.

"You want to what? How can you run the business from Nantucket? I need you here." Tiny beads of sweat broke out on his forehead. He raked his hand through his hair several times, and Jill noticed for the first time that there was a smattering of gray along his hairline.

"I have complete faith in you to run things without me physically here. I bet you'll barely notice that I'm gone, and I'll be fully accessible by email and phone and can conference in for the weekly job-order meetings. Depending on my schedule, I might even be able to make those in person from time to time as I'm hoping to be back once or twice every month."

"You want to do this for a whole year?" He looked miserable at the thought of it.

"No, I don't want to. But I don't have much choice, not if I want to respect Grams's last wishes and do what's right for my sisters as well." She put on her brightest smile. "It's just a year. It'll go by in the blink of an eye."

5

Mandy made Cory's favorite dinner, veal marsala, and planned to tell him about Mimi's Place after they'd eaten and maybe had a glass or two of wine. When she spoke to him earlier in the day, he'd sounded exhausted already and distracted. He also said he'd most likely be home by six thirty, seven at the latest.

So she'd planned accordingly. She fed the kids at about six, chicken marsala for them, and then she set about preparing the rest of the meal that she and Cory would share. At six thirty, she put the asparagus on a sheet of tinfoil, sprinkled a little parmesan cheese, salt and pepper, a drizzle of olive oil, and a quick squeeze of lemon. She threw them in the oven, next to a casserole dish of tiny fingerling potatoes that were glistening with butter and starting to brown nicely.

At a quarter to seven, she poured herself a glass of char-donnay and began sautéing the veal cutlets, which only took a few minutes. The sauce came together quickly and was a simple reduction of the drippings scraped up from the bottom of the pan and stirred into a bit of marsala wine, butter, and sautéed mushrooms. It smelled heavenly.

By seven, everything was ready, and there was still no sign of Cory. At a quarter past, she called his cell phone, which apparently wasn't on as her call went immediately into voicemail. By eight, the children were tucked into bed, the veal was cold and congealing, and Mandy's wineglass was empty. She refilled it, to the top this time, and grabbed an asparagus spear to nibble on. Finally, at almost nine, Cory walked through the door.

Mandy glanced up and tried to keep the annoyance out of her voice as she said, "I was starting to worry about you."

Cory shrugged his coat off and hung it in the front hall closet before coming into the kitchen.

"I had to stay late, needed to finish up a proposal for a client meeting first thing tomorrow morning. Something smells good."

"It's veal marsala. When you said you'd be home by seven, I told you it would be waiting for you." She grabbed two plates and reached for the veal.

"Honey, I'm sorry. I totally didn't hear you say that. We were just crazed today. Ashley ordered Chinese takeout for the office."

"Okay then." Mandy was fuming inside but trying not

to show it. "Well, I'm starving, so there's all the more for me I guess."

"I feel like an ass." Cory looked truly sorry, but Mandy said nothing in response, just continued to fill her plate. "How can I make it up to you?"

She smiled back. "Well, there is something I wanted to talk to you about."

Jill walked into her apartment a little after nine thirty that night. She was bone-tired and ready to fall into bed. Billy had wanted to go for drinks and dinner after work to catch up and talk through how they'd manage in the short term, at least until they both got used to her working remotely and probably fewer hours while juggling her duties at the restaurant.

By the end of the meal, he was still apprehensive but supportive and even a little bit excited for her about the whole idea. Especially when she reminded him that Grams's house had four bedrooms. He'd been there a few times with her, but it had been several years since they'd gone.

"Maybe I'll have to plan a weekend trip to Nantucket. You can show me around, and I can do a quality check on the food at Mimi's Place."

Jill assured him that he was welcome anytime, but she wanted to give it a little time first, for her and her sisters to get their feet wet. She didn't admit it to Billy, but she was a little nervous about working in the restaurant. Aside from some bartending years ago at a college bar, she had no experience.

Emma stepped out of the cab into a seemingly solid wall of heat. It was one thing about living in Arizona that she wouldn't miss. Even though it was a dry heat, a hundred and ten was still hot. Peter was home. His car was in the driveway, and he apparently had company. The other car looked familiar, like Tom's actually, but she wasn't a hundred percent sure. She hoped not. She didn't think she was up to seeing the two of them together just yet.

When she walked through the front door, they were sitting side by side on her sofa. She thought of it as hers because shortly after they'd gotten married, she'd picked it out, and it was her dream sofa. A soft vanilla cream shade, it had big puffy cushions that you could sink into. It was a set of two. The other was a larger version and was where Peter usually sprawled out while Emma claimed the smaller one to curl up on. That was where Tom and Peter were sitting, on the love seat.

Peter jumped up as soon as he saw her and ran over to give her an awkward hug.

"I didn't realize you'd be back so soon. I thought you'd stay a few more days to visit with your sisters." He glanced back at Tom. "We're heading out shortly. We were just checking the basketball score." They were both huge basketball fans. Emma had always been bored to death by the game.

"Hi, Emma," Tom said. "I'm so sorry about your grandmother."

"Thank you." She turned her attention to Peter. "I'm actually only back for a few days." She told him about Mimi's Place.

"You own a restaurant? On Nantucket? That's so cool!" Peter seemed genuinely thrilled for her, and Tom, who loved to cook, even seemed enthusiastic.

"What an incredible opportunity. I've always dreamed of owning my own restaurant." Tom was an accountant by trade, so this was news to Emma, though not apparently to Peter.

"If that's what you really want to do, then you need to find a way to make it happen. That's what I did. Do you have any idea how many people talk about writing a book someday? I did it myself, for how many years?" He glanced at Emma.

"At least seven," she confirmed. "Finally, I told him he needed to stop talking about it and sit his butt down in the chair and just do it."

"I found an hour a day, either before or after work, and that added up to a finished book six months later," Peter said proudly.

"Maybe I'll look into an evening culinary school program," Tom said.

"Great idea!" Peter agreed. "And in the meantime, you can practice anytime on me." A look passed between them then, and it reminded Emma that things would never be the same again for her or for Peter.

"Did you say you guys were heading out soon?" She was eager to have the house to herself.

Tom jumped up. "Yes, let's get going. Nice to see you, Emma."

Emma appreciated his politeness but didn't feel she could say the same, so she just nodded and watched them walk out the door.

Facing the two of them hadn't been as much of an ordeal as she'd anticipated, but it was still difficult and draining. Emma suddenly felt exhausted and just wanted to lie down in the peace and quiet of her bedroom. The spare bedroom, actually. The moment she'd heard the news about Peter and Tom, she'd moved into the spare bedroom, which was bright and roomy and decorated in soothing shades of dusty pink and mauve. Sleeping in the bed she'd once shared with Peter was no longer an option.

She collapsed onto the bed and stretched out against the cool satin comforter. She wondered if there was a support group for women whose husbands left them under these circumstances. Probably, though she was lucky that she already had a personal support group in Mandy and Jill. She was looking forward to spending more time with them and was growing more excited about Mimi's Place.

She'd always had a love/hate relationship with restaurant

work. The things she disliked were the long hours on her feet and the occasional cheap or crabby customer. And the nights when she was "in the weeds," when the timing was off and nothing seemed to go right, when all her customers seemed to need her at once. Yes, she'd had her share of those bad nights, but overall, she'd had many more good ones, when she'd successfully juggled many tables, served food that wowed her customers, and even had regulars who would ask for her every time they came in.

What she was most excited about was the chance to actually do some of the things that she and the other waitresses she'd worked with had talked about, ideas for changes they'd implement if they were in charge. Emma realized that the timing was a blessing. She sent a mental note of thanks to Grams for this chance to start over.

———

Cory poured himself a glass of wine and joined Mandy at the kitchen table. In between bites of the veal, which was absolutely delicious after she'd warmed it up for a few minutes, she told him about Mimi's Place and how the three of them were planning to work there. She wasn't asking his permission; she was telling him. But she still hoped for his approval; it would make things easier and less stressful. The last reaction she expected was amusement. Cory apparently found the situation quite funny.

"You're going to run a restaurant? How? You don't have

a drop of experience." He leaned back in his chair and took another sip of wine before continuing. "Do you know that something like four out of five new restaurants don't make it to the one-year mark? The odds are against you."

Mandy knew that there were several restaurant stocks in his hedge fund, so he'd clearly done some research on the market. They always did before taking on any investments, but she still found his attitude frustrating. Clearly, he didn't think she could do it.

"Mimi's Place isn't a new restaurant. It's been around for years and has a great reputation."

"Sure, it's well established, but do you have any idea how healthy it is? Have you seen the financials?"

"Not yet," she admitted. "We're sitting down next week with Ray, the manager. He's going to walk us through everything."

"I'm not trying to be negative," he began. "It's just that the restaurant business is known to be particularly tough. It's not at all uncommon for even established restaurants to go under if they're not totally on top of the market and make the necessary changes to keep up. There's a lot more competition now."

"I know. We're really excited about this though. It seems like perfect timing for me especially. You know how anxious I've been to get back to work."

Cory frowned. "And you know that we don't need the money. Profits are up again over last year's record year. You don't have to work."

Mandy sighed. She'd lost count of how many times they'd had this discussion or some variation of it. "It's not about the money. I need to feel useful, to get out there and do something challenging."

"And you think running a restaurant is the answer?" The annoying smirk was back on his face. This was a big joke to him.

"I don't know if this is the answer. But I know that I want to find out."

The next day, Mandy went to Grams's house. The houses that were walking distance to town were so old that they were considered antiques. They were all on small lots and close to their neighbors. Her grandmother's house dated back to the late 1800s. The hardwood floors were slightly uneven, and the windows were small, but the ceilings were high, and the rooms felt spacious. Her grandmother had renovated it years ago, modernizing the kitchen, and she'd painted the brick fireplace white, which gave it a beachy look.

Mandy wanted to get it ready for Jill and Emma. She put freshly washed sheets on the beds and stocked the fridge with essentials like Diet Coke, milk, eggs, a cooked rotisserie chicken, coffee, bagels—and of course, chocolate. That should hold them for a few days until they got settled.

It was a little strange when she first walked into her

grandmother's house. Even though it was immaculate and hadn't been touched in close to a year, Mandy could still feel Grams's presence. Walking through the rooms, she thought her senses were playing tricks on her, because now and then, she could swear she caught a whiff of cigarette smoke. Grams had been a heavy smoker, a pack a day from age sixteen she'd once said, and her brand of choice was Virginia Slims. She thought they had a refined look and a more delicate taste. She'd made weak attempts to quit several times over the years, but it never lasted long. Grams often admitted that she loved smoking and never really wanted to stop.

Mandy paused when she walked into Grams's favorite room. Her cozy library/den was just off the kitchen, and the walls were lined with built-in bookcases that held an eclectic mix of books, from fiction and biographies to cookbooks of all kinds. For as long as Mandy could remember, Grams had collected cookbooks. She'd rarely cooked from them, but she'd loved reading them all the way through and getting ideas. Tucked into the far corner of the room was an antique rolltop desk where Grams kept her correspondence. There was an address book, stamps, and what looked like an old diary. Intrigued, Mandy settled herself into the leather padded chair and opened the diary.

A while later, she rubbed her neck, which was starting to feel a bit stiff, and glanced at her watch. She couldn't believe the time. Almost two hours had gone by! No wonder her neck was cramping up. She'd been completely engrossed in Grams's diary. She couldn't stay much longer though. It was almost time to pick the kids up from school. But she needed to know what was going to happen next. Grams's diary was fascinating. She'd had no idea what her grandmother's life was really like.

The diary began in her high school years, and Mandy was at the point where she had graduated from Radcliffe and was starting to spread her wings in Boston. That meant she was living at home in her family's Beacon Hill town house and had just landed her first job out of college as a teacher at a North End elementary school. Mandy put her feet up and began reading again.

I have to admit that I'm both thrilled and a bit terrified to be starting my new job tomorrow. My parents are especially pleased about the location. I'll be able to walk to work, and it's a pleasant walk too, ten minutes tops. And of course Father approves because, he says, "The North End is such a safe area. Nothing bad happens there. The Italians won't stand for it." Those were his exact words. I asked him to further explain, and he just said, "They protect their own." I just love the North End. Always have. Just think, after school's out for the day, I'll be able to stop by Mike's Pastry on my walk home for a cup of coffee and something sweet. Wish me luck!

Grams sounded so young and so full of excitement. Mandy turned the page, and the next entry was dated a month or so later.

Dearest Diary, I'm so sorry that I've neglected you. But I have a wonderful excuse. Two, actually. I love my job! The kids are wonderful, and I've made a great friend in one of the other teachers. She and I have been tearing up the town, going from one party to the next. It seems like there's been so many fun events lately. But best of all, I met someone wonderful!

Jay is a true Italian, born and brought up right on Hanover Street. We met at Mike's Pastry. I was buying some cannoli to bring home for dessert, and he couldn't decide what kind of Torrone to get and asked my advice. Well, you know how I feel about Torrone, that delicious nougat candy? I told him that the vanilla almond dipped in dark chocolate was the way to go. We kept chatting, and he asked me to dinner the following night, and we've been dating steadily ever since.

I've never felt this way about anyone before. He reminds me a bit of Jimmy Stewart but with darker hair and prettier eyes. They're a soft blue-gray, and his smile just makes me melt. I think about him constantly. We seem to have this amazing connection, where we're able to talk for hours about anything and everything. Do you suppose this means I'm in love? I'm pretty sure that whatever it is, he's feeling it too.

The entry ended there, and reluctantly Mandy closed the diary. She couldn't put off leaving any longer, even though she really wanted to read more. Especially to see who this mysterious Jay was. Unless it was a nickname, it wasn't her grandfather, who Grams had been married to for over sixty years. His name was Charlie. Maybe Emma or Jill would know.

Mandy put the diary back in its spot on the desk and got up to leave. She was tempted to take it with her, but somehow it didn't feel right to remove it from Grams's place. Especially since Emma and Jill were going to be staying here. She'd just have to make a point of dropping by regularly to visit with her sisters and sneak off to read a few pages here and there.

6

Emma spent the next two days packing up her old life and getting rid of everything that didn't bring her joy. She donated more than half of her clothes to Goodwill and only kept two large suitcases of her favorite things. Tom's car was old, and they came to an agreement on a price for Emma's vehicle, a reliable Honda Civic. She didn't have the time or the energy to drive it across the country. She found a similar used one online that was a year older, but the miles weren't bad, and it was in her favorite color, navy blue. She spoke to the owner, who was an older woman who had been the sole owner of the car. Emma liked what she heard and had a good feeling about it.

"I'll take it."

The woman sounded surprised. "You don't want to take it for a test drive, dear?"

"I have the same car now. I know that I'll love it." They agreed on a price and worked out an approximate time for Emma to pick it up.

Peter insisted on driving Emma to the airport. She was on a red-eye flight that would get to Boston in the morning, and she would fly on to Hyannis and pick up her car. They were quiet on the drive, which was about forty-five minutes. They made meaningless small talk, but it didn't flow as easily as it used to. Emma still loved Peter, but it was difficult to feel anything but sad when she was around him.

"I hope you're not too angry with me," he said as they pulled onto the airport exit.

Emma sighed. They'd both danced around really talking about this. There wasn't a whole lot left to say.

"I'm not angry with you. It would be easier if I could be," she admitted.

He nodded. "I know. I just hope you know how much I do really love you, Emma. You were an important part of my life."

A part of her life that was over now.

"Are you happy now?" She glanced at him, and he'd never looked so good. He was tan, his hair had grown out a little, and he looked relaxed and confident at the same time. She realized that he was deeply happy in a way that he never had been with her.

His eyes were warm as he smiled at her. "I am. I want you to be happy too, Emma. I hope you know I'll always want good things for you."

She looked away as he pulled up to the terminal and was annoyed that her eyes stung a bit. She didn't want to cry in front of Peter again. She willed them away and got out of the car. Peter pulled her two bags out of the back and set them on the curb and pulled her in for a hug.

"You're still my best friend, Emma. I'm going to miss you. Please keep in touch. Let me know how your new adventure on Nantucket goes."

Emma smiled slightly. Peter was so sincere, and she was going to miss him too.

"I will."

Emma fell fast asleep soon after the plane took off and slept surprisingly well considering that it was her first red-eye flight ever and Jill had warned that she was never able to sleep on a plane. She had an hour layover in Boston before her flight to the Cape, and that gave her time to wake up with coffee and a breakfast burrito at one of the food stands.

Once she landed at the Cape Cod Airport in Hyannis, she got her luggage and took an Uber to pick up the car. She was relieved to find that it was exactly as shown online. After chatting for a few minutes with the owner and looking over the paperwork showing that the car had been well maintained, Emma handed her a check. She put her luggage in the trunk and headed off to see an insurance agent and then to the motor vehicle department. A few hours later, that was all squared away, and Emma stopped into Trader Joe's to pick up some snacks for the house and a few bottles of wine.

She made her way over to the Steamship Authority for her 2:45 reservation on the slow boat as they called it, the one that took vehicles. It would get her to Nantucket by five, which was perfect. Jill was going to be flying in a little earlier and said she'd meet her at the house.

The boat was crowded but not as bad as in the summer months when you had to make a reservations weeks ahead. Emma drove onto the boat, parked, and then went to the upper level to relax. She smiled as several dogs of all sizes passed by with their owners. She'd bought a hot tea just before boarding and settled into a seat by a window and prepared to dive into a new book on her Kindle.

She waited though until they were out of Hyannis Harbor. She watched as they slowly chugged by Baxter's Fish and Chips, which had good fresh seafood and great sightseeing. Emma had loved to go there and sit at one of the outside tables and watch the busy boat traffic go by as she ate a lobster roll and shared fried clams and onion rings. There was often someone playing on the piano, and there was a lively happy hour crowd.

They passed by Tugboats, another fun restaurant at the Hyannis Marina. Emma shifted her gaze to the many beautiful homes that lined the water's edge. A few minutes later, they reached Nantucket Sound, and the homes faded behind them. Emma lost herself in her book, and the time passed quickly. She sensed when they were almost there and looked up to see Nantucket Harbor ahead and the picturesque lighthouse welcoming them.

Seeing Nantucket from the water always took Emma's breath away, and a familiar feeling of calm settled over her. Even though she'd been living away from Nantucket for years, it still felt like coming home whenever she returned to the island.

She stood and went to go to her car. Ten minutes later, she drove off the ferry and onto the cobblestone streets of downtown Nantucket. Traffic was heavy with people arriving to pick up or drop off friends or family at the ferry. Emma rolled her window down and breathed in the clean fresh air. It was a bit windy, and she could smell the salt water as a breeze tossed her hair. She sat in traffic and glanced at the wharf with its many cute shops and the gorgeous condos and townhomes that sat directly over the water. The waterfront area was so pretty. There was really nothing else like it. Emma had to admit that while she'd enjoyed living in Arizona, it was nice to be home on Nantucket again, at least for the next year.

Moving into Grams's place was strange. Jill arrived a half hour before Emma, and as she walked around going from room to room, it seemed a bit surreal to think that they were going to be living in Grams's house and running a restaurant that they'd never even known was hers. Why had she kept it a secret all these years? Jill wondered if anyone at Mimi's Place knew the truth or if they just thought Grams was a happy, regular customer all these years. It had never been a secret that it was her favorite restaurant.

Jill paused in front of a framed picture of her and her sisters with Grams in the middle. She remembered when they took that picture. Emma had used a tripod and set it up in the dining room, with the curtains open so you could catch a glimpse of the snow falling outside. Once she was satisfied with the setup, she set the timer and raced to jump into place. It took five or six tries to get it right, but the end result was worth it. The picture was great, and they all looked happy and content. Emma and Mandy were newly married, and Jill had just moved to Manhattan and gone into business with Billy. Grams looked thrilled as usual just to be surrounded by her girls. Jill's eyes teared up thinking about her. She loved her grandmother's house, but it felt so empty without her.

Emma arrived moments later, and they decided to walk downtown to the Club Car on Main Street. Over a bottle of chardonnay and an appetizer of fried calamari, they caught up with each other.

"So how did it go with Billy? Was he upset about Mimi's

Place taking you out of Manhattan?" Emma reached for a piece of bread out of the basket that had just landed on their table.

"He's not thrilled. He counts on my being there, to bounce ideas off each other and to help keep everyone focused."

"He's a good-looking guy," Emma commented, taking another bite of calamari.

"He's hot, and he knows it." Jill laughed. "Billy loves attention and gets plenty of it."

"How come the two of you have never hooked up? I've often wondered about that." Emma smiled before taking a sip of wine.

Jill hesitated a moment. Other people asked her that often, but it had been years since either of her sisters had raised the question.

"Me and Billy? I've always thought that would just be weird. We're like brother and sister, great friends, not to mention business partners. I don't think either of us wants to risk losing any of that."

"That makes sense. So does he have a girlfriend then?"

"Why? Are you interested?" Jill teased.

Emma laughed. "No, just curious. I don't remember you mentioning one."

"That's because none of them last long enough to qualify for girlfriend status. Billy dates all the time, but he hasn't had a serious relationship in years."

"That sounds familiar," Emma said wryly.

Jill sighed. It was true. Her love life was virtually nonexistent. She dated a little here and there, but it never seemed to go anywhere. No one had knocked her socks off in a very long time.

"I might work a little too much," she admitted. Which was an understatement. On a typical day, she was at her desk by seven thirty and stayed 'til at least six, and a few times a week, she and Billy would grab a drink after work, and usually one or more of their employees would join them. Theirs was a social job, and by the end of the day, they were still energized and not ready to go home yet. A drink or two helped them to unwind and laugh about their crazy days.

It also meant that she wasn't getting out as much with her other friends, and more often lately, she had been content to do absolutely nothing on a weekend, which of course led to even fewer dates.

"You definitely have a point. So now that you're single again, we'll have to get out there and see what kind of trouble we can stir up."

Emma looked horrified at the suggestion. "Oh, I don't think I'm even close to ready for that. Honestly, I can't imagine dating again. It's been so long. Everything is so different now. I wouldn't know where to begin."

"It's still the same. Just take baby steps. Ease your way into it. Don't even think about it right away. Just get out there and discover things that interest you. Maybe take a class or something."

Emma relaxed and even seemed a bit excited at the suggestion. "I'd love to do that. Maybe a cooking class or pottery or something might be fun."

"Get your feet wet with that, then we'll move on to ladies' night." Jill grinned at the initial look of shock on her sister's face. But then Emma nodded.

"I'll see what I can find for classes. Maybe something we both will enjoy."

"So, Brody, looks like we're part owners of a restaurant now. Crazy, huh?" Paul Taylor set his coffee cup down and reached to scratch behind the ears of his oversize orange cat. Brody purred as he rubbed against Paul's leg. They'd been together almost twelve years. He'd adopted Brody soon after he and Patsy divorced and he took the job at Mimi's Place. He would have loved to have a dog too, but he knew with his work hours, it wouldn't be fair to the animal. Cats were easier.

He glanced out the window, half seeing the distant ocean view from his cottage. His place was small, but it suited him; he didn't need a big place. When he and Patsy split, she stayed in their house, and he moved into this cottage. It had been in the family for years as a rental property, and the location was ideal, just a short walk to downtown and the waterfront.

He'd been content enough running the kitchen at

Mimi's Place. He liked the people there and had never felt the urge to go elsewhere. And then he learned that he'd been left a share of the restaurant. It was unexpected and fascinating. As the chef, he had of course known who the secret owner was, and he adored her. He'd known her long before he took the chef position, from when he and Emma used to date in high school. Emma's grandmother always welcomed them in for an afternoon visit, and she always had homemade brownies.

Paul smiled thinking of the condition in the will, where all three granddaughters had to work together at the restaurant for a year or else it would all go to him. Paul knew she didn't really want that to happen and was pretty sure she simply wanted the girls to spend some quality time together.

He'd seen Mandy around town now and then but hadn't seen Emma or Jill for many years. He'd heard that Jill had some kind of high-powered job in New York City, and it didn't surprise him. He imagined it suited her well, and he wondered how she felt about having to work at Mimi's Place for a year. And Emma—well, last he knew, she'd married and was living on the West Coast. She probably wasn't too keen on having to spend a year on Nantucket working with him. He wondered if her husband would join her. He hadn't thought about Emma in years. It would be interesting to see her again.

It didn't sound like any of them had any significant restaurant experience, from what Ray had said, so he was curious to see how that would play out. Hopefully they could all work well together. Paul was happy to let them handle front of the restaurant stuff and leave the food and kitchen area to him. He wondered what would happen when the year was up.

Would they want to sell, and if they did, would he want to take out a loan and buy their shares? It was a risk and a lot to think about. If they all wanted to sell, it might give him a nice little nest egg, and maybe the new owners would keep him on as the chef, or he could always go somewhere else if need be. He wasn't too keen on that idea though. He liked being at Mimi's Place.

Brody jumped into his lap and purred loudly. Paul gave him what he wanted, the under-the-chin rub. "We'll be okay, Brody, whatever happens." Brody responded by head-butting Paul's hand and purring even louder. Paul finished his coffee and got ready to head into the restaurant a little earlier than usual so he could meet with Ray and the girls.

———

Mandy met Jill and Emma at Mimi's Place that morning at a few minutes before nine thirty. They were greeted warmly by one of the young waitresses and ushered to a small dining room at the back of the restaurant where Ray was waiting for them. He was sitting at a small round table with a pile of guest checks and a handheld calculator in front of him. He stood up when they entered the room.

"Ladies, it's my pleasure to see you again. Please have a seat." He gestured to the dark wood chairs around the table. "Make yourselves comfortable."

"Can I bring coffee or tea for anyone?" the blond waitress who had seated them offered.

"Coffee would be great. Thank you. All three of us, I think?" The others nodded, and Jill thought she detected a note of curiosity. She wondered if the staff had been told about the change in management yet.

"This is Samantha, one of our best servers. Samantha, meet the new owners of Mimi's Place." Ray introduced each of them, and Samantha told them how pleased she was to meet them. She brought them all coffee, and once she'd left the room, Ray spoke up again.

"I had a quick meeting this morning and let the staff know about the changes. I also begged them to go easy on you." His eyes twinkled with that last bit, and they could tell that he was kidding. "I understand this came as a bit of a surprise to the three of you?" He glanced around the table with a warm smile.

"That's an understatement," Emma said, and Mandy and Jill both nodded in agreement.

"How long have you known about Grams being the owner, if you don't mind my asking?" Mandy pulled her chair in a bit closer, eager to hear his response.

Ray rubbed a finger absently against his chin as though he was trying to decide how best to answer. "I've known for many years. As manager, there were certain things that had to be communicated directly, you know. But I always respected your grandmother's wish for privacy. She had her reasons, and she wanted to be treated the same as any other paying customer."

Unfortunately, it was clear that Ray's loyalty to their grandmother would keep him from divulging any of her secrets.

"Well, ladies, shall we begin?"

For the next two hours, Ray gave them a crash course on running a restaurant. He stressed that no one expected them to learn overnight and that he just wanted to give them an overview of how they did things at Mimi's Place.

"The only way you'll really learn is by doing. You'll learn on the job, and that's how it sinks in. Plus, it's not like you'll be going it alone. I'll be here to help for a while, and Paul is looking forward to working with all of you." He glanced around the restaurant and then at his watch before adding, "He should be here any moment." He added a bit more cream to his coffee.

"I'm supposed to be cutting back on this stuff, but really, at my age, what's the point? So where was I? Right. I was planning to finish up here this week. But I've only been here part-time for many years now. Gary, my assistant manager, has been doing a fantastic job, and he'll be the one that will be here walking you through everything. Paul has been running the show in the kitchen for the past twelve years now and doing a right fine job of it. He'll be joining us shortly. You all know Paul?"

"Of course," Emma began. "He was in my year in school." She didn't add that she and Paul had dated during their senior year, and after she ended things with him, they hadn't spoken since.

"Where did he work before this?" Mandy perked up now that they were discussing people instead of the restaurant itself.

"Paul came to us from Patsy's Bistro."

"That's a wonderful place! Cory and I used to go there often. Why did he leave?"

"Patsy and Paul were married for a few years. When they got divorced, Paul left. They were college sweethearts who grew apart. Luckily, they never had kids." He looked up and smiled as Paul walked into the room. "Speak of the devil. Paul, we were just talking about you."

"Oh no. Should I come back later?" His voice was deep and amused. He was taller than Emma remembered, though she realized he could have kept growing a bit after high school. He was a few inches over six feet and had the same thick dark brown hair. He met her gaze and smiled, and she remembered how she'd always loved his eyes. They were a pretty mix of gray and green.

"Have a seat. I was just telling the girls that you run the show here and that they'll be in good hands."

Paul sat in the empty chair next to Emma. He looked

around the table at everyone. "It's great to see you all again. I'm very sorry for your loss. Your grandmother was a special lady. I'm honored that she chose to remember me this way, and I'm looking forward to working with all of you. Mimi's Place is a great restaurant." He smiled and glanced around the table before adding, "Do any of you have restaurant experience?"

Emma spoke up first. "I do. As a server, mostly."

"That's great. Was it around here?"

"It was ages ago, actually, at the Barnacle on the Cape. I worked there several summers while I was in college. A group of us rented a place in Dennis Port."

"I worked part-time as a bartender during college. It was a fun job," Jill said.

Emma knew Jill had loved working at the Prickly Cactus. It was where she'd met Billy. They'd often worked the same shifts and became fast friends.

"That's great!" Paul seemed pleased that they had some restaurant experience, even if it wasn't managerial. He glanced at Mandy, waiting to see what she had to say.

"I don't have a drop of experience, unless you count organizing charity dinners and events," she said wryly.

"Actually, I would count that. We do a lot of parties and banquets here. Organizations like the Rotary Club, for example, come in regularly for their meetings, and there's the occasional wedding as well."

They chatted a bit longer and decided that it might make more sense and be less overwhelming for the staff if one of them went in at a time, rather than three people hovering around, getting in the way.

Paul's first impression of the women was positive. They seemed open and eager to learn. He'd worried a little that Jill might want to be in charge and make changes that he wasn't keen on, but he didn't get that sense after meeting with them. For sisters, they all looked so different. Mandy had blondish-brown hair and a ready smile. Jill was vibrant and striking with her long, almost black hair, and Emma was petite and slim with big brown eyes and shoulder-length light brown hair. He knew Mandy was married with children but didn't know much about Emma's or Jill's personal lives. He knew the transition was likely to be more difficult for both of them though, as they lived far from Nantucket.

As they stood to leave, Emma came over to him.

"So strange that we're together again. How have you been, Paul?"

He smiled, and Emma noticed that tiny lines danced around his eyes, but it looked attractive on him.

"I'm good. This should be an interesting year. How are you feeling about it? You've lived out west for years now?"

Emma laughed. "Interesting is the word for it. I have mixed feelings to be honest. A part of me is excited for the adventure, but I'm also nervous." She took a deep breath. "There's a lot of change for me right now. I'm getting a divorce, so staying on Nantucket for a while is a good thing."

He looked surprised. "I'm sorry to hear that."

"It's been hard, but it's for the best." She decided to change the subject as she wasn't ready to go into any details. "We had no idea that you worked at Mimi's Place or actually that my grandmother even owned it." Emma smiled. "She must have thought highly of you."

Paul's cheeks turned a little red. "Your grandmother was quite a woman. I'm honored that she chose to remember me this way. I certainly didn't expect it."

"Did you know she was the owner?"

"I did. A few of us met with her occasionally, and of course she came in to eat regularly."

Emma looked around the restaurant. "She really did love it here."

Paul followed her gaze. "She's not the only one." Emma wondered how she and her sisters would feel about Mimi's Place in a year.

Emma nodded as they reached Jill and Mandy. "It was really great to see you again, Paul. I'm sure we'll be talking again soon."

Jill's phone started to ring incessantly, and she dug around in her purse to find it. "Billy, did you hear back? Will they go up on the salary?"

Paul watched Emma and her sisters walk away as Jill chatted on the phone, oblivious to everything else. He tried to picture them all working in the restaurant and smiled. It was going to be interesting, for sure.

7

Emma was the first to start at the restaurant as Jill was still trying to iron out work issues and get her laptop connected to Grams's internet. She arrived at Mimi's Place at ten thirty and was going to be learning from Gary, the assistant manager, all about the front of the house operations. Downtown was busy with people walking along the cobblestone streets, many wearing sweatshirts with Nantucket emblazoned across the front. Though it was early, several were also carrying multiple shopping bags from the stores that lined the street.

The restaurant was quiet when she walked through the door. The only sounds were a faint radio in the kitchen and the hum of the dishwasher. She could see some activity— kitchen workers bringing in crates of produce and cartons of milk. Gary was waiting for her at the front desk with the book of reservations in front of him.

"This is one of my favorite times of day," he said with a smile. "The calm before the storm. When we prepare ourselves for what's on the lineup for the day. Coffee?"

"Thanks, I'd love some." Emma accepted the mug and added a bit of cream and sugar before joining Gary to look at the book.

"Today should be fairly straightforward. We have the Garden Society luncheon group coming at one. They come once a month, and there's only twenty or so of them. They're a breeze. You'll be amazed though by how much they drink in the afternoon. As long as their cocktails are flowing, all is well."

"Grams used to be in that group, I think."

"She was indeed."

"I did a little serving during school but never really handled the reservations or hosting."

"Well, the serving experience will come in handy." Gary looked pleased to hear it. "One of the biggest challenges with manning the front desk is controlling the timing and flow of customers to the tables. When possible, you try to avoid seating several parties in the same station at once, as that strains both the kitchen and the server."

"I used to hate that. We called it being 'in the weeds,' when all your tables needed you at once."

"It's not pleasant for the guest either, so we try to stagger new tables as much as possible and work in reserved ones as well. And then of course we have our special guests. We'll go over who they are and what you need to know."

"Regulars you mean?" Emma asked.

"Regulars yes, but there are also special guests who don't come in often, but we need to be aware that they are VIP status and make sure they are well taken care of. For instance, tonight we have Senator Jameson and the mayor coming in. They are VIPs."

"Got it." Emma smiled. "I imagine if things didn't go well for them, that kind of PR would be terrible."

"Exactly."

As Gary walked her through the reservations and pointed out any regulars or customers with special requests, the kitchen door suddenly opened, and the most delicious smell wafted out. Involuntarily, Emma's stomach growled, and she quickly took a big sip of coffee.

"Are they making eggplant parm?" she asked wistfully. It was one of her favorite dishes, and the scent of the roasted eggplants and rich tomato sauce was intoxicating.

"It might be a lunch special. Jason mentioned doing an eggplant rollatini today, like parmesan but rolled up and filled with ricotta. A bit like a savory cannoli."

Emma sighed, then realized that the look on her face must have spoken volumes, because Gary chuckled and said, "I think perhaps you need to try a little so you can describe it to a customer if they ask."

"Yes, in case a customer wants to know. What a good idea." Emma had a feeling she was going to like Gary. He disappeared into the kitchen and returned a moment later with two small plates, each with an eggplant rollatini smothered in sauce. They sat at the bar rather than risk dirtying one of the dining room tables that were covered in elegant white linen. They ate quickly, with Gary glancing at his watch every few minutes and continuing his tutorial between bites.

"How long have you worked here?" Emma inquired. She guessed that Gary was in his midforties and wondered what he'd done before coming to Mimi's Place.

"Forever," he said with a smile, and Emma liked the way his whole face lit up when he talked about working at Mimi's Place. "Actually, it will be twenty years next month. Time flies."

"Every year does seem to go by more quickly. Grams always said that it would once you got older. I never understood what she meant until recently. What did you do before Mimi's Place?"

"I was in college until we had some financial issues at home, and I had to get a job. Times were tight then. There were almost no jobs available to a kid like me without a degree and no experience of any kind. Your grandmother took a chance on me. My mother had been one of her students many years ago, and they were neighbors. I knew she put in a good word for me here, but I never knew until recently that she was actually the owner."

"We still can't quite believe it ourselves," Emma said with a chuckle.

"Mimi's Place has been really good to me. I started out in the kitchen, washing dishes. As you probably know, that's just about the lowest rung on the ladder in a restaurant. I was so grateful to have the job. I got lucky when one of the busboys was out sick. I filled in for him, and that went well. I think I've done just about every job here, except cook of course. I'm terrible in the kitchen. Ironic, isn't it? You'd think I'd learn by osmosis, but I think cooking is like singing. You either have the talent or you don't."

"I like to cook," Emma admitted. "I like to play around with recipes and try new dishes, but it's easier to cook for yourself. I couldn't imagine doing it for an entire restaurant." Emma actually thought it seemed terrifying. She used to marvel at the intricate dance the chefs in the kitchen did. How they coordinated the timing of multiple dishes and parties mystified her.

"In a well-run restaurant," Gary continued, "the front of the house and back of the house work in harmony. If it gets too chaotic out here, it can screw up the flow in the kitchen, and then we have a real mess. Fortunately, we have a well-oiled machine, and that rarely happens. Not on my watch anyway."

"I remember coming here for lunch with Grams, and the dining room would be absolutely packed. The energy was so exciting, with all the well-dressed customers and the hustle and bustle of food coming out of the kitchen and tables being cleared. It was always a treat, coming here with her."

Gary frowned and then smiled so quickly that Emma almost doubted what she'd seen.

"Is it still busy like that at lunch?" By the look of the reservation page, it seemed like they had a busy day ahead.

"Sometimes. Not often enough though," he admitted. "There's more competition now, more restaurants. Some of the newer ones are more appealing to the younger 'foodie' crowd. We've fallen off the radar some."

Emma took an objective look around the restaurant. The colors were warm and inviting, the table linens crisp, but the carpet was uninspired, a bit faded, and worn in spots. Emma wondered if it was just a symptom, a contributor to the overall ill health of the restaurant. She made a mental note to pay close attention to everything throughout lunch, at how many customers came in, what they ordered, and how happy or unhappy they seemed to be. She knew that Mandy had taken a copy of the restaurant's financials home to look over with Cory. They were both great at understanding the ins and outs of financial statements and profit and loss statements.

Jason, the lunch chef, came out of the kitchen a half hour later and handed a slip of paper to Gary with the day's luncheon specials.

"What did you think of the rollatini?" he asked Emma.

"Incredible. So delicious. Thank you."

"My pleasure." He turned to Gary. "What time does the Garden Society want their soup?"

"Not until one thirty. They want a full half hour with their cocktails before we interrupt them with food."

"Of course they do." Jason shook his head and strolled back into the kitchen.

"Has he been here long too?" Emma asked. She guessed that Jason was closing in on sixty.

"Not too long. Five years maybe? He worked all over the North End before moving here. I think he is a native Boston Italian. You can tell by his specials."

"Rollatini, braciole, and escarole and white bean soup with Italian sweet sausage. Oh, braciole, isn't that the meat that's stuffed and rolled up and then cooked for hours in a sauce?"

"That's it. Evidently the theme for today is rolls. You'll have to try a little of the braciole later this afternoon when we slow down. It sounds like a cliché, but it really does melt in your mouth."

The lunch service flew by. Gary had Emma take all the calls that came in. After each reservation, he checked the book and showed her how to plan and how to stagger them so that the guests wouldn't have to wait when they arrived and wouldn't feel rushed as they ate. It was a balancing act. Emma was grateful that Gary was being so patient with her and double-checking everything, because twice she needed to call a customer back and change the time slightly.

She was straightening out the pile of guest checks when one caught her eye. At the top of each check, the waiter always indicated the table number and size of the party. "Wow, this guy must have been really hungry." The amount of food he ordered would have fed two to three people comfortably.

"Let me see." A somewhat worried look came across Gary's face as he read off the items the guest had ordered. "Braciole and the rollatini plus the eggplant parm off the regular menu, escarole bean soup, Caesar salad, stuffed mushrooms, a side of ziti with marinara sauce, plus tiramisu and cheesecake?" He raised his eyebrows at Emma. "I suspect we had a food critic in today, and regretfully, I should have picked up on this while he was here. He must be new. I usually recognize them when they come in."

"Do you think we have anything to worry about? I'm sure everything he had was delicious."

"It's not just the food. Normally when someone orders like this, out of the ordinary for one person, we take note and assume that they may be a food critic or travel writer of some sort. So we'll just take extra care to make sure there are no glitches and that service goes smoothly."

"I think he was in during the busiest part of the lunch rush. I remember seating a single dark-haired man at the small table by the window. He seemed pleasant enough."

"We'll see." Gary smiled at Emma, but she could still see a hint of worry on his face.

8

Jill was having the day from hell. Just about everything that could possibly go wrong did.

She tried to dial in to the office for the Monday morning job-order meeting, but her phone kept disconnecting due to construction on the next street over. By the time it was working again, the meeting was long over. Her computer was driving her crazy too, due to Grams's painfully slow connection. She had called the cable company first thing that morning to upgrade to the high-speed network, but the earliest appointment they could give her was a week away.

By lunchtime, she just couldn't take it any longer. She packed up her laptop and cell phone and headed down the street to her favorite local coffee shop, which offered great sandwiches and soups and, best of all, free Wi-Fi. She called her office, had Jenna forward all her calls to her cell, then settled into an empty corner where she could plug in her laptop and hopefully not bother anyone. Interestingly, she noticed there were others also working on laptops and talking on cell phones. This could work.

She was in the middle of an interview with a star candidate when another call beeped through, and Billy's number flashed. She ignored it, figuring she could call him back when she was done. She thought it was rude to answer another call in the middle of an interview. But when he called again five minutes later, she apologized to her candidate and clicked over.

"What's up? Is something wrong?"

"No, I just wanted to see what you were doing. You didn't answer the first time I called." Billy was all charm, and she wanted to kill him.

"That's because I'm working. I'm on the line with a great candidate and only answered now because I figured if you called twice like that, it had to be important, an emergency even."

"What, talking to me isn't important?" he teased.

"I have to go. I'll call you later." She clicked back to her candidate, apologized again, and finished the interview. A minute later, her phone rang again, the main number from her office.

"Jill, it's Jenna. Just wanted to give you a heads-up that Roger Anderson just called in looking for you. I told him you were in a meeting and would call him right back. He said your candidate no-showed for his interview."

"Thanks. I'll find out what happened and call him right back."

After a half hour of tracking down the missing candidate, who somehow got the interview day mixed up, and rescheduling with the client, Jill finally had a chance to call Billy back.

"I thought you were ignoring me."

"No, just putting out fires, as usual. What's going on?"

"It's weird without you here. The energy level is down."

Jill chuckled. "Are you trying to say you miss me?"

"We all miss you."

"That's sweet, but I'm right here. I'm still working. This morning was just a glitch, and it was my first time dialing in. Once I'm regularly part of the meetings, even from a distance, it will be better."

"I suppose. It has to be, right?"

"It will be. I'll talk to you tomorrow. Go bill up a storm, would you please?"

"You got it."

Jill hung up the phone and then, feeling suddenly restless, took a walk up to the pastry counter and gave in to temptation. She settled back at her table and took a bite of the cherry strudel pastry. She wouldn't make a habit of it, but just for today, she felt she deserved a little treat. She didn't admit it to Billy, but she was already missing being in the office too. She missed the fast pace and the constant hum of people on the phone. After only a few days, she was missing everything—Billy most of all.

"So how was your day?" Mandy asked brightly. She'd just arrived at Grams's house and had a bottle of red wine and a casserole dish with something that smelled amazing.

"Fabulous," Jill lied. "What is that?" Mandy had called earlier and said she was bringing them dinner and was anxious to hear how things had gone for both Emma and Jill.

"Veggie lasagna. It's a new recipe. Low-cal but still tons of flavor. We'll see, I guess, right?"

"Well, it smells delicious," Emma said and started getting plates and silverware from the kitchen. They filled their plates and poured the wine, then settled comfortably at Grams's dining room table.

"So," Mandy began, "Emma, tell us everything. How was your day? What was it like? Should I be nervous about tomorrow?"

"No, don't be nervous. Gary is a doll. He'll walk you through everything," Emma assured her and told them all about her day, ending with the realization that they may have been visited by a food critic.

"Do you remember his name?" Mandy asked.

"Why? Are you up on who the local food critics are?" Jill asked, and Emma chuckled. She'd been wondering the same thing.

"I may recognize the name." Mandy seemed serious, so Emma tried to recall the name. It wasn't anything out of the ordinary.

"I don't remember his first name. Last name may have been Connor."

"I don't think he's a food critic." Mandy chewed her bottom lip for a moment, then continued. "He may be a consultant that Cory hired. I just didn't think he'd start so soon."

"Start what? Why would Cory hire a consultant to eat a bunch of food at our restaurant?" Jill sounded annoyed at Cory's interference but also curious to know what he was up to.

Mandy helped herself to another slice of lasagna before settling back into her seat and filling them in on news that she knew they wouldn't be happy about. "Well, you know how we brought the financials home to look through? I took the initial look and was concerned enough to ask Cory to review everything and advise us on what we should do."

"What's wrong?" Emma asked.

"Well, I was planning to tell you all this over dinner anyway, so here's the scoop. Mimi's Place is barely breaking even. For the past seven years, profits and overall revenues have been steadily decreasing from year to year, and expenses have gone up. Not a good combination."

"But nothing seems to have changed," Jill said. "Every time I've been there, it's been busy."

"Well, think about when we usually go," Mandy pointed out. "Almost always for a special occasion, which means a busy Saturday night, their best night."

"You're right." Emma looked thoughtful. "It's funny you mention that about nothing changing. It's like time has stood still there. The menu hasn't changed much over the years. I also noticed earlier today that while the room still has that cozy atmosphere, the carpet is looking a bit worn, and overall, it feels a little faded."

"So what did Cory suggest?" Jill asked, reaching for more salad.

"The Gordon Ramsay approach. You know that old show of his? Not the chef competition, the other one where he evaluates and fixes restaurants that aren't working?"

Emma smiled. "*Kitchen Nightmares*. It's a great show. Peter and I used to love watching it."

"That's it. So Cory did something similar. He knows a great restaurant consultant, someone his old company used when they were thinking of investing in a restaurant chain. He hired him to make a series of visits, try the food, see how the place operates, and then put together a recovery plan with ideas we can implement to turn things around."

"That sounds expensive." Emma's voice held a note of worry. "Where will the money come from?"

"Well, as Cory says, you have to spend money to make money. This will be investing in the business." Mandy could see the others were less enthused.

"Yes, but Emma has a good point. Where does the money come from for this investment?" Jill asked.

"Cory is paying for the consultant. But he also discovered that Mimi's Place has a line of credit that has barely been touched, and that's what we can tap into for any money we need to put into the restaurant changes."

"Oh good." Emma seemed relieved.

"Do we have any idea what we've gotten ourselves into?" Jill asked.

"Well, let's look at it like an adventure." Mandy smiled, reaching for her wine.

"You always did look on the bright side," Emma commented as she topped off her wineglass and, without asking, refilled Mandy's and Jill's glasses as well. "I admit, I did enjoy today at the restaurant. I loved the energy and the overall atmosphere and of course, the food."

"To an adventure." Jill lifted her glass, and the other two joined her, tapping glasses lightly.

—————

Mandy enjoyed working her lunch shift. Gary walked her through everything the way he had with Emma the day before, and she was happy to see that it was fairly busy and stayed steady throughout the afternoon. Or at least that was how it seemed to her. Gary apparently felt differently.

"Well, we were a little off again today. Lunches just haven't been as busy as they used to be."

"Really? Why is that, do you think?"

"Hard to say. The restaurant business is fickle. There's no real rhyme or reason to it. You can plan for a busy night and then be dead and vice versa. There's more competition than there used to be, for one thing. Plus, I think a lot of the business crowd comes less frequently than they used to.

They go for more casual lunches. Faster service so they can get in and out quickly and back to work. The days of the three-martini lunches are long gone."

"That makes sense," Mandy agreed. She pulled a menu from the stack at the front desk and browsed it for a moment. The selection was mouthwatering, as Mandy loved all things Italian, but looking over the dishes, she saw a familiar sameness there. Nothing new or surprising.

"When was the last time the menu was updated?" she asked.

Gary thought for a moment, then chuckled. "It's been years. Paul and Jason do their daily specials, but this has been the menu pretty much the entire time I've worked here. The only thing that has changed every few years is the prices."

"That's interesting." She thought of some of the restaurants that she and Cory frequented, where the menus seemed to change with the seasons.

"Why mess with success, I suppose?" Gary said with a smile as he reached to answer the phone. "Mimi's Place, how may I help you?"

"You may need to fire people," Cory said while buttering a piece of bread. He and Mandy had just sat down to dinner. They were eating outside on the deck so they could enjoy the ocean view and keep an eye on the kids. They had eaten earlier and were now in the backyard playing cornhole. They loved the simple game where they took turns tossing small beanbags at wooden angled boards that had a hole in the middle. It wasn't as easy as it looked, but it was a fun game, and Mandy smiled at the sound of their occasional laughter.

She had just finished telling Cory about her first day and how the menu was virtually untouched over the years.

"That's a bit unusual, don't you think? Plus, we haven't even heard from the consultant yet. He still has a few more visits before he'll make any recommendations, right?" she asked.

"Yes, but more than likely, that will be one of his suggestions. It usually is. There are always ways to cut back, and losing a few people makes a big impact quickly."

"I don't like it. We don't want to come in and ruffle feathers right off the bat. We need these people. Grams would not approve of layoffs." Mandy knew she'd hate it.

"I'm just planting the seed so you're not shocked when it's suggested as part of the recovery plan."

"Well, we'll see what else he suggests. We don't have to do everything he says, or not all at once anyway."

"Of course not," he agreed.

"Plus, we don't want to be shorthanded for the wedding." One of the highlights of her day had been when a young woman and her mother stopped in for lunch, and on the way out, they said they'd decided to book their wedding reception at Mimi's Place.

They were planning on around two hundred people, which would fill the entire restaurant when they opened the adjacent function room. It had an accordion-style folding door that could be opened to make for one giant room. Mimi's Place did a good number of weddings, and Mandy listened intently as Gary walked the two women through all the different options. This kind of event was right up her alley, and she felt confident that she could help make it a special day by making sure everything went smoothly.

"I'm going to run back to the office for a bit," Cory said as Mandy finished clearing the table and stacking the dishes in the dishwasher.

"Now? Why not just work here?" It was almost eight, and she felt about ready to drop. She was looking forward to putting on her softest pajamas, getting the kids tucked into bed, and curling up with a book for a bit before climbing into bed herself.

"I left the papers I need at the office, and I'll be able to focus there and get things done more quickly."

"Okay. Don't stay too late though." She kissed him on the cheek and watched as he walked out the front door. He was obsessed with work and had been as long as Mandy had known him. She foolishly thought that when he opened his own business, he'd have more flexibility and more time to relax, but it was exactly the opposite. He worked more hours now than he ever had before.

9

Jill's first shift at Mimi's Place was on Friday night. They'd agreed that while they'd split shifts so that one of them was always there, Jill would only work nights and the occasional weekend lunch shift so that she could still focus on her real job during the day. When she arrived at four o'clock sharp, Emma was on her way out, and Gary was finishing up as well, filling in Gina, the bartender and occasional night manager, on the reservations they'd taken earlier that day.

Jill had met Gary previously but not Gina. She was relatively new to Mimi's Place.

"It'll be a year next month," she said when Jill asked how long she'd been there.

"Where did you work before this?" She was curious about Gina's background. The girl was absolutely gorgeous with olive skin and wavy, almost black hair.

"I was at Via Mollo for ten years," she said proudly, and Jill was impressed. Via Mollo was one of the best Italian restaurants in Boston. Which made her wonder why Gina would leave there and come here. As much as they all loved Mimi's Place, it seemed like a step down.

"What made you decide to make the move? Via Mollo is a wonderful restaurant." Via Mollo had great food, but their service was exceptional. Customers really felt pampered.

"It was time. I wanted a change, a more relaxed environment. I fell in love with Nantucket, and I like the people here."

Jill was fascinated at the expressions that raced across Gina's face as she spoke. Hesitation initially, and a hint of wariness in her eyes that gave Jill the sense that there was more there than Gina was willing to say. When she spoke of liking the environment and the people at Mimi's Place though, her smile reached her eyes and lit up even more when she gave Jason a thumbs-up as he walked by. His face flushed a deep crimson, and Jill chuckled. "I think you just made his night."

"Jason's a doll. He brought me a sample of tonight's special, the short ribs, just before you arrived, and they melted in my mouth. We should run in the kitchen and get you a quick taste too." Gina twisted her hair into a loose knot, securing it with a pen from her apron pocket, and then ran an earthy red lipstick across her lips. "Okay, let's go."

They went into the kitchen, which was quiet as the dinner rush hadn't started yet, but the cooks were busy getting ready, making trays of dinner salads and checking sauces and other prep items on their stations. Jason was gone, but Paul was behind the line.

"Can we get a sampling of the ribs for Jill? I told her she had to taste them. Jason outdid himself."

Paul grinned. "Sure thing. Here you go." He handed Jill a small plate with a one-inch-square boneless short rib sitting on creamy mashed potatoes. Jill had eaten a sandwich before heading in for the night so she wasn't hungry, but she still inhaled the short ribs. The sauce was rich and silky with a hint of red wine.

"These are incredible. Do you have short ribs on the menu?"

"No, they're just a special. They're pretty popular though. We have them often," Paul said.

Jill practically ran to keep up with Gina all night. Her style was very different from Gary's—just as professional but oozing charm. Watching Gina interact with the customers, Jill realized that she was a huge asset. Her training from Via Mollo gave her sophistication but also a warmth that the customers responded to. It was something that she often saw in the best restaurants, a very subtle way of seeming to know and recognize every customer that walked through the door, even if it was their first time in the restaurant.

"Mr. and Mrs. Dennison, we're so happy to have you here tonight. We have a fantastic quiet table by the rear window for you that I think you'll love. It will be ready in just a moment."

"Oh, that sounds wonderful." Mrs. Dennison turned to her husband. "I'm so glad we finally made it here. The Kelleys have been raving about this place recently."

Gina led the couple to their table moments later, and Jill complimented her once she returned to the front desk.

"I love how you make everyone feel special when they arrive, even if it's their first time. People seem to really respond to that."

Gina looked pleased with the compliment. "Thanks. It's something I learned at Via Mollo." She looked around the dining room. They had a moment of calm before the wave of people were due to arrive.

It lasted about a minute before the first disaster of the night happened. Tina, the bartender on duty who had been with the restaurant for years, hurt herself cutting fruit garnishes. The sharp paring knife slipped and went into the soft skin at the vee at the base of her thumb. It went through almost to the bone, and she must have nicked a vein, because the gushing wouldn't stop, and Tina nearly passed out at the sight of all the blood. Gina took charge immediately and called a cab to take her to the emergency room at the Nantucket Hospital to get it stitched up.

"Great, now I need to call Stacy in, and she worked a double yesterday. I hate to do that to her."

"I can do it," Jill said.

Gina raised her eyebrows but looked hopeful. "When was the last time you tended bar?"

"A number of years ago, but I was good and fast, and I doubt it's changed very much."

Gina glanced at the reservations book. It wasn't full by any means, which was surprising considering it was the weekend.

"Okay. Let's give it a shot. If you need help though, just give me a shout, and I'll figure something out." She spent the next ten minutes showing Jill the layout of the bar and how to work the register. It was a fairly small bar, with twelve stools and a service area. Jill studied the different wines and descriptions from the bar menu and then poured herself a shot of cola. A bit of sugar and caffeine was definitely in order.

Any nervousness she felt quickly melted away once the customers started coming in and the waitresses lined up at the service bar. Jill stumbled a little at first until she got her bearings and remembered the location of the various liquors and wines, and then she was in the zone where you don't think about things, you just react and produce. She'd always been good at multitasking, juggling customers and multiple orders at once. These were the skills of a good bartender, someone who had a feel for when a customer was ready for a refill or in the mood for a bit of chitchat. Bartenders and waiters tended to do well in the world of headhunting, where multitasking was a given and people skills a must.

Gina stopped by an hour into dinner service to give her a compliment. "You're really good."

She sounded so surprised that Jill couldn't help but

laugh. "I used to have a blast bartending in college. I really missed it for a while."

"Well, you're a natural. We can use you behind the bar any time you're willing." And then she was off, back to new arrivals coming through the door.

Most of Jill's business came from the service bar. Only half of the barstools were full, and they were mostly just people waiting for a table to open for dinner. But a new arrival settled in while she was making a tray of martinis for one of the waitresses. A single guy about her age, if she had to guess, and quite good looking with dark wavy hair and a square jaw.

He had a notebook in front of him and was flipping through the pages as she walked toward him. He looked up and smiled, and Jill caught her breath for a moment. He was seriously hot. Dark brown eyes that were almost black, a strong nose that looked as though it had been broken at least once, and those tiny laugh lines around the eyes that looked so much better on men.

"Hi there. What can I get for you?"

"A Harpoon IPA, please, and a dinner menu."

Jill handed him a menu and poured his draft beer, taking care to have just the right amount of creamy foam on top. "Here you go. We have a few specials tonight as well. Lobster ravioli and braised short ribs. Soup is a butternut squash bisque with asiago croutons."

"How do the short ribs look?" he asked casually, and Jill smiled, thinking of the ribs.

"They're great. Meaty and tender in a silky reduction sauce that has incredible flavor. They're served on mashed potatoes."

"I'll have that, the lobster ravioli, a side of broccoli rabe, and the soup to start. Oh, and an order of the antipasto misto."

"I'll put that right in for you." Jill punched the order into the computer, then set silverware, a napkin, a place mat, and a bread plate in front of the relatively thin man who'd just ordered a massive quantity of food. She waved at Gina to meet her in the kitchen.

"What is it? Is everything all right?" Gina looked puzzled as the rush was pretty much over and the bar practically empty.

"Just a heads-up. That guy at the bar just ordered a lot of food. Two meals, two appetizers, and a side dish. Mandy said the same thing happened the other day, and Gary emphasized that you'd want to know in case he's a food critic or something."

"Doesn't look like one to me, though you never know. I'll tell Paul so he can make sure everything looks perfect."

Jill poured a cup of the soup, topped it with the croutons, and dropped two hot rolls into a small basket, along with a few pats of butter. She returned to the bar and set everything down in front of her very interesting customer, who was busy jotting something in his notebook.

"Here you go. Enjoy."

"Thanks." He smiled briefly and continued to write.

Jill wandered off to the other end of the bar where two older gentlemen looked ready for a bit of conversation and another cocktail.

An hour later, she cleared away the last dinner plate from the mystery man. He ate silently and sparingly, eating maybe half of everything on his plate. "Can I pack any of this up for you?" It seemed a shame to throw so much food out.

He hesitated for a moment before saying, "Sure, pack it up."

"Dessert?" she asked, assuming he'd say no, but again, he surprised her.

"Yeah, I'll have a cannoli and a slice of the tiramisu. And an espresso please."

"Sure thing." Jill carefully made the espresso for him, adding a sliver of lemon rind as garnish, then went into the kitchen to pick up his desserts.

"Two desserts, huh?" Paul said. "Did he seem to like his meals?"

"I think so. He's taking the leftovers with him."

She wasn't surprised to see that once again, just a few bites were taken out of each dessert.

"I hope you enjoyed everything?" Jill was curious for any information she could get. So far, he hadn't given anything away.

"The food was very good. Portions a little big though, but no one ever complains about that, I'm sure." That was the most he'd said all night. Jill was about to get the conversation rolling when he nipped it in the bud. "I'll take a check, please."

"Of course." She turned to the computer, pulled up his check, and printed it out. Out of the corner of her eye, she saw him hold a slim cell phone up. He was taking pictures of the carpet. That was when it clicked, and she knew that he wasn't a food critic.

"Do you know Cory Lawson by any chance?" she asked, putting the check into a soft leather folder and placing it in front of him.

He seemed surprised by the question. "I do know Cory, but I'm sure I'd remember meeting you."

"No, we haven't met. I'm his wife's sister. She was telling us about you the other night. That Cory had hired a restaurant consultant."

He grinned and held out his hand. "Macaulay Connor. My friends call me Mac. Nice to meet you."

"Jill O'Toole." She shook his hand and enjoyed the feel of his warmth against hers. He had a firm handshake, very much in control.

"I'll call next week to set up another visit. I like to do the first few sort of incognito, to get a true sense of the food and the restaurant's rhythm on a given night. Next time I come in, I'd like to meet your staff and get a good look at the kitchen."

"Great, I look forward to it," Jill said brightly, though inwardly, she had mixed feelings. She was looking forward to seeing Mac again but worried about what he might find and what he might want them to do at Mimi's Place. Though she wasn't as financially astute as Cory, she knew enough about running her own business to know that sometimes you had to make difficult choices.

10

By the following week, they had settled into a regular schedule of sorts. Mandy worked the lunch shifts, so her hours were mostly when the kids were in school. If she knew ahead of time that she was going to need to stay longer, she could always put them into extended day session or, in a pinch, call one of her sisters to pick them up. Jill worked mostly evenings and usually helped at the bar. She liked the way the night flew by, especially when they were busy.

Emma was still trying to figure out where she fit best in the restaurant. Because she'd previously worked both as a server and behind the bar, she was able to jump in wherever they had a hole that needed to be plugged, even in the kitchen where she manned the salad and dessert stations, plated cheesecakes, and chopped vegetables for the salad.

Her schedule varied depending on what was going on each day and was mostly nights with a few days here and there. She was starting to enjoy having her days free and spending time wandering around Nantucket. It was both familiar and new and different at the same time as it had been so long since she'd lived there. One of her favorite discoveries was a tiny coffee shop just off Main Street. She'd stumbled into My Favorite Cup when walking around one day.

Although the coffee was excellent, what Emma really liked was the feel of the place. It was very cozy and artsy, with original art and photographs on the walls, posters for creative events, and eclectic furniture, none of it matching. She settled into a worn and buttery-soft leather chair, set down her steaming coffee and toasted bagel, and plugged in her laptop. All around her, people were tapping away on keyboards or chatting into cell phones. There was an interesting assortment of people—several power-suit types, checking email on their phones, while the rest of the clientele seemed to be a mix of tourists, moms with small children, and more creative types, the group that Emma felt a part of.

She ate most of her bagel while her laptop was booting up and thought about the project she was embarking on. She'd decided to start a blog of sorts to go with her website. She had a very basic website that one of Peter's friends had designed for her about a year ago. It had some of her best photographs along with a bio and contact information. When she was in Arizona, almost all her work came through word of mouth, so the website was just a formality, a place people could go to easily get her contact information by simply googling her name. She worked on her site for a while, and once she had everything looking the way she'd envisioned it, she turned her attention to her next project.

Her other idea was for another blog, a food/photo blog, that would feature her recipes and photos of dishes she tried to create and possibly pictures and features on Mimi's Place. She hadn't run that idea by the others yet though. They were due to catch up Sunday afternoon for brunch. Mandy had suggested they get together to go over the consultant's preliminary suggestions and to compare notes on how the first full week had gone.

Emma figured the food blog would be a no-brainer, especially since the website for Mimi's Place, like its menu, hadn't been updated in several years. She wrote a couple of sample posts and was deliberating which font to go with when a sudden bump of her chair caused her coffee to spill a bit.

"I'm so sorry. Let me grab you a napkin." The tall man in front of her was apologetic and strangely familiar. Emma placed him in an instant.

"Veal parmesan, extra sauce on the side, right?" He'd come in twice for lunch last week—once alone and another time with what Emma guessed were several coworkers.

"Yes! Great memory." He quickly grabbed a paper

napkin from a nearby coffee stand, blotted up the small amount of spilled coffee, and then held out his hand and introduced himself. "John Bigley. The accounting firm I work for is a block away, just off Main Street. Guess you could say I'm a regular."

"I'm Emma. My sisters and I are the new owners of Mimi's Place, and we definitely appreciate our regulars." He still seemed a bit nervous, so she tried to make him feel at ease. "Don't worry about the coffee. I only spilled a drop, and it was getting cold anyway. I've been here awhile, and that was my third cup. I'm well caffeinated." She smiled and was glad to see him relax a bit. He was kind of cute if you liked the clean-cut preppy type.

He was about six feet tall and was wearing a pale blue oxford shirt tucked into well-worn jeans. His hair was sandy blond and very short, as if he'd just had a cut. He was probably about her age, and if she was looking, he was the type she might go for. But of course she wasn't—looking, that is. And because of that, she wasn't nearly as nervous as she would have been otherwise.

"Are you sure? I was just heading up to get in line. I'd be happy to pick up a hot cup for you," he offered.

"No, I'm good, thanks. I'm going to be heading out shortly." She looked at her watch and sat up in surprise at the time. Several hours had flown by since she'd first arrived at the café, and she was due at the restaurant in a half hour. "I didn't realize how late it was. I have to run."

"Right. Well, I'll see you next week, I'm sure."

He went to join the coffee line, and Emma gathered up her stuff. She was going to have to race to make it to Mimi's Place by three and relieve Mandy, who had to pick up the kids. It was a juggling act, but between the three of them, they were managing to make it work so far.

———————

Paul worked one lunch shift each week to give Jason a day off and also to give himself a night off. He was writing out the daily specials list when Mandy walked into the kitchen and looked around until she saw him and made her way over to him.

"I have something I need to tell you." Mandy paused and seemed somewhat hesitant.

"What is it?"

She took a deep breath before continuing. "So my husband, Cory, hired a consultant to come in here a few times and then make some recommendations for how we can improve the business."

Paul immediately felt defensive. "What's wrong with the business?"

Mandy met his gaze. "Have you read over the financials?"

"No, not yet." They were in a folder with all the other paperwork that he'd been given, and he hadn't looked at them yet. He'd never been a numbers person.

"Well, sales are down, and costs are up, and this is what

Cory does, evaluates businesses. He hired the guy as a gift for all of us."

Paul still wasn't sure if he liked the sound of it.

"What kind of changes is he going to want?"

"I'm not sure. He's going to come in a few times to eat, and he'd like to be able to walk around the whole restaurant, including the kitchen, just to see everything. This is all he does, help restaurants reinvent themselves. And it's just going to be observations and suggestions. We'll review everything, and then the four of us will decide what, if anything, we want to do."

Paul relaxed a bit. "Okay, he can walk around. I suppose it will be interesting to see what he has to say." He'd suggested updating the menu a few times over the years, but when Ray ran the idea by Rose, she never wanted it changed. Instead they agreed to allow him to be as creative as he wanted with the specials. When an item like the short ribs was consistently popular, he just kept it in the regular rotation, and that had seemed to work fine. But maybe it was time for some changes, including an overhaul of the menu, if sales were down as much as Mandy implied. He'd have to open that folder when he got home and take a closer look.

When Emma arrived at the restaurant, Mandy was organizing lunch checks at the front desk. She looked up and smiled when she saw Emma.

"Thanks for agreeing to come in a bit earlier. Brooke is starting a new dance class today."

"No problem. How was lunch? Was it busy?" Emma glanced around the nearly empty dining room, which wasn't really a good indicator since they were in between lunch and dinner.

"It wasn't too bad. We had a bit of a rush earlier. Gary experimented with putting a sign outside listing the day's specials, so it may have been that, or just warmer than usual weather. You never know, right?"

Mandy left a moment later, and Emma poked her head in the kitchen to say hello to Paul. "I heard your lunch specials were a big hit," Emma said, helping herself to a roll and butter.

"We'll see how they do tonight. That will be the real test," Paul said, but he was smiling, and Emma could tell he was pleased. "We're also adding a butternut squash tortelloni with toasted walnuts, prosciutto, and a cream sauce with a little gorgonzola."

"Yum." Emma bit into her roll, and then her stomach did a giddy dance as Paul pushed a small dish of the pasta special toward her. "I really shouldn't," she protested weakly and dug her fork into the creamy sauce. As anticipated, the contrast of flavors and textures was delicious.

"Now you can sell it to the customers."

And she did. Emma loved when she was asked what was good and what she'd recommend. She didn't hesitate to give her honest opinion. If there was a dish she loved, she raved about it. If there was one that she was less crazy about such as the surf and turf, which in her opinion had a too small and thin steak, she'd truthfully say something like "It's an excellent steak, but if you're very hungry, it's not an oversize portion. You might enjoy the New York strip instead."

As it happened, she said exactly that when Mandy's consultant came in again and insisted on ordering the surf and turf anyway, along with the steak she did recommend and the pasta special. By now, most of the employees knew he was some kind of consultant, and since no one knew what he was likely to suggest changing, they all still treated him as if he were a food critic, walking on eggshells to make sure everything went as smoothly as possible. He stayed for several hours, didn't bother to take his leftovers home and, after eating, spent a bit of time in the kitchen, observing quietly and browsing through the walk-in refrigerator and oversize pantry area.

He finished up with a draft beer at the bar and must have written at least a dozen or so pages of notes. Emma knew he was there to help them, but she still couldn't help feeling a bit nervous, especially if one of his suggestions was to trim the staff. She wanted to make sure that the positive work environment that Grams had been so proud of stayed intact.

At the end of the night, when most of the staff had left, Emma joined Gary and Paul at the bar for an after-shift drink. Paul ended up working a double as his sous chef called out sick. Talk turned to the consultant as both Gary and Paul were curious about him.

"What did he think of the food?" Paul asked.

"He seemed to like everything, but I think he liked the pasta the best. It was the only meal he finished."

Paul smiled. "That's good to hear."

Gary's phone buzzed, and he glanced down at a text message and frowned.

"I have to run. Maria needs me to stop at the store on the way home. I'll catch up with you both later." He took a big sip of his beer, then dumped the rest of it in the sink and headed out.

Paul sipped his draft beer and looked at Emma thoughtfully.

"So how is it going? This is a huge change for all of you."

Emma nodded. "It is. It's probably the most challenging for Jill, as she still has her business going in New York and is trying to juggle that during the day. For Mandy and me, it's actually a godsend. We both needed something new. I love the fast pace. And during the day, I can still do some of my photography."

"I didn't know you were into photography. Did you do that full-time?"

"No. I was a teacher in Arizona. I always did photography on the side. I actually had an idea for how I might be able to tie it into the restaurant." She told him about her website and food blog. "What do you think of me taking some pictures of you and your signature dishes and maybe sharing a recipe or two on the blog? I could link it to social media like Instagram and Facebook. It might be a way to help get the word out."

Paul looked intrigued. "I like it. Let me think about what might be a good dish to start with, and you can pop by to take some pictures. Do you like to cook too?"

"I do. Just as a hobby though. The thought of doing it for hundreds of people like you do is intimidating." Emma took a sip of her chardonnay. "I never knew you wanted to be a chef. I thought you might go into the family business after college." Paul's family ran a clothing store on Main Street.

He made a face at the thought. "I hate retail. I sort of fell into restaurant work. After graduating from college, I spent the summer working in the kitchen at the Straight Wharf. It was just supposed to be temporary, but I fell in love with it and decided to go to culinary school. That's where I met Patsy, and a year later, we were married."

"That was fast." Emma knew he'd married but didn't know the history of it.

"We probably never should have gotten married," Paul admitted. "We're very different. Patsy is loud and passionate and the life of the party. She was fun to be around. When she got pregnant, it seemed like the thing to do."

Emma was surprised. "Oh, I didn't realize you had children."

"I don't. She miscarried a month after we got married. It became apparent not too long after we started the restaurant together that we weren't well suited. Patsy was somewhat difficult to work with. I'm sure I was too. It just wasn't a good match."

"I'm sorry that didn't work out. Divorce is hard."

"Yeah, it is. It was a long time ago for me though." He grinned. "I'm over it now. I'm sorry that you are going through it. You were married a lot longer than I was."

Emma sighed. "Almost fifteen years. And I thought we were happy. Well, happy enough. Looking back now, I realize we were probably more like roommates, but we were always great friends."

Paul opened his mouth as if he was going to ask a question but then thought better of it and took a sip of his drink instead. She guessed he'd been about to ask why they got divorced.

"He left me for another man. His best friend from college. I had no idea, none. I think I'm still a little bit in shock."

Paul set his drink down and met Emma's gaze. "Em, I am so sorry. Jeez. I can't imagine."

"I know, right? How could I not have known?" She explained how Peter and Tom had reconnected when Tom took a job in town. "He said they'd experimented in college but realized it was more than that when they saw each other again."

"So how are you doing? That must be difficult to process."

Emma laughed. "That's an understatement. It makes you question everything. In a weird way, I suppose it's a little better than if it had been another woman? I don't know. I'll just say I'm in no hurry to get into another relationship any time soon."

Paul nodded. "I bet. It was close to a year before I dated after the divorce."

Emma wondered if there was anyone serious in his life now. She noticed there was no ring on his finger, but she knew that some people didn't always wear their rings when they worked with their hands.

He must have seen the question on her face. "I still don't date much. Nothing serious anyway. It's hard with the hours I work. I have a cat though. He's good company."

Emma smiled. She remembered that Paul had always loved animals.

"I'm tempted to get a cat too. I'll have to run that by Jill as we're both staying at my grandmother's place."

"If you do decide to get one, let me know. I can give you the name of the shelter I went to."

"I'll do that." Emma glanced at the clock and tried to hold back a yawn. She was enjoying catching up with Paul, but it had been a long day. "I should probably get going. I didn't realize how late it was."

Paul took the last sip of his drink. "Same here. I'll walk you out."

———

Mandy pulled into her driveway at a little past five. As the garage door opened, she was surprised to see Cory's car already there. He was rarely home from work this early.

"Kids, go get changed, and start your homework," she said as they walked through the door. "I'll call you when dinner's ready."

Mandy hung her coat up and headed into the kitchen. The house was silent except for the sounds of the children as they ran upstairs. The door to the downstairs study/office was open a crack, and it was so quiet that Mandy thought the room was empty and that Cory must be up in his bedroom. But then she heard a familiar chuckle and his voice, but he was talking so softly that she couldn't make out any words. She poked her head in the door, and when Cory turned, she waved hello.

"Excuse me," he said to whoever was on the phone and looked up at Mandy. "I'll be off in a minute." He seemed annoyed at the interruption.

"Take your time. I just wanted to say hello and that dinner will be in about a half hour." Without waiting for a reply, she backed out of the room and closed the door behind her. He was so grouchy lately.

She got busy in the kitchen, heating up leftover spaghetti sauce and meatballs and putting a pot of water on the stove to boil the pasta. Once the spaghetti was ready, she fixed plates for the kids and for herself and Cory and set everything on the table, along with butter and a loaf of soft Italian bread.

She called upstairs to the kids when dinner was ready

and knocked softly on the door to Cory's office. A few minutes later, they were all gathered around the table and had a nice family meal. Brooke excitedly told Cory about her new dance class, and Blake announced that he'd made an A on his math test earlier that day. Mandy relaxed and dug into her pasta. Once everyone finished and the kids had bolted from the table, Mandy poured herself a small glass of red wine and offered some to Cory.

"No, thanks. I need to get back to work for a few more hours. That will just put me to sleep."

"I thought it was odd that you were home so early. I should have known you weren't done working."

"There was too much commotion at the office, construction on the floor above us. I've actually been home since noon, just working from here."

"You work too much," Mandy began. "Isn't it time that you hired someone that can take on some of the stuff that bogs you down?"

Cory ran a hand through his hair and sighed. "We were just talking about that this morning. Both of us are feeling burned out and agreed that we need to delegate more. Soon though. I'm actually heading out to a conference next week for a few days and might do some informal recruiting there to get the word out."

"What kind of conference?" Cory had never gone to a conference before, so it was a bit of a surprise.

"It's an industry networking and strategy brainstorming kind of thing. It was recommended by my old boss at BBH, and I'm really looking forward to it. It'll be nice to have a few days 'off' so to speak."

"Will you close the office then? How will you manage?" Mandy wondered out loud.

"We're not both going. Patrick will hold down the fort for a few days, and I'll fill him in on everything I learn when I get back. Plus, it's in Vegas." His smile reminded Mandy of an excited little boy. "I've always wanted to go there."

11

Jill ordered a glass of chardonnay as soon as the flight attendant came through the cabin. She'd worked the lunch shift that afternoon, then quickly showered and changed and raced to make a five thirty flight. She was meeting Billy for dinner and spending the next day at the office. Fridays were usually a quieter day, and Jill knew that her presence would hopefully kick things up a notch. The JetBlue flight from Nantucket to New York was just over an hour, and she was looking forward to relaxing and calming her nerves.

She was actually nervous about seeing Billy, which was ridiculous since they were so close, but her new feelings for him were confusing and exciting and terrifying all at once. Billy had never really given her "that vibe" before, the one you get when you know a guy is interested, but she would have thought it strange if he had, given that they were such good friends and business partners. She'd never given him the slightest inclination of interest either, so she knew she had to do this carefully, to test the waters first.

She actually thought it might help that she was working in Nantucket for a while. Having some distance from Billy and the day-to-day environment of the office would give her some privacy and also the necessary time to sort out her feelings. She also hoped that Billy might miss her being around and perhaps be open to seeing things in a new light. The first step in her plan was going to take place that night. She was meeting him for dinner at one of their favorite restaurants, Rosa Mexicano, at the Upper East Side location. The restaurant was dark and cozy, and the upscale Mexican food was delicious.

Jill wore her favorite dress. It was a deep ruby red and flattering with a formfitting cut that was a bit shorter than usual and showed off her legs, and she was wearing a pair of very cute high heels. She'd blown her hair dry just before leaving for the airport, and it fell in fluffy, layered waves just past her shoulders. She'd kept her makeup light, just a coat of rich black mascara to make her lashes lush and her eyes pop and her favorite glossy rose lipstick that had magic lip-plumping abilities. She wanted Billy to notice her in a new way tonight.

Jill took the last sip of her wine as the plane started its descent. Within minutes, they were on the ground, and after jumping in a cab, she was at the restaurant right on time. Billy was already there, waiting for her at the bar.

"Hello, gorgeous!" He pulled her in for a hug and a kiss on the cheek. "Have a seat and a margarita. I think we have a few more minutes until our table is ready."

Jill settled herself in the seat next to Billy and took her coat off.

When he saw her dress, Billy whistled softly and said, "You look fantastic. Nantucket seems to be agreeing with you."

She smiled. "Thank you. I can't wait for you to visit soon. Remember, we have several guest rooms at Grams's house."

"I'm counting on it. Not next weekend, but maybe the weekend after, if that works for you?"

"I'll plan on it. So fill me in on what's going on. How are things?"

For the next twenty minutes, just up until they were called for their table, Billy filled her in on what was going on in the office, how the month was looking, and what issues he needed advice on. The minutes flew by as Jill realized that even though she was connected via the internet and phone, she was still missing the pulse of the business and being up on the day-to-day operations of the office. She and Billy spoke a few times a week, and it didn't feel like enough.

"We need to talk more often."

"Well, it's not like you're down the hall. Things are different now," Billy said.

"I know, but it's a work in progress. If we talk more often, I'll have a better sense of what's going on and how I can help."

"Okay, let's make a plan then to connect at least once a day, to debrief and say hello." Billy lifted his margarita, and Jill did the same, tapping her glass against his.

The hostess came a moment later and led them to a cozy table for two, tucked away in a secluded alcove. Jill sunk into one of the plush oversize chairs that were more like mini sofas, covered in a soft brushed suede.

Once they were both settled, Billy flipped open his menu. "So on to more important matters. What are you going to have?"

Jill was about to answer when the waitress appeared and told them about several specials. When she left to get them another round of margaritas, Jill said to Billy, "Too many choices, and they all sound good. What are you getting?"

"Well, the guacamole to start, don't you think?" That was a given, as they always ordered it. The server made it table-side, crushing fresh avocados in a stone bowl, along with tomato, onion, cilantro, and jalapeño to taste. Jill loved watching them make it, and it was how she'd learned to do it herself as well.

"I'm going to have the chili rellenos, I think." She'd had them the last time she was there and had been craving the plump peppers bursting with gooey cheese and raisins and sauce ever since.

"I'm going to try the seafood enchiladas. Just to be different."

The food was amazing as usual, and when they finished,

they adjourned back to the bar for Mexican coffees, a mix of liqueurs, coffee, and fresh whipped cream.

Jill had a warm glow going by this point and a hint of courage. She found herself laughing more than usual and touching Billy's arm to make several points. He seemed a bit confused by her behavior.

"Do you want to come back to my place for a drink?" she asked as they walked out the front door.

Billy raised his eyebrows and said, "I think someone has had her limit. Let's get you in a cab and home. I'll see you in the office tomorrow." He touched her arm gently and guided her into the nearest cab. "I'll catch the next one." They were going in opposite directions.

"Okay. I am kind of tired." And she was suddenly bone-tired. The week had caught up with her. Just going home and going to bed was very appealing. Tomorrow was another day.

Morning came way too quickly. Jill drank several glasses of water and was halfway through an extra-large dark roast coffee when her cab pulled up in front of the office. She'd had more to drink the night before than she usually did, and it was just enough to ensure that she wasn't at a hundred percent. And she needed to be.

The office was starting to buzz a little as she walked through the hallways and toward her office. People were arriving, settling in, and a handful, the early risers, were already on the phone. Heads turned in surprise when she walked past, as her appearance was not expected. Fridays were generally the most laid-back day of the week, but Jill knew that with both she and Billy on the floor, that wouldn't be the case.

In her company as well as the larger firm she and Billy used to work at, the intensity level was always higher when the managers were in the office, and especially when they were actually "working a desk" along with their employees. That was one thing that she and Billy were both in agreement on when they decided to start their company. They would never be hands-off managers—telling people what to do but not actually doing it. They wanted to lead by example, showing them how to do it.

Jill wasn't at her desk for more than a few minutes when she was asked to put out the first fire of the day. She sipped the last bit of her coffee as two of her employees peeked into Billy's office first, and when they saw he wasn't in yet, they walked back toward hers. That was understandable, of course, as they were now used to going to Billy first.

"What's up guys?" Jill asked as Tony and Nicole hovered outside her door.

"We hate to bother you so early, but do you have a minute? It's kind of important," Nicole asked.

"Of course. Come in. Have a seat."

Once they were settled in the two chairs in front of Jill's

desk, Nicole glanced at Tony nervously, and he began to talk.

"You know the MacGregor placement, the big one?"

"Of course, you both did a great job on that." The two exchanged glances, and Jill guessed they'd run into an issue. There were so many moving parts to any placement, some more so than others, that you really couldn't consider your work done until the person had actually started and stayed in the role for several months.

"Well, he's due to start on Monday," Nicole began. "Today was supposed to be his last day."

Tony leaned forward and added, "His boss took him to lunch and presented a ridiculous counteroffer. Told him he's important to the success of the company and they can't do it without him. He's incredibly flattered and confused."

"He called you and told you this?" Jill asked, and they both nodded.

"He's your candidate, right, Nicole? Did you have a talk with him at the beginning about this?" Jill asked. It was what she trained all new people to do, to defuse the possible counteroffer issue from the outset. If people expected to receive one, it wasn't usually as effective when it actually arrived.

"Yes. I told him to expect a counteroffer. I also stressed that they wouldn't want to lose him and that this is very inconvenient for his company. He assured me that they'd never give him one because he asked for a raise and promotion a few months ago, and they turned him down flat, said there was no money budgeted. And when he gave his notice, they didn't do anything then, so I thought we were safe."

"Then you can relax. He's probably just flattered. If he's smart, he'll realize what's going on."

"So what do we do now though?" Tony did not look at all relaxed.

Jill felt for them. She had been in their shoes many times and knew well the feeling of panic when something that was supposedly all set threatened to go south. She had a good feeling about this one though. It sounded like they'd done things the right way. Covering everything ahead of time was essential in smoothing over rough patches that developed.

"How did he leave things with you?" Jill asked Nicole, who seemed a bit calmer.

"He said he was flattered but had to give their offer serious consideration. That it would only be fair. He's calling me this morning."

"Okay. Sit tight then, and wait for his call. If you don't hear from him by noon, call him. If you need to, remind him why he was looking and that in most cases, nothing will change. He'll likely be regretting his decision if he stays."

Nicole grinned and then said, "I said all of that to him last night."

"Great, then you should be good. If not, I'll be here. Keep me posted."

Jill walked them out of the office and then wandered to the kitchen to find more coffee, feeling like she'd barely had a drop. She was filling her mug and sensed Billy before she actually saw him.

"How are you feeling this morning?" he asked softly as she turned to leave the kitchen.

"Tired. Maybe a little hungover," she admitted.

"Well, you're in good company. The day will go quickly. Before you know it, we'll be ready for after-work drinks."

"Ugh…I don't know about that."

———————————

Funny how what she didn't think was possible at eight thirty in the morning seemed like a good idea at the end of the day. By six, Jill and Billy, along with Tony, Nicole, and a half dozen others from the office, were at their favorite bar around the corner. It was a tiny place, just below street level in an elegant old hotel. They loved it because when they first opened the office, it was where they celebrated at the end of their first day, and they'd been coming back ever since.

The bar was small and dark but plush, with soft leather-cushioned chairs and a polished cherrywood bar. The lighting was low, the drapes were deep burgundy, and black suits dominated. From where they sat, taking up the corner of the bar, Jill could see people scurrying past on their way home from work. Well, she could mostly just see their feet, but she'd always loved the view, catching glimpses of some pretty spectacular shoes.

As usual, the hours slipped by even though Jill wasn't drinking. She was too tired and admittedly still a little hungover from the extra drinks she'd had the night before. Soda water and lemon with a splash of pomegranate juice was her drink of choice. By nine, everyone else from the office had moved on, and she and Billy were dining on burgers and fries. Jill rarely ate burgers, but sometimes they hit the spot.

"Nothing like a greasy burger to soak up any lingering alcohol effects, eh?" Billy said before taking another bite.

"It's not fair that you don't seem the least bit hungover." Jill picked up a fry. They were dusted with olive oil, salt, and rosemary, delicious on their own but better still with ketchup.

"You're just jealous. Tell me, why is it that you haven't had a single bite of that burger yet? You always eat your fries first." Billy was just about done with his.

Jill smiled. "Are you still hungry? I'll be lucky to finish half of this." She put half of her burger on his plate. He often finished what she couldn't eat.

They chatted easily as they finished eating. Jill had worried that she'd been too flirty the night before, but Billy didn't seem to think anything of it. It was like it had never happened. And as they laughed and chatted, she realized that maybe she'd been fooling herself. She and Billy were the best of friends, and it was clear that he didn't see her in any other way. She must have been temporarily out of her mind to think otherwise. If anything was going to happen between them, it would have happened by now. She told herself that it was just that she hadn't dated anyone in so long. And maybe it was time to do something about that. Time to find someone to get her mind off her nonromance with Billy.

12

Cory flew out of the Nantucket airport at eleven on Sunday for his conference. Mandy dropped him off at the airport and wished him a safe trip. The tiny airport was always so busy with regular flights to Boston and New York. Mandy was amazed by the rows of private jets and that there was so much wealth on their small island.

"I should get in around four on Thursday." Cory kissed her goodbye, and she watched him walk off. There was a spring in his step. He was clearly looking forward to this conference and going to Vegas for the first time.

On the way home, she stopped at the market to pick up some laundry detergent. She hadn't realized that she was almost out when she went shopping earlier in the week.

When she got home, she went up to her bedroom to throw a load in before meeting Jill and Emma later that afternoon for brunch. Jill was flying back from New York, and Emma was picking her up at two. They were meeting after that.

Mandy did the sheets and towels first, and when they were in the dryer, she emptied out Cory's gym bag to add his clothes to the wash. Along with his T-shirt and shorts, a folded bill tumbled out. She picked it up and stared at the name on the envelope. It was a cell phone bill addressed to Scott Lawson. The address was Cory's office, but he was the only Lawson there. And the cell phone number was unfamiliar. Scott was Cory's middle name though. It didn't make sense.

She felt her chest tighten and the beginning of a panic attack building and sat down for a moment. She took a series of deep breaths and tried to will the feeling to go away. She hadn't had a panic attack in years, but she couldn't think of any good reason why Cory would need a second cell phone or a different name on the bill. She set the envelope on the bureau and planned to ask him about it when he got home.

––––––––––––

Emma and Jill were just sitting down when Mandy met them at Black Eyed Susan's, the eclectic restaurant on a cobblestone street in downtown Nantucket. They all ordered coffee and didn't really need to look at the menu. Jill and Emma both got the French toast, and Mandy got the Portuguese scramble with cheesy grits. While they waited for their food, Mandy filled them in on what the consultant had recommended.

"He had a lot of positive things to say. The food and service were both solid. He liked just about everything that he tried, but he did suggest that the menu itself could use an update to make it more fresh and modern."

Jill and Emma both nodded. None of them were surprised by that.

"He also suggested we give the restaurant a 'facelift.'"

"That sounds expensive." Emma took a sip of her coffee, and it was clear she was worried about the money.

"What would that entail?" Jill asked.

"I don't think it would necessarily be too expensive. New carpet, definitely. What's there is worn and needs replacing. And a fresh coat of paint on the dining room walls."

"It does look a little dingy," Emma agreed.

"He also suggested that we hang some new artwork, maybe on consignment from local artists."

"Oh, that's a great idea. It would keep costs down too," Jill said.

"Right. I thought that was a great suggestion." Mandy paused before continuing, because she knew the consultant's next one wasn't going to be popular. "He also suggested that we look for ways to cut back on staff. Maybe not have as many servers on and see about less help in the kitchen too."

Jill frowned. "What do you think about that idea?"

Mandy laughed. "I hate it. And I think Grams would have hated it too. We don't have to take all the consultant's suggestions. Of course, Cory would be all for cutting staff. He guessed that would be one of the recommendations." "I don't think we should make any drastic changes with the staff either. What else did he say?" Emma asked.

"His other suggestions were marketing related, such as implementing more promotions and maybe a loyalty program."

"How would a loyalty program work? That sounds intriguing," Jill asked.

"It could be whatever we want. As an example, he suggested something like after ten meals, they get a free entrée. And that we should make sure we get the word out on social media and see about online advertising and coupons that we can give to local hotels and bed-and-breakfasts and, of course, an updated website."

"Those all seem like good ideas. We should probably run all this by Paul too—he will have a say in everything," Jill said.

Mandy nodded. "I agree. I figured we could discuss and then meet with him at the restaurant. He might have some other ideas, and I have one too." Mandy had been thinking of ways to get the word out more about Mimi's Place and had an idea she was excited about.

"What are you thinking of?" Emma asked.

"Once we replace the carpet, do some redecorating, and have a new menu all set, I thought maybe we'd have a big grand reopening party and invite a lot of the local businesses and our regular customers too. We can do a cocktail hour type of thing, with a cash bar but provide complimentary appetizers so they can all see the place and try the food—and Paul can introduce any new items."

"I love that idea," Jill said enthusiastically.

"I do too," Emma agreed. "And I can help with some of the social media marketing. I was thinking about starting a blog and linking to it on Facebook."

"That would be great," Mandy said and then paused before changing the subject. "So there is something else. Not about the restaurant." She hadn't been planning on saying anything, but she couldn't stop thinking about the bill she'd found, and she was curious what her sisters would think.

"I was doing laundry earlier and found something odd in Cory's duffel bag." She told them about the second cell phone.

Emma and Jill exchanged glances and were both quiet for a moment before Emma spoke. "You said Scott is his middle name? I hate to be negative, but given what I'm going through, there's only one explanation that comes to mind. Have you considered that he might be having an affair?"

Before Mandy could answer, Jill chimed in. "Have you noticed anything different about him lately? Has he lost weight or started dressing better? And is he away more, late nights, working weekends?"

Mandy sighed. "Honestly, it never crossed my mind, ever, 'til I found that bill. I thought things were fine, I guess."

"Didn't you say you dropped Cory off at the airport earlier today?" Jill leaned forward. "And he's going to Vegas. Maybe it's not just a work thing?"

"Hmm. He did seem unusually excited about going. But to be fair, he's never been to Vegas before. He's always been a workaholic, but he is working more late nights at the office. He says he gets more done there."

"If he's there." Jill said what Mandy had been wondering since she'd found the envelope.

"He has been hitting the gym more lately too. I didn't think anything of it."

"How are things with you two?" Emma asked.

"We've been together so long that I thought things were fine. Good enough. We don't really do much as a couple and haven't for years. I focus on the kids, and Cory focuses on work."

"You don't do date nights?" Jill looked surprised.

Mandy laughed. "What is a date night? Usually when I suggest going out, Cory's too tired, and we settle on getting takeout, and an hour later, he's fast asleep on the sofa."

"What do you think he is up to?" Emma asked.

"I can't think of any other possible explanation. I was in denial about it all afternoon, but there is just no good reason why he'd need a phone under a different name."

"Are you going to ask him when he gets home?" Jill asked.

"I put the bill on our bedroom dresser, so he will see it. And yes, I am very curious to hear his explanation."

Cory called to check in a few times while he was away, and Mandy had to restrain herself from asking about the bill. She wanted to do that in person so she could look into his eyes and see his expression.

She'd had a lot of time to think about her marriage while Cory was away in Vegas. She still loved him, and it was beyond painful to think of him with someone else. She didn't want to believe it, but she didn't want to be naive either. Thinking about the past six months, she saw a few things differently. Like the extravagant gift he'd given her on her thirty-fifth birthday a few months ago.

He'd had a sleek white Mercedes convertible delivered, and when she stepped outside, the car was in the driveway wrapped in a big red bow. She'd been shocked. Even though they could easily afford it, Cory had never given presents like that before. She'd been thrilled at the time; it was so unexpected, and it was a beautiful car.

But now she wondered if it was because he'd been cheating then and felt guilty. He'd worked a lot of late nights the week before her birthday. And he'd been grumpier than usual with her. He'd been short with her more recently too, easily annoyed. But when she'd asked what was wrong, he'd said nothing and that everything was fine. But obviously things were not fine.

His flight was due in at four on Thursday, but around noon, he called to let her know he'd be coming in later and that he'd just grab an Uber from the airport and would see her around nine. That was when Mandy decided to do what she'd been thinking about all week.

She went upstairs and opened the mysterious cell phone bill. There were only three phone numbers on it. She punched in a code to block the caller ID on her phone and dialed the first number on the list. The call was answered after the first ring by a woman with a perky voice. "This is Margie."

"I'm sorry, I think I dialed the wrong number." Mandy hung up quickly and looked back at the bill. There were several calls to Margie in the first two weeks of the month. She took a deep breath and dialed the next unfamiliar number.

This time, the call went to voicemail. "You've reached Sharon Jones, and I'm sorry I missed your call. Leave a message."

Sharon was mostly in the second half of the month. And in the last week, there was one more number. She dialed it and waited. It rang four times, and she thought it was about to go to voicemail when a breathless voice answered.

"Hello?"

Mandy froze for a moment. "I'm not sure I have the right number. Is this Nancy Smith?"

"No, it's Anna Davis."

"I'm so sorry." Mandy hung up and sat down on the bed to catch her breath. She was out of tears. She'd cried enough so far, and now she was mad. She grabbed a piece of paper and jotted down their names so she wouldn't forget.

It was a quarter to ten by the time she heard Cory's Uber pull into the driveway. The house was quiet, as the kids were in bed. Mandy had curled up in the living room, watching a movie and sipping a glass of chardonnay. She was trying to stay calm, but since nine, she'd been watching the clock and jumping every time she heard a car outside. She was dreading the conversation with Cory. Mandy had never enjoyed conflict or arguments of any kind. She liked everyone to be happy and get along.

The front door opened, and Cory walked in with his travel bag slung over his shoulder. He looked tired and smiled when he saw her.

"I wasn't sure you'd still be up. I thought I'd be home earlier."

Mandy looked at him carefully. "How was your trip? Did you have a good time?"

He grinned. "We did. Vegas was a blast. I can't believe I waited so long to go there."

"Your conference was good too?" She had no idea what it was about or who he was with.

"It was fantastic. A great exchange of ideas and good networking."

"Who else did you say went?"

"Jim and John from the Boston office and Daisy. It was a good group."

"Daisy went?" Cory hadn't even asked her if she wanted to go. Not that she did, but she was surprised to hear that Daisy went with them.

"Didn't I tell you? She's working in the Boston office now too, training to be an analyst. She loves the business."

"No, you didn't mention that. I had no idea about Daisy. I thought she liked not working and doing her charity stuff."

"I think she got a little bored with all that and was looking for something more challenging."

"Well, I can certainly relate to that." Mandy couldn't keep the sarcasm out of her voice, and Cory just nodded.

"I'm going to head upstairs and unpack. I'll be back down in a bit."

She watched him go, waited a few minutes, and went up after him. He was just about finished unpacking when she walked in the room. And he hadn't noticed the bill on the bureau yet. He looked up and smiled when he saw her. Mandy went to the bureau, picked up the bill, and handed it to him.

"This fell out of your gym bag when I was emptying it to do laundry."

He looked surprised but just took the bill and stuffed it in his briefcase.

"Thanks."

"So who is Scott Lawson?"

There was a long, uncomfortable silence. Mandy waited with her arms crossed. Cory looked down, and she could sense his wheels turning, trying to come up with an explanation. Finally, he laughed.

"Yeah, it's a funny story. I thought I'd lost my cell

phone, but I was also pretty sure it was going to turn up so I didn't want to get a new phone with the same name and number. This way, I figured I'd just have a backup phone. And I was right. Turned out I left my phone in the Boston office. Patrick overnighted it to me the next day. But in the meantime, I couldn't be without a phone. You know how that is."

"What's funny is if that is true, you never mentioned it to me."

Cory just stared at her, saying nothing. Did he really expect her to buy that ridiculous story?

"Who are Margie, Sharon Jones, and Anna Davis?" Mandy glared at him.

A look of shock flashed across his face. But he quickly recovered and tried again.

"They're new high-net-worth clients." But he didn't look her in the eye. He just stared at the floor, saying nothing.

"I'm not an idiot, Cory. You didn't call anyone else. I don't know who they are, but they're not new clients. What's really going on?"

Finally, he sighed. "Okay, I messed up. I'm sorry. I used that phone and my middle name for a discreet dating site. Nantucket is a small place, so I had to be careful."

Of all the things she imagined him saying, going on a dating site wasn't it.

"A discreet dating site? You were online dating?"

"Well, not exactly dating. It was no secret that I was married. That's why it's called discreet."

"So you were hooking up with random strangers? Why?" Mandy stepped back and wondered who this person was that she was married to.

"None of it meant anything. It has nothing to do with you. It was just something I needed to do. It's hard to explain."

"Well, try. I'd love to know why my husband thought it was a good idea to find other women to sleep with online."

"It was just a release. And the thrill of doing something forbidden. I'm not proud to admit that, but it's true. I didn't care about any of those women. I love you. I won't do it again, I promise."

Mandy's jaw dropped. "You're serious? You expect me to forgive that and act as though it never happened?"

A panicky look crossed Cory's face. He wasn't used to people saying no. "I swear I'll make it up to you. I don't want to lose you."

"You should have thought of that before you got your second phone and placed that ad. I think you should leave."

"Now?"

Mandy sighed. It was after ten. "No. You can stay here tonight. But tomorrow, you need to go. I can't forgive this, Cory. It's too big." She sniffed and looked around for a tissue. She tried to keep the tears back, but they fell hard. Cory took a step toward her and looked like he wanted to hug her. She sidestepped him and walked toward the door.

"I'm so sorry, Mandy. I never intended to hurt you." He did sound sorry, but she knew he was probably more sorry that he got caught than anything else.

"I'm going to sleep in the guest bedroom tonight," she said.
"You don't have to. I'm happy to sleep there," he offered.
But Mandy didn't want to sleep in their bedroom tonight. There was too much Cory in that room, and she wanted to be far away.

"No, you have it. Enjoy your last night in our bed, alone."

The next morning, Mandy was in the kitchen making a cup of coffee when Cory walked up to her and looked like he'd been crying too. She was surprised to see it, but it didn't change anything. She'd cried more last night than she'd thought possible until she finally fell asleep.

"Can we talk about this? What can I do to make it up to you? I'll do anything." He flashed the smile that used to melt her heart. It only made her want to cry again, and she'd told herself she was done crying.

"There's really nothing to talk about. I'm not going to change my mind. It's over."

He sighed. "I thought maybe you'd think more about it and want to try to save our marriage. I'd even be willing to go to counseling."

"I don't see how counseling can fix this, Cory. How can I trust you again? And what kind of example would I be setting for our children?"

He was silent for a moment before saying, "They'd never need to know. We could pretend this never happened."

"Maybe you could, but I couldn't. You should call a Realtor and see about getting yourself a rental or buying something, whatever you prefer. In the meantime, there are plenty of hotels and bed-and-breakfasts for you to choose from. Just let us know where you decide to stay, and we can figure out some kind of visitation for the kids."

He nodded. "Okay. I'll go pack a suitcase. I can get the rest of my stuff this weekend, maybe?"

"That's fine."

"Maybe we could just separate for a while, take a break, and then maybe revisit things?" His tone was hopeful, but Mandy shook her head.

"I don't think I'm going to change my mind, Cory. I'll let you know if I do. Right now, I just can't be around you."

He nodded. "Okay, we don't need to rush into anything. But whatever you want to do, I'll support. Again, I'm really sorry, Mandy."

Mandy felt the tears threaten again, and she tried to channel her anger to keep them at bay. She did not want to cry again in front of Cory. He wasn't worth crying about. She picked up her coffee cup and turned to head into the sunroom.

"Bye, Cory. Let me know when you get settled somewhere."

13

Mandy was relieved that Cory didn't take long to pack a suitcase. He was out the door before the kids were up, which she was grateful for. She wasn't up to explaining anything to them just yet. They were bound to be upset, and Mandy hoped to disrupt their lives as little as possible. They would have to spend some time with Cory, most likely on weekends, and given that he was rarely around and always working, they might end up actually seeing more of him this way—though she knew it was going to be a huge change for all of them. She felt like she was going through the motions and that the full impact of what had happened hadn't really hit yet.

She woke the kids up, and once they were eating breakfast, she jumped in the shower and stayed in a few minutes longer than usual, letting the hot water soothe her. After dropping the kids at school, she called Emma, knowing she'd be up early.

"Did you talk to Cory last night?" Emma asked as soon as she answered the phone.

"I did. It's—well, it's worse than I could have imagined." Mandy's voice broke, and she felt the tears coming again.

"Where are you? Can you stop by here on your way into the restaurant? I'll start the coffee now."

"I'm about five minutes away. I'll be right over."

Before heading to Emma's though, Mandy made one more phone call. Her doctor's office answered on the first ring, and Mandy took a deep breath. It was the most awkward and uncomfortable phone call she'd ever had to make. She'd googled the night before though, so she knew what she needed to ask for.

"Hi, this is Mandy Lawson. I'd like to come in as soon as possible for an STD test."

———

When she walked into Grams's house, Emma and Jill held the door wide open and pulled her in for a group hug. Emma handed her several tissues as they walked to the kitchen and sat down with their coffees.

"I have some cinnamon crumb muffins if you're interested? I just had one," Emma offered.

Mandy shook her head. She had no interest in food.

"No, thanks. I ate earlier." Sort of… She'd finished half a

piece of toast that Brooke had left on her plate. Even that was hard to get down.

"So when you're ready, tell us about Cory," Emma said gently.

Mandy took a deep breath and told them.

"A discreet dating site?" Emma looked horrified.

"He thinks he can do whatever he wants. His success has gone to his head." Jill was clearly disgusted.

Mandy nodded. "I think that's very true. Everyone has put him and Patrick on a pedestal, the golden boys that can do no wrong. Cory has always been a risk taker, but he pushed it too far this time. He really seemed shocked that I wouldn't consider forgiving him. He even offered to go to counseling. I could tell he was pretty proud of himself for that."

Jill shook her head. "I'm so sorry, Mandy. I have to admit, I'm shocked. I thought you guys were so solid, the perfect family. Looking back, were there any signs?"

"Yes, but I didn't see it at the time. You know the convertible he gave me for my birthday? That was very much out of character for Cory. I think it may have been a guilt gift. He was working really late the week before my birthday. All those nights he worked late or went back to the office after dinner—well, he may have been doing something else."

"So now what? Do you want to try to save the marriage?" Emma asked.

Mandy sighed and grabbed a fresh tissue. "I'm not sure

that I can. The trust is gone. Cory packed a bag and moved out this morning. I told him I'd let him know what I want to do."

Jill nodded. "It's a horrible situation, but maybe it's best to be decisive about it. I would imagine it would be harder to try to make it work."

"A small part of me wants to try to fix it, but I feel physically ill now when I look at him. I'm not sure we can come back from something like this. It's just the shock of it all. It was so unexpected, though I guess I missed other signs too. He's been short with me more often and hasn't been all that fun to be around. I just assumed it was work stress."

"You should get tested, just in case," Jill said.

Mandy nodded. "I called the doctor's office earlier, and I'm getting that done as soon as I leave here. It's just a quick blood test."

"What can we do to help?" Emma asked.

Mandy looked at both of her sisters, and her eyes welled up again. She was so grateful that they were there.

"There's really nothing to do. I'm just glad you're here and that we have Mimi's Place. It is a blessing really and will give me something to focus on."

"If you need help with the kids or anything, please let us know," Jill offered.

"Yes, definitely," Emma agreed.

Mandy smiled as a thought came to her. "You know there is something. When I got this place ready for you, I found a diary on Grams's desk and started reading it. I think I mentioned it. Have you guys seen it? It was a fascinating peek into her life. If you don't mind, I'd love to borrow it. I'll have more time for reading now with Cory gone."

"Of course. I haven't seen it. Have you, Jill?"

"No. I didn't know Grams even had a diary."

"When I finish, I'll bring it back so you can read too. Oh, and we have our meeting with Paul later today."

Emma looked concerned. "Are you sure you're up for that?"

"I'm looking forward to it. To seeing what Paul thinks and to get started on these changes. I'll need a project to focus on now more than ever."

———————

Paul came in early to meet with Mandy, Emma, and Jill about the consultant's suggestions. They grabbed coffee and went into the function room side of the restaurant so it would be quiet. Mandy walked through the list of recommendations, and Paul was surprised to find himself agreeing with most of them, except for cutting staff. They were all in agreement that Grams wouldn't have supported that idea, and they didn't plan to either.

He especially agreed with the suggestions to get new carpet in the dining room and to hang local art on the walls. As they went through everything though, he couldn't help but notice that something seemed a little off about Mandy.

"What are your thoughts on changing the menu?" Mandy asked.

Paul grinned. "I agree that it's long overdue. I tried to add my own spin through the specials, but other than that, the menu really hasn't changed much over the years."

"I thought it might be good to have a grand reopening party of sorts," Mandy said. "We could invite the regulars, local businesses and hotels, and serve samples of some of the new menu additions—whatever you decide on. If you are up for it?" She seemed excited about the event, and Paul had no doubt she'd do a great job organizing it.

"We thought it might be a good way to thank the regulars and get the word out about the new menu," Jill added.

Paul agreed that it was a smart idea and a good chance for him to show them what he could do. It would be a fun challenge. "I like it. I have some ideas on menu items. Let me think about this and get back to you with what I have in mind. Sound good?"

"That sounds perfect," Jill said, and Emma nodded in agreement.

Mandy took a deep breath. "Good. I am looking forward to this event. It will give me something to focus on." She glanced at her two sisters and then at Paul and hesitated for a moment as if she wasn't sure whether to continue.

Emma reached out and grabbed her hand, and Jill nodded. Paul knew then that his initial sense that Mandy wasn't quite herself was on target. Something was wrong.

"I might as well tell you, since you are our partner and

word is going to be out soon enough anyway. Cory and I are separating." She didn't go into why, and Paul didn't need to know. His heart went out to her. He'd gone through a divorce himself, and it was hard.

"I'm so sorry, Mandy. Let me know if there's anything I can do to help. I've been there."

She smiled gratefully, and he could see that her eyes were slightly red.

"Thank you, Paul. I appreciate that."

As far as he was concerned, Mandy was better off without that guy anyway. He didn't know what Cory had done, but Paul didn't like his attitude. He'd been in the restaurant a few times before with work colleagues, and Paul had heard from the waitstaff that Cory was a difficult customer. He was demanding and full of himself.

He spent a lot of money though—expensive bottles of wine, after-dinner drinks, appetizers, and dessert. Paul knew that Cory owned some kind of financial services company and made an obscene amount of money. There were a lot of those types on Nantucket.

Most of them had second homes on the island and visited them just a few weeks a year, but when they did, they expected to be catered to. Many of them hired personal chefs for their stay. Paul had worked a few of those gigs before he landed at Mimi's Place. It was relatively easy money being on call to cook whatever a rich family wanted—from peanut butter sandwiches to clambakes on the beach and elegant dinner parties. Some of the people were nice, but others were difficult and full of themselves, like Cory. Mandy seemed too down to earth and nice for someone like that.

"Okay, so I think we're all set then?" Jill asked.

Mandy nodded. "I'll start working on a plan for the event and run the details by you all in a few days."

"And I'll let you know some thoughts on the menu soon too." Paul was looking forward to trying some new things and was excited to create a menu that would showcase what customers loved about Mimi's Place, along with some fresh new dishes.

14

Paul slept in until a little after nine, brewed himself a cup of dark roast coffee, and settled on his sofa with Brody by his side. He didn't have to be at the restaurant until later that afternoon, and he was looking forward to a relaxing day. He took a sip of the hot coffee and debated between diving into a new book he'd bought or going for a walk. He glanced out the window. The sun was shining, and it would be a good walk to the beach and back. He liked to walk the beach and watch the boats come and go, but he could always do that later in the afternoon.

He reached for his book, the newest Longmire mystery, and before he could open it, his phone rang. It was Jason, his lunch chef.

"Hey, Jason."

"Paul, sorry to call so early, but I'm afraid I don't have

good news. It's the damndest thing. I was out walking the dog this morning and wasn't paying attention I guess. I fell, hard, and they say my ankle is broken. The good news is I'm getting surgery on it tomorrow. But I can't put any weight on it for six weeks. I hate to leave you in a jam, but the doctor says I won't be cleared to work until it heals up."

Paul set his coffee down. "That's rough. I'm sorry, Jason. Don't worry about it. We'll figure something. Keep me posted on how the surgery goes and when you're ready to come back."

"Will do. Thanks, Paul."

Paul ended the call and scratched Brody under his chin.

"Well, so much for hanging with you today, buddy. I'm going to be working doubles until I find someone to pick up Jason's shifts."

Mandy walked into the kitchen a little after eleven and did a double take when she saw Paul. He explained about Jason's ankle.

"What do you usually do when something like this happens?" she asked.

"We have people pick up the shifts usually, as two of the guys swap off doing lunch shifts on the weekends, and it's not a big deal when it's just a few days. But Jason is going to be out a good six weeks or so. So I'd love to find someone if I can."

"We can post an ad online?" Mandy suggested.

Paul nodded. "Sure, if you want to do that, please do. I have a few calls in to guys I know to get the word out. See if anyone knows of anyone looking for work. You never know."

Mandy nodded. "I'll work on that now. I have some time before people start coming in. What do I need to know about the role and the pay?" They chatted for a few minutes about the responsibilities of the role and hourly salary range they could do. Mandy turned to head off to put the ad together.

"Wait. You have to try this. It's today's special. A lobster and scallop quesadilla." Paul had put one in the oven before Mandy walked in. He slid it onto a plate and added a side of sliced avocado, sour cream, and pineapple salsa.

"Oh, thank you. That looks delicious. And I'm starving. I haven't eaten a thing yet today."

Mandy left with her plate of food, and Paul quickly made another quesadilla for his own lunch. He used a nutty Gruyère cheese and sweet red peppers, and the pineapple salsa was perfect with it. His cell rang as he swallowed his last bite. It was his friend Randy, who was a chef at a seafood restaurant on the wharf.

"Hey, Paul, I got your message. I might have a lead for you. It's just a temporary gig, right?"

"Yeah, probably about six weeks or so. Though maybe there's a possibility for longer. I've been thinking it wouldn't be a bad idea to have a backup person that can float around and fill in wherever needed."

"Hmm. Well, I know of someone who might at least be a good fill-in for you. Zach worked for me for about three months. He was in a similar role for us, filling in while my regular sous-chef was on maternity leave. I think he was hoping she wouldn't come back. She did though, and unfortunately, I couldn't keep him on. He's a little quirky, but his food is good."

Zach sounded ideal. Paul and Randy chatted for a few more minutes, and as soon as they hung up, Paul gave Zach a call. He explained the job, and Zach seemed into it. Normally Paul would have someone come in and formally interview, but since he'd worked for Randy, that was good enough for Paul. He offered him the job, and Zach agreed to come in the next day to work the lunch shift. Paul would work with him for a few shifts until he was comfortable with the menu and the kitchen. He let Mandy know when she brought her empty plate into the kitchen, and she laughed.

"That was fast. I didn't even have a chance to post the ad."

Paul smiled. "Hopefully we won't need to. Zach is starting tomorrow."

15

"Mandy, meet Zach Crane. He's filling in for Jason."
Mandy had just walked into the kitchen the next day and
this time wasn't surprised to see Paul there.

Mandy smiled and held out her hand. "Welcome, Zach.
Are you from Nantucket? You look familiar?"

He nodded. "I was a few years behind you both. My
family moved off-island, retired to Florida. I stuck around."

Zach was wiry, with longish wavy brown hair and dark
stubble. He was maybe five eight or so, and he didn't smile
when he shook Mandy's hand. He had an intense energy
around him. Mandy vaguely recalled him from high school.
He hadn't been into sports or arts. She'd seen him smoking
outside with his friends who also rode motorcycles. That
wasn't so common on Nantucket, so it stood out in her
memory. His voice was raspy, and she guessed he was still a

smoker. But as long as he didn't smoke in the kitchen, she didn't care about that.

She heard the front door open, and before she turned to go, she asked, "Any specials I should know about?"

Paul nodded. "Grilled swordfish, and Zach came up with the sandwich of the day." He glanced at Zach, and at the mention of food, he smiled. "It's a Brazilian chicken sandwich. Grilled chicken breast, avocado spread, green beans, cheddar, and hot sauce."

"Oh, that sounds intriguing," Mandy said.

"I'll have Zach make you one so you can describe it," Paul offered.

"I'll get right on it." Zach grabbed a soft roll and split it in half as Mandy headed out to the front desk.

It was only a quarter to twelve, a bit early for the lunch rush, and the customers who came in were just looking to buy gift certificates. She took care of that, and a few minutes after they left, Zach brought the sandwich out to her.

"Here you go. Hope you enjoy." He set it on the desk and disappeared back into the kitchen.

Mandy took a picture of the sandwich before taking a bite. It looked impressive. Paul occasionally picked up Portuguese sweet rolls from a local bakery, and Zach used them for this sandwich. It was a six-inch or so soft bread that had been split and grilled in butter, then spread with avocado and warm grilled chicken. The green beans added a little crunch, the cheese a bit of creaminess, and the hot sauce a welcome kick. The flavors all worked together beautifully.

Mandy quickly posted the picture online on all social media, mentioning that it was today's lunch special, along with the swordfish. She tried to describe the sandwich in a way that would do it justice and hoped her enthusiasm would come through. She inhaled the rest of it, returned the plate to the kitchen, and told Zach and Paul how much she'd enjoyed it.

The lunch rush began soon after noon and went for an hour and a half. Gina manned the bar, which was steady. They had a regular crowd that liked to come in for lunch. It was a mix of tourists and locals on their lunch break. At about one thirty, Gina came to the front desk.

"Mandy, can you keep an eye on the bar? I need to run out to my car for a minute. I just popped a button on my pants and have a safety pin in my glove compartment."

Mandy tried not to laugh. "Of course, take your time. It's slow now."

Gina grinned. "Thanks, I'll be back in a minute."

There was no one waiting to be seated, so Mandy wandered over to the bar. There were just a few people sitting there, an older couple who were eating swordfish and a single guy with a soda and menu in front of him. He texted something, then set his phone down and glanced around the bar.

Mandy smiled. "Did you place your order with Gina yet?"

"Not yet. I got interrupted by a text message." He grinned. "I'm not really sure what I'm in the mood for today. Any suggestions?"

"We have a really good special. Well, two actually. The grilled swordfish is always good, but there's also a sandwich. I had one earlier for lunch." She described it to him.

"Sold. I'll have that."

"Great." Mandy took his menu and punched the order into the computer. She recognized him as one of their lunch regulars. He was about her age, and he came in once or twice a week, sometimes with a friend, sometimes alone. She guessed that he worked nearby. He was a handsome man, with thick blondish-brown hair and a stocky build. Not that she was looking, not that way. She shuddered at the thought.

"I'm Mandy," she introduced herself. "I'll let Gina know. She should be back in a minute."

"Nice to meet you. I'm Matt. Matt Flynn. You're one of the new owners? Gina filled me in that there are a few of you now."

"Yes, my sisters, Jill and Emma, and I and also Paul, the chef. Do you work nearby?"

He nodded. "I do. I have a boat business down at the wharf. Sightseeing, deep-sea fishing, and private charters mostly and some restoration work."

"My grandfather used to be in that business. He always loved wooden boats especially."

Matt's eyes lit up at the mention of wooden boats, and they chatted for a few more minutes until Gina returned.

"Thanks so much, Mandy."

"No problem. It was nice chatting with you, Matt."

16

Later that night, Jill worked the evening shift and was surprised when Macaulay Connor, the consultant Cory had hired, strolled in and took a seat at the bar. His dark brown hair was wavy and a little too long, but she'd always liked that look. As she walked toward him, a hint of his cologne drifted her way, and it smelled really good. She set down a cocktail napkin in front of him.

"Nice to see you again. Would you like something to drink?"

He recognized her and smiled. "Hi, Jill. What do you suggest for a local IPA?"

"It's Macaulay, right?"

He nodded. "Yes, but call me Mac."

"Okay, Mac. We have two local options from Cisco Brewers. Indie Pale Ale or Whale's Tale."

"I'll try the Whale's Tale."

She returned with his beer and asked if he'd like to see a menu.

"Yes, I'm starving."

Jill handed him a menu and ran through the specials. As soon as he heard short ribs, he said, "I'll have that. It was excellent when I tried it before."

"Anything else?"

He laughed. "No, one meal should do it tonight."

Jill put his order in and went to take care of several new customers. The bar quickly grew busy as people started coming in and wanted drinks while they waited for their tables. When Mac's short ribs came out from the kitchen, Jill set them in front of him and saw that his beer was almost empty.

"Would you like another?"

He nodded. "Sure, thanks."

She checked to make sure his meal was to his liking and then left him alone to enjoy it. She didn't like to bother people with chitchat while they were eating. And the bar was busy enough that she didn't really have time to stop and chat anyway.

There was a lull though when he finished, and she went to clear his plate.

"Did you save room for dessert?" She remembered that he seemed to enjoy all their desserts.

"I'm pretty full, but it's hard to pass up the tiramisu here. It's one of the best I've had."

"It really is good. It should be right out."

Jill returned a few minutes later with his dessert, and no one else needed her, so she decided to linger.

"Your job sounds great, getting paid to go out to eat at all different restaurants. How did you get into that?"

He grinned. "It doesn't suck. I grew up working in restaurants, actually. My family owns Connor's Grille in Manhattan."

Jill's jaw dropped. There were multiple locations for Connor's Grille, and it was one of her and Billy's favorite places to take clients. It was similar to the Capital Grille, but they liked the environment better at Connor's.

"I've been there many times. It's our favorite place in the city for steak."

"Thanks! I knew I wanted to do something food-related still. After I got my MBA, I joined a consulting firm that had a restaurant practice, and it was a good fit."

"My sister went through your report with us, and there were some great suggestions. I knew you were finished, so I was surprised to see you here. Do you have another project on Nantucket?"

"No, but Nantucket is one of my favorite places, so I'm staying the rest of the week to take some vacation time and relax. It's a nice time of year, not too crowded."

Jill thought for a moment. "I suppose you've already done the touristy things like the whaling museum?"

"No, actually. I've never gone there. Is it worth going to?" The whaling museum was near the pier and was one of Jill's favorite places to bring people when they visited Nantucket.

"You really should go. I take everyone that visits there, and they always love it."

"Maybe I'll do that then. What other restaurants would you recommend while I'm here?"

Jill didn't have to think about it. "Definitely Millie's if you're in the mood for something sort of casual but really good. It's fresh California-style Mexican. Great fish tacos. And for breakfast, Black Eyed Susan's is always good. Those are my two favorites." She set his check down when he finished his dessert. "Here you go."

Mac fished his wallet out of his back pocket and threw a credit card down. She picked it up and returned a minute later with his credit card slip and card.

"It was really nice to see you again. Enjoy the rest of your vacation."

Mac looked thoughtful, picked up the pen, quickly scrawled his signature on the charge slip, and added a very generous tip.

"I don't know what your schedule is like, but is there any chance you might want to show me around the whaling museum tomorrow and grab a bite at Millie's after?"

Jill was surprised and pleased by the invitation. She thought about her schedule. She wasn't working the next night and could finish up her recruiting work a little early.

"Sure, I'd love to. I'm off tomorrow night, but I do have

my consulting work during the day. I could finish that up by around three or so."

"Great. Let me know your number, and I'll touch base with you tomorrow afternoon."

They exchanged cell phone numbers, and as Jill watched Mac leave, she realized she was still smiling and very much looking forward to playing tourist with him.

———

The next afternoon, Jill was rushing to finish up early when her phone rang and it was Billy. She glanced at the clock; it was almost two thirty. She'd talked to Mac an hour earlier when he called to confirm, and they made plans to meet in front of the whaling museum at three. It was about a ten-minute walk from Grams's place, and Mac was staying nearby at the Jared Coffin House.

"Hi, Billy. What's up?"

"Nothing in particular. Just calling to check in and hear your voice. How's your day going?" Jill could picture Billy in his office, leaning way back in his chair with his feet on his desk.

"It's good, busy. I talked to a few good candidates this morning and already got two interviews set up for the new search."

"Nice! You sound busy. Am I interrupting anything?"

Jill glanced at the clock again. She had about ten minutes before she needed to leave, and she wanted to freshen up a little, add some lipstick and brush her hair and teeth.

"No, not really. I'm just heading out shortly so I can't talk long."

"Oh, where are you off to? Got a hot date?"

Jill smiled at the teasing laughter in his voice. "Actually, I do. You know that consultant I told you about that came into the restaurant a few times and wrote up a report for us on ways to improve? Well, he came in again last night. We got to talking, and I'm going to play tourist with him and show him the whaling museum."

"Oh! He doesn't live on Nantucket?"

"No, he's just here for the rest of the week on vacation."

"So you probably won't see him again after that then?" Billy sounded pleased that Mac wasn't going to be around much longer.

"Probably not. But he does live in Manhattan, so you never know."

"No kidding?" Billy was quiet for a moment before adding, "Well, have fun then. Say, we need to firm up a date for me to come out there. I'm still thinking maybe next weekend, if that works for you? Or the weekend after?"

"Next weekend works. Why don't you come Thursday night? We can work from here Friday, and then you can fly back Sunday night."

"Perfect. Well, I better let you go get ready for your big date. Talk to you later."

"Bye, Billy."

As Jill hung up the phone, she smiled thinking about how surprised Billy sounded to hear she had a date. She really hadn't dated in a long time, so it was understandable. She was glad they'd set a date for his visit. It would be fun to play tourist with him too, and she knew her sisters would be glad to see him.

Mac was waiting for her outside the whaling museum and smiled when she walked up. The museum was around the corner from the wharf where the ferries came in, and there were always a lot of people walking by. Jill caught a whiff of the slightly salty crisp sea air and breathed in deeply, appreciating the fresh, clean air. It was a nice change from the hustle and bustle of Manhattan.

"Thanks for agreeing to do this with me. You've probably been to the museum a million times."

Jill grinned. "I haven't been yet this year. And it's always more fun when I'm going with someone who has never been before."

They went in and spent the next hour and a half roaming the several floors of the museum. Mac was suitably impressed.

"I have to admit, this was better than I expected. There's a lot to see here." The museum was full of interesting history and replicas of ships, whales, scrimshaw, and so much more.

It was just after five when they finished up and walked outside.

"Can we walk to Millie's?" Mac asked. "If not, my rental car is right here in the lot by the grocery store. I was running an errand earlier."

"We need to drive there. It's not too far and right by the ocean."

Mac led the way to his rental car, a red Jeep Wrangler. Jill directed him, and ten minutes later, they arrived at Millie's. It wasn't crowded yet as it was still early, and they went to the upstairs bar area, where the views were better, and settled at a high-top table.

Jill ordered a margarita on the rocks and Mac another local beer, this time Cisco's Indie Pale Ale. They both ordered the fish tacos and shared an appetizer of guacamole and chips. While they snacked on the chips, Mac entertained her with funny stories about some of the other restaurants he'd evaluated. While he talked, she couldn't help think what a catch he was. He was around her age, midthirties, came from a successful family, was smart, funny, and handsome. Yet as they ate their dinner and got to know each other, as much as she enjoyed his company, she didn't feel much of a romantic spark. He seemed like a really great guy though.

"So enough about me. When you're in Manhattan, not running a restaurant on Nantucket, what do you do?"

"I'm a recruiter, a headhunter, in the financial services space."

"New York is a good place for that. Do you like it?"

Jill smiled. "I do. I love it actually. My friend Billy and I used to work together and left to open our own small firm. I miss the energy of Manhattan and being in the office," she admitted. "But I'm enjoying being here too. It's nice catching up with my sisters. We don't see each other often enough. Do you have any siblings?"

"I do, one of each. Both work in the family business. My sister manages the office, and my brother runs the front of the house at our flagship location. I'm the oldest."

"Are you always traveling for your job?" Jill imagined he probably was and knew she'd hate that aspect of it. Every once in a while would be fine, but more than that, no.

"I do travel a fair amount, but it seems to go in spurts. There are months when all the clients are local, which is nice."

"I'm traveling back to New York once or twice a month now, which is more than I've done before. I don't know how you do it."

He grinned. "It's really not that bad. And I get to meet interesting people, like you. In fact, if you're up for it, we could go out again one of these times when you're back in town."

Jill did enjoy talking to Mac. He was charming and funny and good company overall. So she didn't hesitate to say yes. Maybe she needed to give it more time, give him a chance for the attraction to grow.

"I'd like that."

His eyes lit up. "Great. Just get in touch whenever you want to get together, and we'll make a plan."

When they finished eating, Mac insisted on paying, and when he pulled up to Grams's house, he parked and walked Jill to the door.

"Thanks for showing me around today. Millie's was great, as you said, and I'm glad I finally saw the museum."

"I'm glad you did too, and thanks for dinner. It was fun."

"My pleasure." Mac pulled her in for a hug and kissed her lightly on the cheek.

"I hope I get to see you again soon?"

"I'll be heading back in a few weeks. I'll get in touch then."

"Perfect!"

17

Mandy was grateful that she had the restaurant to focus on, because otherwise, she suspected she would have been tempted to crawl back into bed and stay there after dropping the kids at school. She did give in once, when she wasn't expected in the restaurant, and spent the entire day lounging on her living room sofa, watching classic sitcoms and romantic comedies and eating the things in her freezer that she usually avoided—mac and cheese and ice cream. She thought she was all cried out, but it turned out she was wrong and had to buy more boxes of tissues. She never knew when it was going to hit her and the tears would fall.

Sometimes it was the littlest thing, like once when she was folding laundry and a picture fell off her dresser. She picked it up, and it was of her and Cory on their wedding day. They looked so young and in love that the pain of it made her gasp, and she had to sit down. When she finally calmed down, she stuffed the picture in a drawer so she wouldn't have to look at it and finished putting the socks away.

Cory called the day after he moved out to let her know where he'd landed. He'd made one phone call to a local real estate office, and they hooked him up with a stunning, three-bedroom rental in Brant Point, their neighborhood, one of the most desired areas of the island. He'd said it was on the water and had everything he and the kids needed, so he could keep them on the weekends. The location was good though a little too close for Mandy's liking, only a few streets away. But she realized it would be convenient for the kids.

She still hadn't had the conversation with them yet. She was dreading it but knew she had to do it soon. They probably sensed that something was up. She'd been quieter than usual, and Cory had been gone all week. She'd simply told them that Daddy was busy with work, which they didn't question. He was always busy with work.

Cory was all apologies when he'd called to tell her about the rental and again asked if she'd consider taking him back. He seemed surprised that she kept saying no. She knew him though, and even though she'd told him it wasn't going to happen, Cory was probably going to keep asking, hoping that eventually she'd say yes. That strategy usually worked for him. But she didn't think it was going to work this time. Mandy did briefly consider taking him back and seeing if they could move on and try to get past it. But she quickly dismissed the idea, because she knew the trust was gone, and oddly enough, she no longer found him even remotely attractive. The thought of being physical with him was repulsive. So that made it a little easier to say no.

What she was still struggling with was why it had happened. Cory had said it had nothing to do with her, but she couldn't help think that it had to be partly her fault, that she hadn't been enough or did something that pushed him away. Maybe they'd just grown apart as Cory's work consumed him more and more and they began to spend less time together. It was Mandy and the kids all the time, and Cory off doing his own thing. And it wasn't like she hadn't tried to get him to do more with them, with her especially. But he rarely agreed. He was either too busy or too tired from work. So she had to keep reminding herself of that when she worried that she was somehow at fault.

It was hard though. She'd never felt so alone before. The sprawling house seemed empty without Cory in it. His energy was big, and the house was quiet without him. Her first instinct was to move, to get out, but she knew that was selfish. This was the only home her kids had ever known, and she couldn't take that away from them. She knew that if they divorced, it was going to be stressful for the kids too. Not to mention an unexpected change, and she would do whatever possible to ease that stress. So they weren't going anywhere.

She decided to tell the kids after she picked them up

from school. They came bounding into the car, all excited to tell her about their day. While she was waiting in the parking lot, she'd called in an order for takeout from Millie's. The kids loved tacos, and it would be a fun treat for them and she wouldn't have to cook. The food was ready when they reached the restaurant, and once they got home and were all sitting around the dining room table eating an early dinner, she told them what was going on.

"So I have some news that might seem a little strange. Your father and I have separated, and he's going to be staying somewhere else. He got a place not far from here. On the water, so that should be fun for you guys."

Brooke set her taco down and looked confused and angry.

"Why?"

Mandy sighed. "Sometimes people are happier apart than together. Your father and I got married young, and I think we've grown apart. We have different interests. Other than you kids, of course."

"Is it us? Did we do something?" Blake asked. His lower lip trembled slightly, and Mandy immediately got up and gave him a hug.

"Of course not, honey. This has nothing to do with you kids. Your father loves you both very much. It's between me and him."

"He doesn't love you anymore?" Brooke looked dubious.

Mandy hesitated. "We both love and respect each other, but we've decided that this is best for us right now."

"I don't understand this at all." Brooke's eyes watered, and Mandy gave her a hug too.

"I'm so sorry, honey. I don't really understand it either, to be honest. But it's what we need to do. You'll see your father this weekend."

"We have to go stay with him? And leave you? I don't know if I want to do that."

"It will just be for one night. He'll come get you on Saturday and bring you home on Sunday. It will be fun to see his place." Mandy tried to sound positive and didn't want to say anything negative about Cory. The kids didn't need to know he'd cheated.

"I don't like this at all." Brooke took a final bite of her taco and seemed to have lost interest in the other one on her plate.

"I don't either," Blake said. But his appetite didn't seem to be affected.

"I'm sorry, kids. I know it's going to be a change for all of us. But we'll figure it out. Brooke, finish your taco." Mandy understood though. She hadn't felt like doing much of anything all week. "If you both finish your dinner, we'll have some ice cream and maybe watch a movie. Sound good?"

"What kind of ice cream?" Brooke asked.

"Mint chocolate chip. I picked some up yesterday."

That got a smile out of her. It was Brooke's favorite flavor.

"Okay, but I get to pick the movie."

Mandy smiled. "Deal."

Later that evening, after they'd all snuggled together on the sofa watching a movie and the kids were sound asleep in bed, Mandy found herself wide awake. She couldn't find anything she wanted to watch on TV and looked around for a book to read before remembering that she still had Grams's diary in her tote bag. She fished it out, climbed into her pajamas, and curled up in bed to read for a bit.

She thought she'd probably just read for a few minutes until her eyes grew heavy, but the opposite happened, and she read for over an hour. And learned more about the mysterious Jay.

Dear Diary, Jay asked me to marry him! Of course I said yes. It was the most romantic thing. He took me to our favorite restaurant in the North End, Cantina Italiana, and instead of our usual wine, he ordered a bottle of champagne, and I didn't think anything of it. I had no idea. I just thought he wanted something different. But once it was poured and we put our orders in, Jay got down on his knee and held out the most beautiful ring I've ever seen. It was his grandmother's, and it's so delicate and pretty. I can't stop staring at it.

The rest of the night was magical. I barely remember eating my pasta, we were so busy making our plans for our life together. We decided

*that we'll aim for a New Year's Eve wedding, so
that gives me six months to plan. I'm so excited
that I don't think I'll sleep a wink tonight.*

The next few entries were more about the wedding
planning and her grandmother's search for the perfect
dress. The search was put on hold though when the United
States entered the war and Jay promptly enlisted.

*Dear Diary, We're at war now. And Jay and his
friends went down as soon as it was announced to
sign up. I understand why they did of course, and
I support it, but I wish he wasn't going. I won't be
able to fully relax until it's over and he's home. The
wedding, of course, is on hold until he comes back.
It might be sooner or later, no one really knows. It's
a scary time for all of us.*

Her grandmother's worry was evident in the next few
entries, which spanned several months.

*Dear Diary, It looks like this blasted war is never
going to end. I write to Jay every week and hear
back maybe once a month if I'm lucky, and it's a
relief every time. He says he's well, but I know he's
anxious to get home too. I have these awful dreams
sometimes, nightmares really where he never comes
home. It's my biggest fear. But I try to stay focused*

*on my job, and I pray for him every night and
every Sunday in church.*

There were a few more entries, and then nothing until nearly two years later.

*Dear Diary, I know I have ignored you. I just
haven't felt like writing for the longest time. My
biggest fear has come true. A telegram arrived
saying that Jay is missing in action and presumed
dead. His plane was shot down. I held out hope
that maybe it was wrong information, but his
parents are having a service this Sunday, which
makes it real. I feel like I've lost a piece of my soul.
I don't think I will ever be able to love anyone the
way that I loved Jay. I miss him so much.*

Mandy closed the diary through blurry eyes. Now she knew who Jay was to her grandmother, and her heart hurt thinking of the pain she must have felt. She was only halfway through the diary, so she looked forward to reading more and learning about when her grandparents met and about Mimi's Place.

18

Barbara came over Sunday night for dinner. She'd been away on vacation with her husband, Ryan, so Mandy hadn't wanted to bother her with the Cory drama while she was relaxing in the Bahamas. But when Barbara called earlier to check in once she arrived home, Mandy filled her in, and Barbara was suitably horrified.

"What are you doing tonight? Do you want to go out for a drink? We need to talk this through."

Mandy sighed. She would have loved to go out and relax over a glass of wine.

"I can't. Cory just dropped the kids off an hour ago. But why don't you come to dinner? I'm making lasagna, and there will be plenty. Once the kids eat, we can chat."

"Perfect. I'll bring the wine."

Barbara pulled Mandy in for a tight hug when she

arrived and handed her a bottle of Duckhorn Cabernet, which was one of their favorite wines.

"You deserve the good stuff," Barbara said, looking around for a wine opener.

Mandy pulled it out of a drawer and handed it to her.

"Thank you."

She watched as Barbara expertly opened the bottle, found two wineglasses in a cupboard, filled them, and handed her a glass.

Mandy took a small sip. As usual, it was delicious, a big, bold cabernet, and she knew it would taste even better once it opened up a bit. She called the kids in for dinner, and they gathered around the kitchen table. When everyone was done eating, the kids went into the living room to watch TV. Mandy put the leftover lasagna in the refrigerator and the dishes in the sink, then she and Barbara brought their glasses of wine and settled at the kitchen island.

"So how are you really doing?" Barbara asked gently.

Mandy forced a smile. "Well, the good news is I got the results back from the STD test, and it was negative."

"That's great news!" Barbara sounded so enthusiastic.

Mandy's eyes immediately welled with tears, and she sniffled with embarrassment.

"I thought I was doing better than this. I thought I was all cried out. It's just… It's hard. I really didn't suspect a thing. Not until I found that phone bill."

"You said he's been kind of a jerk though lately. How

long ago did that start?" Barbara took a sip of wine and looked furious on Mandy's behalf, which she appreciated.

"Probably about a year, actually. But it really got worse about six months ago. Everything I did seemed to irritate him."

Barbara nodded. "Yet he says there was nothing you did?"

Mandy shook her head. "That's what is so frustrating about this. He said it was just him. But I know there must have been something broken in our relationship for him to do what he did."

Barbara looked thoughtful. "Or maybe it's just that he is broken. I mean, Cory had it all. Beautiful family, money, and a company where people constantly praised him. He was super successful. Maybe it just went to his head?"

Mandy nodded. "Maybe. He said something to that effect, just that it was a challenge and the thrill of doing something and getting away with it. But if things were really good with us, I don't think it would have happened." That was what Mandy couldn't get past. She kept going over and over their relationship, trying to figure out where things first went wrong.

"What do you think it might be then?"

"I'm really not sure. I think it may be all that, but also I think maybe we just grew apart too. For years, we've kind of been on separate tracks, me with the kids and Cory with work. It consumes him. He works such long hours that by the time he comes home and eats dinner, he's usually asleep on the sofa an hour later."

Barbara lifted her glass. "I know you guys would have us over and come to our place now and then, but did you ever go out on date nights? Just the two of you to dinner?"

Mandy laughed. "Not in ages. It's not like I didn't try. But every time I suggested it this past year, Cory was always too tired. He was often too tired for other activities too." She made a face. "I didn't think much of that before, but it makes more sense now."

"I'm sorry, but he's an ass," Barbara said sharply and lifted her glass for another sip.

"Don't be sorry. I fully agree. I called a divorce attorney on Friday. We have a meeting tomorrow."

"Good. At least find out what all your options are," Barbara said.

"It's all so ugly. But I kind of want to just move forward and get it done. I don't want to change my mind. Cory keeps asking me to give him another chance." When he'd dropped the kids off that afternoon, he'd pulled her aside to tell her how awful he felt, and he really did seem sorry. He'd looked as sad as she felt. But she'd told him she couldn't do it.

"Do you think you could? You don't have to rush anything." Barbara added a little more wine to their glasses.

"I know. I don't want to rush this, but I don't want to be in limbo either, and I know if I gave him a second chance, I would be." Mandy took a sip of wine, and they were both quiet for a moment. She set her glass down. "It's funny, but he actually physically repulses me now that I know he's been with other people. He tried to pull me in for hug, and

my stomach clenched. I used to be so attracted to him."
Mandy felt a wave of sadness sweep over her. She took
another sip of wine. "My emotions are all over the place."

"I'm sure they are," Barbara said sympathetically.

"I'll talk in more detail with the divorce attorney when
I meet with her in person, but we spoke a bit on the phone.
She said I should ask to keep the house. She also said that if
I wanted to really go after Cory, I could do something called
a forensic audit and uncover all his personal and company
finances and demand a percentage of the company."

"Definitely the house." Barbara picked up her wineglass.
"Do you want to do an audit? Do you think Cory is hiding
anything with the company?"

"I don't think so. I'd never even heard of that before. She
said it's just an option to consider if Cory makes an unusually low agreement offer. I hope I don't have to do that. It
sounds stressful, and I don't really want to own part of his
company. That would tie me to him. I'd rather just have
a lump sum, whatever the lawyer thinks is fair, once they
look over all the financial details."

Barbara nodded. "It will be in his best interest to be
generous. I'm sure Cory doesn't want an audit or the legal
stress either."

Mandy sighed again. "Honestly, it makes me feel stressed
just thinking about it."

Barbara's eyes radiated sympathy. "How are the kids
handling it? They seemed good. Do they know why you're
splitting?"

"No. I didn't want to tell them. They're too young. And Cory was fine with that."

"Of course he was," Barbara scoffed.

Mandy smiled. "The kids are good though. They were upset when I first told them, and they don't understand, but they know Cory's just a few streets away. I guess that's a good thing."

Barbara frowned. "A little close for comfort. It's just a rental though, right?"

"Yeah. He'll probably buy something once everything is finalized, and hopefully it won't be as close by."

Barbara grinned. "You'll want a little privacy for when you start dating!"

Mandy laughed. "I can't even imagine. That is so not on my radar. I don't know that it ever will be. Not any time soon anyway. I'm just grateful that I have Mimi's Place to focus on."

"You know, it might do you good to talk to someone. I know a good therapist. I can text you her contact info."

Mandy hesitated. She'd never thought of herself as someone who would need to talk to a therapist. It seemed like an admission of failure. But maybe it would help.

"You don't have to decide on that now. I'll text you her info, and if you want to call, great. If not, no worries." Barbara smiled and leaned forward. "So tell me about this event you want to do. Ryan and I will be sure to come in soon. It's been a while since I've been there."

Mandy appreciated the change of subject. She'd needed

to vent but was ready to move on and talk about something happier. They chatted for another hour before Barbara headed home and Mandy got the kids up to bed and followed soon after. She was utterly exhausted and fell fast asleep not long after climbing into bed.

19

Billy's flight from New York arrived Thursday night a little after six. Jill smiled when she saw the familiar tall, lean figure get off the plane and walk toward her. He left his power suit at home and looked comfortable and still very handsome in faded jeans, a navy button-down shirt, and a chocolate-brown leather jacket. He grinned when he saw her and pulled her into a bear hug that lifted her in the air.

"Is Nantucket ready for me?" he asked as he set her back down.

She laughed. "That remains to be seen."

They walked to the luggage area where a baggage handler was wheeling out a rack of bags. Billy spotted his duffel bag and grabbed it.

"You just have the one bag?"

"I'm only here for a few days. Though you'd probably need a bag just for your shoes?" He knew her well.

She smacked his arm. "Very funny. Let's go."

They put Billy's bag in the back seat of Grams's white Volvo sedan, and Jill drove them home. The house was quiet when they walked in.

"Where's Emma?" Billy asked.

"She's working tonight. We'll see her later or tomorrow morning. Mandy says hello too. We thought we might all do brunch with you on Sunday before you head out?"

"Great. It's been a long time since I've seen them."

"Are you hungry? I thought we could get some takeout and just relax in tonight. Maybe go sightseeing on Saturday and out to a restaurant after work tomorrow?"

Billy set his bag down and flopped into a chair at the kitchen table.

"That sounds good to me, and I could eat."

Jill laughed. She knew that was Billy's way of saying he was starving. She fished a Thai takeout menu out of a drawer and handed it to him. "Take a look, and let me know what sounds good. I have some wine and cheese and crackers we can snack on for now."

She opened a bottle of cabernet, poured a glass for each of them, and set out a plate with a container of creamy pub cheese, a block of cheddar, and an assortment of crackers.

A few minutes later, she called in the order for Thai delivery and settled at the table across from Billy, who was slathering pub cheese on a cracker. They talked shop for the next hour while they waited for their food to be delivered. Billy caught her up on everything going on in the office, and once they finished dinner, they opened a second bottle of wine and spent the rest of the night laughing and talking about everything under the sun. Jill realized how much she'd missed Billy's company. More than anything, they really were best friends and often finished each other's sentences.

The thought crossed her mind, when their hands accidentally brushed against each other and Billy immediately jumped and apologized, that there was absolutely no vibe between them. And there likely never would be. But if Billy was never going to be more than a best friend and business partner, she was okay with that. And she was looking forward to working with him the next day.

When Emma got home a little before eleven, she poured herself a glass of wine and joined them. They were still sitting around the kitchen table. Jill put out some fresh cheese and crackers in case anyone felt like snacking again. Billy and Emma immediately reached for them.

"Was it busy tonight?" Jill asked.

Emma nodded, her mouth full. "We were steady. It seemed pretty good for a Thursday night. Paul tried out a few new menu items as specials, and they went over well."

"Oh, what did he make?" Jill suddenly felt hungry at the mention of food and reached for a cracker and a slice of cheese.

"A lobster pot pie, lobster mac and cheese, and tater tots

smothered in short ribs, melted cheese, and sour cream. They were all ridiculously good."

"Luxurious comfort food. I like it." Jill thought it all sounded amazing, and she knew how good the short ribs were.

"Can we go there for dinner tomorrow night?" Billy asked.

"We could. I'd love to get your feedback on the restaurant too."

They chatted for almost another hour before Emma started yawning, and it started a chain reaction.

"I'm going to head up." Emma stood and rinsed her glass in the sink.

"I think I'm about ready to call it a night too," Jill said.

"Sounds good to me," Billy agreed.

Jill led Billy upstairs to one of the extra bedrooms and showed him where the linen closet was.

"Jump in the shower whenever you feel like it tomorrow. I'll be up early, and coffee will be ready when you are."

Billy grinned and pulled Jill in for a hug. "The service is good here! Thanks for everything. I'll see you in the a.m."

Even after a late night and several glasses of wine, Jill was still an early riser and rolled out of bed the next day a little before six. Emma and Billy were still sleeping, so she made her way quietly downstairs, fired up her laptop, and made a cup of coffee. She always loved the early morning hours when she could savor her coffee while she browsed the news online and looked through her email.

Billy came down an hour later, laptop in hand. He'd already showered and was in an old T-shirt and sweats with damp hair.

"Help yourself to coffee. Sugar and K-Cups are by the machine, cream is in the fridge, and coffee mugs in the cupboard by the sink."

Billy silently made himself a cup of coffee and joined her at the kitchen table.

"If you're hungry, there are bagels and eggs."

"I'm good with coffee for now, thanks."

"I was thinking we can do a Zoom call with the office at eight thirty and have a mini job-order meeting. What do you think?"

He grinned. "Great idea. They were teasing me yesterday about taking today off and slacking. I told them we were working here today."

Jill set up the Zoom call and had everyone in the New York office dial in at eight thirty, and after a few minutes of joking around, they had a lively and productive meeting. Billy had a new client and several really hot jobs, and as he talked about them, everyone, including Jill, got excited to work on the searches and to see who they might already be working with who could be a good fit.

When Emma came down to the kitchen a little after ten, she stopped short when she saw both Jill and Billy on their phones and typing away on their computers. She made herself a coffee and a bagel and took both of them back upstairs to get away from the chaos in the kitchen. Jill had to laugh, knowing how loud they could get and how energetic. At times, Billy paced around the kitchen, gesturing with his hands while talking to a candidate.

When they were both off the phone, they had several fires to put out and situations to discuss. It was fast-paced and exciting, and Jill loved every minute of it. She and Billy both fed off the energy of the other, and it made them both work better.

When they stopped for lunch, Jill made turkey sandwiches, and they ate quickly while they worked. The rest of the day flew by until about four o'clock when the madness stopped and they both took a breath and called it a day as Emma left to head into the restaurant. They told her to save them a table if she could.

"That was wild," Billy said, shutting his laptop.

Jill was still on a high from a fun, productive day. "It was awesome. We always did work well together. I really miss the energy of the office," she admitted.

Billy frowned. "You know we all miss you too. Can you cut this experiment short? Can't your sisters cover for you maybe?"

Jill shook her head. "No, I really can't. Remember the terms of the will? We all have to be here for at least a year together." She sighed. "It's really not that bad. And a year will go by fast. When I'm able to, I'll come back more often, maybe on a Wednesday night and work in the office Thursday and Friday, then come back here for the weekend."

"Or you could come Thursday night and stay through the weekend..." Billy wore a teasing grin.

Jill laughed. "I'll see what I can do."

"Is it time for Friday happy hour yet?"

"Almost. I haven't showered yet today. I should probably do that, and then maybe we can walk into town and grab a drink at the Club Car and eventually make our way over to Mimi's Place."

"I'm going to take a power nap then. That sofa in the living room is calling to me. I'll be ready to go when you are."

Jill went upstairs and took her time showering and getting ready. She knew Billy was good for a solid hour nap. He could fall asleep anywhere easily. It was a little cool out, so she decided on a soft cashmere V-neck sweater in a pretty burgundy shade and her favorite slim jeans and charcoal-gray cowboy boots. She blew her hair dry and used a curling iron to add a few waves here and there.

Billy sat up when he heard her footsteps coming down the stairs. Her boots were loud against the hard wood floors.

They walked to Main Street and down to the Club Car. It was just a little after five but already getting busy; lots of people were eager for after-work Friday cocktails. Jill found two seats at the end of the bar, and they settled in. Once they had their drinks, a cabernet for Jill and a Jack and Coke for Billy, they looked around at the parade of people walking along Main Street.

"This is a busy place," Billy commented.

"Weekends are always busy here. And I think one of the ferries must have just landed." They saw people strolling along the wharf with luggage. The atmosphere in the Club Car was festive. People were happy to be done with work for the week, or they were on vacation, even if just for the weekend.

"I can see why you like it here. It's a beautiful place," Billy said.

"It really is. As much as I love Manhattan, Nantucket will always be home. It's nice to be here again and to be around my sisters. We really hadn't spent much time together in recent years. We talk on the phone of course, but it's nice to hang out more."

"I bet. Maybe your grandmother knew what she was doing. Even if I don't fully approve," Billy said.

Jill grew silent for a moment, thinking of Grams. "It's strange that she's not here. And that we're staying in her house. I miss her."

Billy reached over and gave her shoulder a reassuring squeeze. "I know. She had a good, long life. Crazy to think she owned a restaurant and none of you knew. What was up with that?"

"I'm not entirely sure. She won it in a bet of some sort. That's all we know. Mandy is reading her diary, so maybe she'll be able to fill us in at some point."

"Hey, I forgot to ask. How did your date go the other night?"

Jill was surprised by the question; it had been over a week, and she'd thought Billy would have asked about it sooner if he was going to ask.

"It was fine. He's a nice guy. He's not from around here, so I probably won't see him again."

"Hmm. I thought you said he lived in New York?"

"Well, yeah, he does. But I'm not exactly living there at the moment," she reminded him.

"Right. But if you start coming home more often, you never know."

Jill didn't feel like talking about Mac, who she hadn't heard from since their date other than a text saying he'd had a good time and reminding her to get in touch with him if she wanted to get together next time she was back in Manhattan.

"Do you want to head to Mimi's Place soon?" she asked.

Billy finished his drink and set it down on the counter.

"Lead the way."

Jill was glad to see that Mimi's Place was busy when they arrived. Every seat at the bar was full. Emma was at the hostess station and smiled when she saw them walk in.

"You're in luck. I just had a cancellation, and their table is ready. You two can have it. It's being set up now."

A moment later, Emma led them to a cozy table for two by a window overlooking Main Street.

They ordered a bottle of Charles Krug Cabernet from Ellie, their waitress, and as she poured the wine, she told them the specials. Two of them were the same from the night before, which Jill was happy to hear.

"We have some menu additions tonight—lobster pot pie, stuffed lemon sole, and an appetizer of tater tots topped with braised short ribs."

"I'll try the lobster pot pie," Jill said.

"And I'll do the New York strip steak, medium."

"Great. Would you like an appetizer to start?"

Billy looked at Jill. "If I get that short ribs appetizer, will you have some?"

She laughed. "What do you think? Of course."

Everything was good. Jill could only eat half of her meal, it was so rich, and she'd eaten more of the short ribs appetizer than she should have.

Billy cleaned his plate and was impressed with everything.

"I can't believe the three of you own this place," he said as he looked around the restaurant.

"The four of us," she corrected him.

"Oh, right. But still, it's impressive."

"It doesn't seem real that we own a restaurant," she admitted.

Emma brought their check over to them when they finished.

"We never talked about this, but Gary said if we come in to eat, it goes on the house account. There's no bill, just a tip for the server. Hope everything was good?"

Jill was stunned. It hadn't even crossed her mind that they wouldn't pay.

Billy grabbed the check. "Tip's on me then. Thank you, ladies."

They walked home, and Jill put her leftovers in the refrigerator. It was still early.

"We could walk back into town and hear some live music at the Rose and Crown if you feel like? It's not too far a walk, maybe ten minutes or so."

"I could use the walk after that food."

They made their way over to Water Street and the Rose and Crown, which was a pub-style restaurant and bar. They often had bands on the weekends, and Jill had seen a listing earlier in the week that they were going to have a blues band. She knew Billy loved blues music. They both did, actually.

The band was just getting ready to go on when they walked in and found seats at the bar. Jill stayed with wine, and Billy went back to a Jack and Coke. The band was excellent, and they stayed and listened to two sets. The bar was more crowded by the time they started their second set, and several people got up to dance when they shifted to a popular country blues song that was climbing the charts.

"Do you want to go join them? This is an awesome song," Billy said. He was tapping his fingers on the bar and swaying in his seat to the beat.

"Sure, let's go."

They joined the small crowd that was dancing and stayed up for several songs. When the music shifted to a slow song and people moved closer together, Jill turned to walk back to their seats, but Billy took hold of her arm and pulled her closer.

"Where are you going? This is a great song too."

He put his arms around her waist, and she leaned into him and put hers on his shoulders. They swayed to the music, and it was nice, though a little strange. For the first time, Jill felt a shift in the air between them. A hint of some kind of vibe was there, and it took her by surprise. But when the song finished and they sat back down at the bar, everything was back to normal, and she wondered if she'd imagined the fleeting sense of attraction.

They walked home a short while later, fell into bed, and spent the next day sightseeing and went out to dinner again, this time to Millie's, and Billy agreed that their Mexican food was as good as Rosa Mexicano, the place they loved in Manhattan. They had a blast, but Jill never got that feeling again and was sure she'd imagined it.

On Sunday, they went to brunch with Emma and

Mandy at the Brant Point Grill. The food was elegant, and they all had mimosas, which were delicious. Billy charmed her sisters with his funny stories about their crazy business.

"How did it go yesterday?" Jill asked Mandy. She knew Cory was coming to get the kids to spend the night at his new place.

Mandy shrugged. "About as I expected it would. It's very strange. Cory is on his best behavior. I think he still believes he can change my mind if he's charming enough. You'd think he'd know better than that. It's awkward for the kids too. Brooke really didn't want to go with him, and Blake follows her lead. She finally agreed about ten minutes before he arrived to get them. So that was fun."

"I'm sorry to hear you've separated," Billy said.

"Thanks. I'm sure Jill told you, it's all a bit sudden. I'm still getting used to the idea."

"If you need someone to go rough him up, let me know," Billy offered with a wink, and Jill loved him for it. He was always great at lightening the mood.

And it made Mandy laugh. "Thanks. You don't know how tempting that is. How about we all have another mimosa? I have the rest of the day free, so I feel like splurging."

The mimosas were light, more orange juice than champagne, and they all agreed a second one was a good idea.

When they finished, Jill drove Billy to the airport and walked him in.

"I'm so glad you were able to come this weekend. It's been ages since you've been here."

"Way too long," he agreed. He pulled her in for a quick hug and a kiss on the cheek. "I had an awesome time. Thank you. Let me know when you'll be back in town and stay the weekend so I can return the favor and take you out."

She smiled. "Will do. Bye, Billy."

20

Mandy was grateful for the leisurely brunch with her sisters and Billy. She'd been looking forward to it, and the time went by too fast. When she got home, it was early afternoon, and she still had a few more hours before Cory would be bringing the kids back. She puttered around in the kitchen, making a batch of stuffed shells for their supper. It was one of the kids' favorite meals, and she felt like pampering them a little. She hoped their second weekend in the new place had gone okay. She knew it had to be strange for them to get used to.

Once the casserole was in the oven, she made herself a cup of chamomile tea, settled on the sofa with Grams's diary, and flipped it open. The next entry was two years later.

Dearest Diary, I know it has been a long time. It has for me too. I never thought I would get over Jay. I was just so sad for so long. But something lovely has happened. I wasn't expecting it at all, but I went to Nantucket with some friends a few months ago. We went for the long Memorial Day weekend, and it was so much fun. But the best part is I met someone special. His name is Charlie, and he's from there. His family runs a boating business, deep-sea fishing and charters.

It's a different kind of love than what I had with Jay. That was unique and special. But Charlie is so sweet, and I really enjoy his company. I think we could have a wonderful life together. He's asked me to marry him and to move to Nantucket, and I said yes!

Mandy smiled, thinking of her grandfather. He really had been a sweetheart, and he'd adored Grams. She read further on about her grandmother's wedding and the big move to Nantucket. And then the birth of her first child, Mandy's mother. When the baby was two, Grams had a visit that turned her world upside down.

Dear Diary, the most wonderful, shocking thing has happened. Jay didn't die. He was held as a prisoner of war, and as soon as he was released, he came to find me. He's so thin now, and he's grown

*up so much. I met him for coffee, and we both cried
buckets. It's so unfair what happened to him, to us.
And of course, I feel horribly guilty for moving on.
But I truly thought he was gone. He doesn't blame
me. He said he understands, but the pain in his
eyes brought tears to mine. He's such a good man,
and I loved him so much. I still do. But Charlie is
also a good man, and I love him too. We've built a
life together.*

    *Jay and I agreed to keep in touch. There's no
reason not to. He's a dear friend, and we both care
deeply about each other. I need to tell Charlie, but
I don't want to hurt him, so I need to be careful
about this. He has nothing to worry about. I'll
never leave him.*

Mandy found herself reaching for a tissue as the front
door opened. She closed the diary and smiled as the kids
came rushing through the door. She got up to meet them
and looked outside. Cory sat in his car, watching to make
sure they made it inside. He waved when he saw her, but he
wasn't smiling. She guessed that her attorney had reached
out to his and that he was surprised she was moving so
quickly. She gave a quick wave back and shut the door
firmly behind her.

    "Are you hungry? I made stuffed shells. Your favorite."

    "I'm starving," Blake cried as he ran to hug her.

    Brooke hung behind and gave her mother a quick hug

when she finished with Blake. "Thanks for making the shells. We haven't had those in a long time."

"Put your stuff away, then come to the kitchen, and we'll eat."

Later that night, once the kids were in their pajamas and they were all relaxing on the living room sofa watching TV, Mandy asked about Cory's rental to see how they felt about staying there. She hadn't asked too many questions the first weekend, just if they'd had a good visit.

"How are you liking your dad's new place?"

Brooke shrugged. "It's okay. Dad took us shopping. We went off-island to Target and got some stuff for our bedrooms. We picked out new comforters. I got a pink one, and Blake picked out a purple one. We got some new books too. It's nice, but it's weird sleeping there. It doesn't feel like my bedroom. You know what I mean?"

Mandy nodded. "I do. I'm glad you got some new things though. That must have been fun. Did you go anywhere else off-island?"

"We went to McDonald's. It was so good. I wish we had one here."

Mandy smiled. The kids loved to go there when they went off-island, and Mandy didn't think McDonald's or any fast food restaurant would likely be approved on Nantucket. Every few years, companies tried and were always voted down.

"Mom, does Dad have a girlfriend?" Brooke asked.

The question shocked Mandy. She couldn't imagine

that Cory would be foolish enough to bring anyone around the kids so soon.

"What makes you ask that, honey?" Mandy tried to keep her voice calm.

"I heard him on the phone a few times talking to someone, and he was talking real soft and smiling a lot. It just seemed weird. I asked him, and he said of course not."

"Well, there you go then. I'm sure it was just a friend."

Brooke nodded. "That's what he said."

Brooke turned her attention to the new show that was starting, and Mandy wondered who Cory was talking to. He'd told her he'd just had a few flings, but could it be something more serious? Did her husband have a girlfriend?

Mandy felt a wave of emotion, a mix of anger and sadness and a steely resolve to move forward with the divorce, as soon as possible.

21

When Emma walked into Mimi's Place for her evening shift, Gary was at the front desk with a concerned frown. His hand was still on the phone. He removed it as he looked up and saw Emma.

"What's wrong?" she asked.

"José just called out sick. So Paul is short-staffed in the kitchen tonight. José was on the salad and dessert station."

"How are we set for waitstaff?" Emma usually floated between helping on the reservations desk, bringing out food from the kitchen, and keeping an eye on the tables.

"We're good there. I'm just debating if I should try to call someone in to take José's place."

"Don't bother. I can do it. I've helped out on that station before."

Gary looked doubtful. "Are you sure? For the whole shift? It might get kind of crazy in there."

Emma laughed. "I don't mind a little crazy. It will be a nice change. I'll head in there now."

"Okay, if you're sure. Thanks, Em."

Emma put her purse away and headed into the kitchen. Paul nodded when he saw her and continued writing the daily specials on the blackboard along with a note for the waitstaff that said "86 swordfish." Emma knew that "86" meant they'd run out of swordfish. She went to the salad station and took a look around to make sure she had everything she needed. When Paul finished writing up the specials, he headed her way.

"Are you looking for something? Can I help?"

Emma smiled. "Looks like I'm actually going to help in here today. José called out sick."

"Oh! You sure about that? I'm happy for the help if you are."

"I'm sure. Before it gets busy, I could snap a few pics of the specials if that's okay? I was thinking I could post them on Facebook, and that might drive some impulse reservations."

"Absolutely. We have a little time before the madness starts. I just took a batch of lobster pot pies out of the oven. Those have been a hit."

Emma pulled her cell phone out of her pocket and followed Paul behind the line where the ovens were. A huge tray of gorgeous pot pies sat on the counter, cooling. They were in individual blue ceramic casserole dishes, with golden brown puff pastry on top in a lattice pattern with bubbling creamy filling peeking out. Bits of lobster, carrots, and celery were visible for a colorful contrast against the nautical blue. Emma snapped a few pics and asked Paul for a good description of what was in the pot pies so she could add that to the Facebook post, along with the price.

"When I get an order for the tater tots with the short ribs, I'll let you know, and you can get a picture of that too. Same with the baked stuffed lobster. It's a two-pounder, stuffed with a Ritz and Royal Lunch Milk Cracker combination, lots of butter, parsley, shrimp, scallops, knuckle, and claw meat. It's chock-full of good stuff."

Emma's stomach grumbled. She usually grabbed a snack before heading in but didn't have time today.

Her face must have given away her hunger, because Paul immediately asked, "Have you tried the pot pie yet? We've run it as a special for a few days now, and it will probably go onto the new menu as a permanent item."

"No, not yet." Emma's eyes grew wide, watching Paul take a plate and scoop a generous amount of a pot pie onto it. He added some roasted potatoes and sautéed spinach on the side and handed it to her.

"It's going to be a busy night. Eat up, and let me know what you think."

"Thank you!" Emma took the plate to her station and happily did as instructed. The pot pie was delicious, with a flaky crust and big chunks of sweet lobster and veggies in a creamy sauce. As soon as she finished, she uploaded the picture to Instagram and to the restaurant's Facebook page along with her mouthwatering description, which also teased the other two specials and promised more pictures to come.

Gary wasn't kidding when he said it was likely to be busy. Soon after their first orders came in, Emma felt like she was running all night to keep up—making salads, plating shrimp cocktail and all the desserts. Before it got too busy, she was able to snap a few photos when the first orders came in for the short ribs appetizer and the baked stuffed lobster. She posted those to the Facebook page too, along with a picture of the specials board.

When the night was over and the kitchen was once again shiny and spotless, Emma and Paul joined Gary at the bar for an after-work drink. Gary seemed pleased as he sipped his draft beer.

"We had a good night tonight. Business was steady." He glanced Emma's way. "Do you know anything about a Facebook page? I had a few calls with people wanting to make sure we still had the lobster specials."

Emma laughed. "Oh good. It worked." She told him about the posts she'd made and the pictures she took.

"That's a brilliant idea. My wife said she always looks restaurants up on Facebook. I never go there, so it didn't even occur to me that we might want to do something on Facebook."

Emma nodded. "I put a Facebook page up earlier this week. I'm like your wife. I always look too."

"Well, let's keep it going. If we can get people into the habit of looking, they might make a point of coming in more often."

"That's the plan," Emma agreed. "And the new specials really seem to be a hit. Either Jill or Mandy, I forget who, called them luxurious comfort food. That could be something we're known for. Who doesn't love comfort food? Especially when it's decadent too?"

Paul chuckled. "That works for me. I was thinking for our party, I could do mini versions of the pot pie to give people a taste. Same with the short ribs app. And a few other things. I have a loaded mashed potato side dish I want to test out soon."

"That sounds up my alley. What's it loaded with?" Emma was envisioning bacon, cheese, and sour cream.

"Blue cheese, sour cream, and an obscene amount of butter."

Emma thought that sounded even more delicious. "I want to try that. It's not very diet-friendly though."

"No. It's not. Comfort food generally isn't." Paul looked thoughtful for a moment. "But maybe I can also introduce a few items that are both. I made a mashed potato the other day that was half cauliflower and used chicken broth instead of butter. It had great flavor but was a good deal lighter."

"That might be popular. Lots of people are trying to cut back."

"It all sounds good to me," Gary said. "I think having both options is a smart idea. Something for everyone. And on that note, I'm heading home. I'll see you both soon enough."

Gary left, and Emma took another sip of her chardonnay. She wasn't in any hurry to get home. Jill was likely in bed since it was nearly eleven, but Emma was still wide awake. She knew once she got home and climbed into bed, exhaustion would take over, and she'd go right to sleep, but for now, she was full of energy. Paul still had half a beer left and didn't seem ready to rush off either.

They sipped their drinks and chatted easily for a while before Emma remembered something she'd meant to ask him.

"What was the name of that shelter you mentioned where you adopted your cat?"

Paul smiled. "Nantucket's Safe Harbor for Animals." A moment later, he added, "I'm off during the day tomorrow and would be happy to go there with you."

"That would be great, actually. Jill's okay with it, so I am anxious to get a cat. I was thinking maybe an older one, five years or more. I know they aren't adopted as often, and I'd love to give an older cat a good home. Plus, I'm thinking that they wouldn't need as much attention as a lively kitten."

"That's true, and cats sleep a lot. I'm sure the shelter is

likely to have some older cats. I can swing by around eleven if that works for you." Paul finished his last sip of beer and put it in the bar dishwasher. Emma did the same with her now-empty glass of wine.

"That works for me. See you tomorrow."

———————

Paul came by at eleven sharp the next day, and Emma was ready for him.

"Are you sure you don't want to come with us and help me pick out our cat?" she asked Jill.

Jill shook her head as her phone started buzzing. "No, I'm slammed this morning. I trust you to pick out a good one. Have fun."

Emma walked outside, and Paul was waiting in his blue Ford pickup truck. She climbed into the passenger side, and a few minutes later, they turned onto Crooked Lane where the shelter was.

A volunteer had Emma fill out some paperwork, including references from her vet. She'd had several cats over the years, and they'd lost their last one just a few weeks before Emma learned about Tom. Losing Bella had been a blow, but she was an elderly girl at sixteen years old. They'd adopted her when she was nine. Emma knew her vet in Arizona would give her a good reference. Once she handed in the completed paperwork, Melissa, the volunteer, led them back to the area where the cats were held.

Emma always hated this part of going to a shelter. Her heart went out to all the animals, and she wanted to gather them up and take them all home with her. But of course, that wasn't possible. It turned out that her decision this time was easy though as there were only four cats currently available. One was a kitten, two were both about a year old, and then there was Izzy, a six-year-old beauty. She was a multicolored Maine coon cat, but a tiny one with a delicate face and a long, fluffy tail.

Izzy looked up as they walked into the room, and Emma was glad to see that the cats weren't in cages but were free to roam the room. The kitten was sound asleep while the two younger cats stretched in a patch of sunlight that came through the window. Izzy was perched on a carpeted cat stand, watching them. As they came closer, she lifted her head and closed her eyes, inviting Emma to pat her and scratch lightly under her chin. And then she hopped down and rubbed against Emma's legs, weaving in and out. Emma wanted to scoop her up and take her right home.

"I'd love to adopt Izzy, if possible."

Melissa looked surprised and hesitated a moment before saying, "She's six years old, you know?"

"I know. She's the one I want."

Melissa's eyes grew damp, and she looked away before smiling and saying, "Bless you. She's a doll, but we've had her for months now. Most people want to adopt the younger cats."

"When can I take her home?" Izzy was still rubbing

against her leg, and Emma bent down to talk to her. "I'll be back for you soon," said softly.

"I'll process your application this morning and will call you as soon as I'm done. You might be able to swing by this afternoon to get her if all goes well."

"Wonderful. Thank you."

Emma was still smiling as she followed Paul back to his truck and climbed in.

"Well, that was easy," he said. "She's a beautiful cat. Do you want to come by for lunch? I was planning to make a pot of seafood chowder, and you can meet my cat, Brody?"

"Sure."

It didn't take long to reach Paul's cottage. It was small but neat, and Emma could see that it had everything he needed and was close to the restaurant. When they walked in, Brody ambled out to the kitchen to greet them. He was a big boy, vivid orange with white along his belly. When Emma scratched him under his chin, he purred so loudly that it startled her, and Paul laughed. "I tell him he sounds like a train. He's enthusiastic, that one." Emma settled into one of the kitchen chairs, and Brody hopped into her lap. They both watched as Paul got busy in the kitchen.

"Can I film some of this?" Emma asked as Paul added diced bacon and onion to a big stock pot and turned the heat up.

"Sure. I'll let you know when it gets interesting."

Emma shot a series of very short videos, documenting the various stages of the chowder making, from the initial sauce to adding the seafood, which was a mix of clams, scallops, shrimp, and lobster with a flour and butter roux to thicken the half-and-half. Paul finished it with a swirl of heavy cream, more butter, sherry, and a sprinkle of fresh thyme.

He poured bowls for each of them, and they ate at the kitchen table.

"What do you think of adding this to the menu?" he asked when Emma was about half done.

She gave him a thumbs-up. "Everyone does clam chowder. This is better and fits the luxurious comfort food brand, if we decide to go for that."

"Works for me. We'll run it by the others."

Emma looked around while she ate. The cottage was small but homey. "Have you lived here long?" she wondered aloud.

"As long as I've worked at Mimi's Place. I moved in right after Patsy and I split. I should probably look into buying something bigger, but this is just so easy and convenient to the restaurant."

Emma nodded. "I can understand that. Easy is good."

Paul finished eating and set his spoon down. "Do you ever wonder what would have happened if we'd stayed together and gotten married?"

Emma shook her head sadly. "I wasn't ready to get married that young. I didn't think you really were either." Even though he'd said that he was. They were in their senior year of high school, and Paul had wanted to get engaged before they went off to college. But as much as she'd loved him then, and he had been her first love, it just didn't feel right.

"I suppose you're right. I think I always thought though that after college, you'd come back, and we'd pick up where we left off."

"We didn't really keep in touch though." Paul hadn't taken their breakup well and stopped talking to Emma at the time. She'd been upset at first, but then she'd moved on.

"You're right. Still, I was surprised when I saw your engagement notice in the paper a month before you graduated from college. I knew it was truly over then."

"I'm sorry, Paul. I had no idea. I fell in love with Peter. We married a few months after graduation and settled in Scottsdale."

"I know. I met Patsy not too long after that."

"And there hasn't been anyone serious since?"

He shook his head. "No. I've dated here and there, but I've mostly focused on work. It's hard with the hours. I've mostly dated other people in the restaurant business. What about you?"

Emma made a face. "Dating is honestly the last thing on my mind right now. I'm still trying to process what happened and how I could have been so blind."

When Emma finished, Paul took her bowl and his and rinsed both in the kitchen sink.

"Thank you for lunch. That was a treat."

He smiled. "Anytime."

Emma's phone buzzed with an unfamiliar number. "Hello?"

"Emma? This is Melissa from Safe Harbor. You're all set to come and collect Izzy today if you like."

"I'll be right there." She hung up and turned to Paul. "Do you mind swinging by the shelter on the way back to my place? Izzy's ready."

"Let's go. We can stop by the pet store and grab a carrier for her too and whatever else you need."

Emma picked out a pretty pink cat carrier and stocked up on wet and dry cat food, litter, and a litter box. When they arrived at the shelter, she brought the carrier in. It was the soft style that unzipped, and both Melissa and Emma were surprised when Izzy immediately hopped down from her perch, sniffed the carrier once, then strolled in, turned around, and flopped down, making herself at home immediately.

"Well, look at that. Usually they fight going into the carrier," Melissa said.

Izzy looked up at both of them as if to say "Let's get going already."

Emma laughed. "She's a smart one. She knows she's going home."

And ten minutes later, she said goodbye to Paul and welcomed Izzy to her new home.

Jill was sitting at the kitchen table typing away on her laptop and looked up in surprise when she saw Emma and Izzy. "Wow, you got one already!"

Emma set the carrier down in the middle of the kitchen floor and unzipped it. Izzy slowly made her way out and sniffed her way around the kitchen.

"Meet Isabella. Izzy for short. She's six and seems very sweet."

"She's gorgeous," Jill said as her phone rang, and she turned her attention back to work.

Emma set up Izzy's food in a corner of the kitchen and the cat box in the mud room, out of the way. She grabbed a magazine and went into the living room to curl up on the sofa. A few minutes later, Izzy found her, after sniffing every corner of the room. She jumped up on the sofa next to Emma and started giving herself a bath.

"Welcome home, Izzy."

22

Mandy threw herself into work and took on arranging all the changes they wanted to make. She researched vendors and, with input from the others, chose a new carpet to be installed in the dining room. She also lined up painters to come the same day the carpet was scheduled to be installed, and she reached out to local artists to see if any were interested in having their work shown on a consignment basis.

They closed the restaurant on a Monday to do the work, which was typically the slowest day of the week. Once she dropped the kids off at school, she met the painters at Mimi's Place. At noon, the carpet guys came, and she oversaw the installation of the new carpet. By the end of the day, the dining room had an overall flattering facelift. The paint dried overnight, and the next day, she hung the various paintings and photographs from local artists.

The grand reopening party was set for the following Monday night. They wanted a night that wouldn't interfere with their busy nights but would also be good for all the local businesses, and many also took Mondays off. They invited all the local downtown businesses, especially those that were in the hospitality industry, like bed-and-breakfasts and hotels, as they would be likely to recommend local restaurants. They also invited all their regular customers either by emailing them or including a note with their checks—an elegant invitation for them to stop by.

Mandy dropped the kids off that evening at Cory's place, and he agreed to bring them to school the next morning. She took extra care with her appearance, wearing one of her favorite dresses in a pretty light blue shade, and curled her hair so that it fell the way she wanted it to. It gave her a boost of confidence to look her best, as the last thing she'd been feeling lately was attractive, given what had happened with Cory.

Not that she was looking for any attention from men, more just to feel good about herself. She was excited and nervous for everything to go well. There was a lot riding on this event. If it went the way she hoped, they'd receive a steady stream of referrals and visits from locals eager to try out the new menu.

When Mandy arrived at Mimi's Place, the only other person there was Paul, and he was busy in the kitchen, getting all the food ready. A delivery from the florists arrived while Mandy was settling in, and she placed the flowers around the dining room. Gary was right behind them, and a few minutes later, both Jill and Emma arrived.

The plan was that the party would be like a big open house, with some food set out on stations where guests could help themselves to cheese and crackers, shrimp cocktail, various dips and chips, and fresh vegetables. Servers would make the rounds with appetizers like mini lobster pot pies, short rib tater tots, and seafood chowder. Paul had also made a seafood stuffed mushroom that he was planning to put on the menu. They were smothered in a rich cream sauce and were already one of Mandy's favorites.

Gina manned the bar, and while they'd debated doing an open bar, they decided instead to go with more food and a cash bar, thinking people would pay more attention to the food that way and would drink more responsibly if they were paying for their own drinks. They did go with a few drink specials and a discounted rate on several wines and beers, which made it easier for Gina as most people took advantage of the specials, and she didn't have to make as many kinds of drinks.

Jill hopped behind the bar to help out too, while Emma, Mandy, and Gary mingled with the guests. Many of their regulars, such as Matt Flynn, were there, and Gary introduced them to ones they hadn't met yet as well as local business owners. Mandy knew a fair number of the guests too, just from living on Nantucket so long, and she introduced Emma to many of them.

"Emma, this is Lisa Hodges. You remember we were in school with her daughters, Kate and Kristen?"

Emma nodded. "Of course. How are you?"

Lisa smiled. "I'm well. This is really lovely. You three have done a wonderful job. My late husband and I used to come here often. I can't wait to bring my friends Sue and Paige in soon. And I'll be sure to spread the word with my guests at the Beach Plum Cove Inn."

"Thanks so much," Mandy said. When she moved on, Mandy explained to Emma that Lisa had turned her waterfront home into an inn.

They were just getting themselves a glass of wine when Mandy spotted someone out of the corner of her eye that she preferred to avoid, but Daisy walked right up to her.

"Hi, Mandy. Nice event." Daisy looked down her thin nose at Mandy and wore a tight smile that didn't reach her eyes.

"Thanks." Mandy looked around but didn't see any signs of Patrick. "Did Patrick come with you?" She was surprised to see either of them. She'd assumed after what Cory had said that they'd both be in Boston, now that Daisy was working with the firm.

"No. I'm here with a friend. We came for the weekend, but Patrick flew back last night. I'm going back tomorrow."

Mandy nodded. "Congrats. I hear you're doing a great job with their firm."

Daisy looked surprised by the compliment. "Thank you. I really am enjoying it. I'm sorry to hear about you and Cory."

The words were polite, but they didn't feel sincere, and

her situation with Cory was the last thing Mandy wanted to discuss with Daisy of all people. Aside from Barbara, she hadn't mentioned it to any of her other friends. She knew how people loved to gossip, and the last thing she wanted was to be the focus of gossip. She knew it would get out eventually though. She wondered how many people Cory had told, besides Daisy.

She smiled stiffly back at Daisy. "Thank you. Would you excuse me? I see someone I have to go talk to."

Mandy darted across the room to greet Barbara, who had just walked in the door.

"You saved me. Daisy was offering her sympathies on my separation."

Barbara groaned. "Ugh. That sounds painful." She looked thoughtful. "Did you say that she's working with Cory's firm now?"

"Yes. She said Patrick was here this weekend too but headed back to Boston early. I was surprised to see her, actually."

"I saw her this morning having coffee with Cory at the Bean. I guess that makes sense if they're working together. They looked awfully cozy though."

"Honestly, nothing would surprise me anymore," Mandy said. "Though it would be incredibly stupid and risky for both of them." Mandy was pretty sure that Cory was smarter than that, considering that Patrick was his partner. Plus, he and Daisy had always seemed happy together. She doubted it was anything more than it appeared.

"Enough about him," Barbara said. "So where are those lobster pot pies that you told me about?"

Several hours later, when the restaurant was empty and everything had been put away and the kitchen scrubbed clean, the staff gathered around the bar, and Gina poured drinks for everyone. It had been an exhausting but also exhilarating night; everyone seemed to love the food and said they'd be spreading the word about the new menu.

They'd finalized the menu just a few days ago, adding all the new items that Paul suggested and that had gone over well with customers when they introduced them as specials.

Everyone seemed enthusiastic about the new branding of luxurious comfort food, which included fresh local seafood and familiar pasta favorites.

"Our reservations for next week are already trending up," Gary said. "People were excited about the party and also made a point to book reservations, which seems like a good sign."

Mandy agreed. "It does. It's hard to resist Paul's food."

Paul's cheeks immediately turned red, but Mandy could tell he was pleased with the compliment. "Thank you. It seems like everything went over well. There's nothing but scraps left in the kitchen."

Jill's phone buzzed, and she glanced down at it and smiled.

"Is that Billy texting?" Mandy guessed.

"No, actually it's Mac. Remember the consultant that I went out with? He just texted wondering when I'm coming back to Manhattan for a weekend."

"Will you see him again?" Emma asked.

"I just might. Why not?" Jill looked happy at the thought of seeing Mac again.

"Mandy, cheers to a great job pulling this all together. You really know how to run an event." Emma lifted her glass, and everyone at the bar did the same.

Mandy lifted her glass too. "Thank you, but this was a group effort. Everyone did a great job."

"To Mimi's Place!" Jill said, and they all clinked glasses.

Mandy was pleased that everything had gone about as well as it could have. It was nice to relax now that it was over. She nodded when Gina waved the bottle of wine over her glass and then topped it off. The cool chardonnay was delicious, and after this glass, she'd be ready to head home and call it a night.

When she got home, the house felt oddly quiet and empty with the kids sleeping at Cory's. Though she was tired, she wasn't ready to go to sleep yet and decided to read in bed for a while. She opened up Grams's diary and started reading. Several years had passed before there was more news on Jay.

Dear Diary, Jay wrote to let me know that he's married, and he and his wife are moving to

*Nantucket! His family owns several businesses
and restaurants in Boston, and they bought one on
Nantucket and gave it to Jay as a wedding gift.
It's going to be an Italian restaurant, called Mimi's
Place, named after his grandmother and featuring
many of her recipes. Charlie and I can't wait to go
try it out.*

And then a few months after the restaurant opened,
there was an entry.

*Dearest Diary, It's so wonderful having Jay and
Brenda here on Nantucket. She's very sweet, and
we've become friends. Charlie and Jay get along
well too. The four of us go out occasionally, on the
rare time that Jay isn't working at the restaurant.
We see him there more often, as Charlie and I have
become regulars. It's a cozy spot, the food is good,
and of course Jay always visits with us.*

A year later though, things took a darker turn.

*Dear Diary, The saddest thing has happened. I
feel just awful. My heart is breaking for Jay. He
and Brenda were so excited about their first baby.
Everything went so well with her pregnancy. She
hardly even had morning sickness, but when she
went to deliver, something went very wrong. I*

don't really understand exactly what happened,
but Brenda died in childbirth, and the baby
didn't make it either. Jay is devastated of course.
I've never seen him look so lost and lonely. Well,
that's not quite true. He had the same look in his
eyes when I first saw him and he learned I was
married. I'm really worried for him.

There were several entries after that, talking about how she and Charlie tried to help Jay, bringing him food and spending time with him, but he was so depressed. He focused on work and eventually seemed a little better, but then everything fell apart.

Dear Diary, Jay just let us know that he's sick,
really sick. The doctors say he has an inoperable
brain cancer, and there's nothing they can do for
him. Chemotherapy won't reach the brain. He said
he feels fine, just has the occasional headache, but
I've noticed that he's lost weight and seems tired. I
wish there was something that I could do.

Dear Diary, We had Jay over for dinner tonight,
and it was a fun night. He seems to be feeling
better and was like the old Jay, laughing and
teasing us as we played cards. He's a very good
card player, though I am too and that surprised
him. I've always loved a good poker game, and

it's kind of fun to be underestimated. Jay actually bet the restaurant on our final hand, he was so sure of himself. But I had a better hand and won. Of course I told him I wasn't going to take his restaurant, as that was ridiculous. He just smiled and said he'd see about that and that when he passed, he would leave Mimi's Place to me. I told him I didn't want to hear that kind of talk, and he wasn't going anywhere.

But two weeks later, Jay left us suddenly. He went to sleep and didn't wake up. And we got a call from his attorney. He really did change his will and left Mimi's Place to me. Charlie and I were shocked. It was the sweetest, most outrageous thing to do. I met with his manager, and he assured me that the restaurant is a well-oiled machine. When I asked if I could be a silent owner and they continue to run it, he assured me that was possible.

I want to respect both Charlie and Jay by keeping my ownership private. I don't want there to be any talk of anything inappropriate— that wouldn't be true or fair to Charlie, and people always assume the worst. Charlie wasn't so sure about that. He thought we could just say we bought the place, but I insisted. I'd rather have people think of us as regular customers than owners. In my mind, Mimi's Place is really Jay's

place. It's a lovely piece of him, and I want to take
care of it as best I can.

Mandy sighed and closed the diary. There were no more entries, and she was happy to hear that her grandfather had supported Grams's decision to keep her ownership a secret. She felt sorry for Jay, who had so much tragedy in his short life. She was glad that they had Mimi's Place renovated and the new menu created. She wanted the restaurant to be a success and to honor her grandmother's memory.

23

The next few weeks saw a steep increase in reservations and sales, which was a welcome relief to Jill, Mandy, Emma, and Paul. The new menu was a hit, and they were seeing a steady stream of new customers coming from local hotels and bed-and-breakfasts. Mandy had some loyalty cards and coupons printed up and distributed them at the local businesses, and they were starting to see them being used as well. The regulars liked the idea of the loyalty cards, which were stamped each time they came in, and then on their tenth visit, they would receive a free entrée. The coupons were good for ten dollars off the bill, and that got a lot of new people in to try the restaurant.

"Mac really did have some good ideas," Jill said Thursday morning while Emma ate her breakfast and they were talking about how successful the coupons and loyalty cards seemed to be.

"Will you see him this weekend?" Emma asked.

"I told him I'd meet him after work tomorrow night." Jill was flying out later that day and planned to work in the New York office on Friday.

"Will you see Billy too? Are you staying through the weekend?"

Jill nodded. "Yes. When he found out I have plans with Mac tomorrow night, he insisted I stay until Sunday so we can go out Saturday night."

Emma raised her eyebrows. "You're sure you're not dating?"

Jill laughed. "No. Billy just thinks he owes me for his recent trip here. It will be fun. We're going to some new restaurant he loves that I haven't been to yet."

"That does sound fun."

Emma finished her breakfast and went upstairs to shower and change. When she came back down an hour later, she stopped short when she stepped in the kitchen and saw Jill staring at Izzy.

"Look at your crazy cat." Jill laughed. She had been so deep into what she was doing that she didn't realize at first that Izzy was trying to get her attention. The fluffy cat had climbed onto the kitchen table and was sitting just behind the laptop with her little nose resting on the edge.

Emma watched as Izzy stared at Jill until she finally saw her and reached out to pat her. "Izzy, get off the table."

Emma tried to sound stern but failed utterly, and Izzy just looked at her and didn't move. Finally, Emma went over and scooped her up.

"She is too cute," Jill said. They'd both fallen in love with Izzy, and it was hard not to spoil her. Jill liked having her around while she worked. Izzy often slept in the chair next to her or brushed against her feet to get her attention.

"She'll miss you this weekend," Emma said.

"I'll miss her too." Jill went to pat her, but then her phone buzzed again as her email dinged, and she had to shift her focus back to work.

"Have a good weekend. I'll see you when you get home on Sunday," Emma said.

———————————

Jill's flight was at six. She was too busy to get out earlier. Billy had wanted her to come into the office and go for an after-work drink, but she wasn't going to get in early enough to do that, and truth be told, she was just as happy to go straight to her own condo and get a good night's sleep and then be well rested to get into the office early the next day.

High winds caused her flight to be delayed a half hour, and it was just after eight by the time her Uber pulled up to her condo building. It was nice to relax in her own place and sleep in her own bed. She woke early the next day, did an online yoga class, and felt energized as she jumped into the shower. An hour later, she walked through the doors of her office. Billy was already there and grinned when he saw her.

"You almost beat me. I got here literally two seconds ago." He gave her a hug, and they caught up over coffee in his office. It didn't take long before the rest of the team arrived. They had their morning meeting, and then it was nonstop action for the rest of the day. Jill barely had time to eat a sandwich at her desk, it was so busy. She loved it though, and it was great to see the team. She wanted to get back to the office at least once a month, twice if at all possible. Now that she was settled on Nantucket and into a routine with the restaurant, it would be easier to take some weekends away.

Around four, Billy came into her office and leaned on the side of her desk. "Are you sure you can't come for just one with us? What time are you meeting your date?" Jill was amused that Billy either didn't remember or just didn't want to say Mac's name.

"Not until seven."

"So you have time to come out with us for a little while. We'll just go around the corner to our usual spot."

It was tempting. And Jill was half wishing that she didn't have plans with Mac and could just relax with everyone after work. "Okay, I'll come for a little while. What time are we heading over?"

Billy jumped up. "Great, I'll let the others know that we're wrapping it up at five sharp. Come to my office, and we'll head out then."

Jill started winding down her day, and by five, she was ready to go. They all headed to their favorite bar and took their usual spots.

"Dill pickle martini for you?" Billy asked once they were settled. It was Jill's favorite cocktail. They made it with cucumber vodka and homemade pickles.

But Jill shook her head. "No vodka for me. I need to pace myself. Just a wine, I think. Cabernet. And a glass of water."

It was fun to hang out with everyone from the office. Jill realized how much she'd missed it. She especially missed the energy and enthusiasm of their newer recruiters. One of their newest, Lara, had just landed her first client and had an offer pending on her own candidate, so it would be what they called a "double-bubble," when you had both the job order and candidate sides of the placement. Like real estate, the placement fees were split between the holder of the job listing and the person with the candidate. And that amount was then split with the house, which was Jill and Billy.

While they were all chatting at the bar, Lara's phone rang, and she looked like she was about to throw up as she went outside to take the call. A few minutes later, she came back, white as a ghost, and seemed a bit in shock.

"What happened, Lara? Did your candidate say no?" Billy looked sympathetic.

But Lara shook her head and took a moment to speak. "No, he actually said yes. He took the job."

A chorus of cheers erupted, and Billy waved the

bartender over and ordered a bottle of their most expensive champagne.

"Congrats on your first double-bubble. It's time to celebrate." Billy handed out flutes of champagne to everyone.

"Awesome job, Lara. To the first of many double-bubbles," Jill said.

The mood was festive as everyone toasted Lara, and she looked like she couldn't quite believe what had happened. Jill was thrilled for her. She glanced at the time to make sure she wouldn't be late to meet Mac. Billy caught her doing it and frowned.

"I wish you didn't have to go. Can't you cancel and reschedule with him? Better yet, don't go out with him at all."

Jill laughed. "What do you have against Mac? I think you'd actually like him. He's a nice guy."

"I'm sure he is. We just don't get to see you often enough."

"Well, I'm looking forward to tomorrow night. Tell me again about the place we're going to?"

"It's small but fancy. Everything is top notch. I don't know what kind of food it is, but it's all good. You'll like it."

"It sounds great. I probably should get going though. I'll talk to you tomorrow."

Jill made her way out of the bar, flagged down a cab, and gave the address of the restaurant where she was meeting

Mac. It was the flagship location of his family's steakhouse. The last time she'd been there was over a year ago with Billy, when they were celebrating a new client and another big placement.

Mac was waiting for her just inside the door and was chatting with a tall man at the reception desk who looked vaguely familiar. She realized why as soon as Mac introduced him.

"Jill, this is my brother, Ryan." The resemblance was strong.

"It's nice to meet you."

Ryan led them to a quiet table in a corner. The lights were dim, and the leather and wood were dark. A small candle glowed in the middle of the table. The overall feeling was comfortable elegance.

Jill wasn't a big meat eater, but now and then, she enjoyed a good steak and ordered the house-aged sirloin that was coffee crusted and served with a butter sauce. Mac got the same, and they shared a side order of creamed spinach and scalloped potatoes. Mac ordered a good bottle of cabernet, and they sipped it while they chatted. It was nice catching up with him. Jill felt like she was with an old friend. There wasn't any nervousness, and they chatted easily. Mac was especially interested to hear about the changes they'd implemented and the reopening party.

"I should have suggested a party. That was a great idea that Mandy had. And it sounds like it went well?"

"It really did. It let us introduce Paul's menu changes to a lot of people, and once they sampled the food, they were sold."

Their steaks were done perfectly, and Jill thought it was pretty much a perfect date except for one thing. Mac was a perfect gentleman. He was funny and attentive and easy to talk to, and they had a lot in common as they swapped restaurant stories. It was a fun night, but Jill still didn't feel any kind of physical attraction. She wanted to want to kiss him, but it just wasn't there. And she was pretty sure that it would have been by now if there was anything there. It was frustrating, because on the surface, Mac seemed ideal for her.

And he seemed interested too. At the end of the evening, as he walked her to the Uber that she'd ordered, he somewhat nervously suggested that they go out again, and she didn't have the heart to say no.

"Thank you for a lovely night and for dinner. It was wonderful. I'd love to do it again."

He looked relieved. "Great. Let me know when you're in town again, and we'll make a plan."

"Will do."

She settled into the Uber and gazed out the window as they pulled into traffic. Her cell phone buzzed, and she smiled when she saw a text message from Billy.

Hope you're behaving yourself. I'll be by to get you at six tomorrow. Sleep well.

Jill put her phone back in her purse. She'd text Billy back in the morning.

Jill stood in front of her closet the next day, staring at her clothes and feeling like she had nothing to wear. She finally settled on black dress pants and a shimmery pewter top that was whisper soft with a flattering neckline. Unlike her date with Mac the night before, Jill was feeling a little nervous about her nondate with Billy, which was ridiculous. She'd accepted that nothing was going to happen between them, but some part of her obviously still held out hope.

When Billy called to say he was downstairs, the butterflies in her stomach danced again, and she tried to ignore them. She made her way downstairs, and he was waiting in the lobby wearing a blazer and tie—which meant the restaurant was expensive. Billy looked sharp. His tie was a deep purple, which looked great against his dark hair.

"You look handsome," she said when she reached him.

He grinned. "Thanks. You clean up pretty good yourself."

She followed him outside to where his black BMW was waiting. Most people in the city didn't drive. It was expensive to keep a car there, but Billy loved his BMW and didn't mind paying to garage it. The restaurant wasn't far, but traffic was heavy, so it took them almost a half hour to get there. Billy turned his keys over to the valet out front, and they went inside.

Jill loved the feel of the restaurant when they walked in. It was intimate and quiet with rich fabrics and plush carpet. Billy gave his name to the hostess, and she looked up their reservation, then led them to a cozy table in the back. It was a semicircle shape, and they sat side by side, looking out on the dining room. The leather seats were soft and comfortable, and the service was excellent. Within moments of sitting, they were greeted by their server and told the specials.

One of the drink specials was a hot and dirty martini, vodka with blue cheese–stuffed olives and red pepper juice. Billy looked her way when their server finished, and Jill nodded.

"I'll have that, please."

"Jack and Coke for me, thanks."

The menu was over-the-top decadence. Everything was rich and seemed to have truffles or cream sauces. It was hard to decide. Billy wanted to share a foie gras appetizer, which Jill loved, but it was very rich, so she decided on a piece of fish for her entrée—salmon with a honey mustard sauce. Billy went with steak, which was his usual choice.

The foie gras was silky and sumptuous, and Jill enjoyed every bite. She couldn't finish her entrée but agreed to help Billy with the dessert he wanted. She was curious to try it too, never having had a Baked Alaska. It was an impressive-looking dish, ice cream on cake, smothered in meringue that was baked in the oven. She had two bites and thought it was just okay, but Billy loved it and ate every bite.

Neither one of them was ready to go home after dinner, so they found a place nearby that had live music. Billy dragged her up on the dance floor, and she was surprised when she sensed that same vibe again that she'd felt briefly on Nantucket. It was like something had shifted between them. But she still worried it wasn't real and was just her imagination playing tricks on her.

They left at the end of the set, and when they walked outside, Jill decided she'd lost her mind as everything seemed as normal as ever with Billy. Until he pulled her aside, leaned over, and kissed her. It took her totally by surprise.

"What was that?" she asked when the kiss ended.

"Just something I've been wanting to do for a while. I hope you don't mind?"

Jill was speechless and finally said, "I don't understand."

Billy ran a hand through his hair and looked frustrated. "I'm not sure I do either. This might be a really bad idea. But I've just really missed you. I didn't realize how much until you weren't here. Nothing has felt right with you gone. And I have to admit, I felt jealous as hell that you were going out with that other guy last night."

"Mac."

"Yeah, Mac. I've just been thinking a lot. And when you were here last, I thought I sensed something from you too, at Rosa Mexicano. Am I losing my mind?"

Jill shook her head. "No, you're not. I feel it too. I've just been torn between wondering if it's a good idea or a bad one. I don't want to ruin our friendship, and we are business partners."

But it looked like all Billy heard was that she felt it too. "I think it's a good idea."

And then he kissed her again, and she had to agree. His lips felt good and right against hers. And unlike with Mac, she really wanted to kiss Billy.

"I don't suppose you want to come back to my place for a while?" he asked.

But she shook her head. "I do. But I don't. This is huge, Billy. We need to be really sure. I think we should take things slow."

He grinned. "I'm sure you're right. But I had to ask. So we'll take it slow then. You'll come back in two weeks, and we'll go on an official date."

"Okay."

Billy drove her home and kissed her good night again before she got out of the car. He waited until she was inside the building before he drove away, which she appreciated. She went up to her apartment, quickly changed into her softest pajamas, and slid into bed. Before drifting off to sleep, her mind kept replaying their first kiss. It was every bit as perfect as she'd imagined it would be.

24

"I heard from Cory's lawyer today." Lindsay Smith did not sound happy. Mandy had just gotten home a few minutes ago, and the kids were doing homework in the living room while Mandy got started on making dinner. She'd just put a chicken in the oven to roast when her cell phone rang and she recognized her attorney's caller ID. She went into the connecting sunroom where the kids would be less likely to overhear her and settled in a big comfy chair.

"Not good news, I take it?" Mandy asked.

"Cory did not come close to agreeing to what we asked for. He said you can keep the house, and he agreed to the child support amount that we requested. But the amount he proposed for a lump sum in lieu of ongoing alimony is ridiculous given his company financials." Lindsay sounded disgusted.

Mandy wasn't surprised though. Cory never had valued what Mandy did, and she knew he would be reluctant to give away part of his company. Mandy hadn't asked for that though. She didn't want to be involved in his company. She just wanted him to be fair.

"So what do we do now?"

"I'd like to remind him that we didn't ask for a percentage of the company, which you would very much be entitled to. I'd also like to remind him that we could ask for a full forensic audit. I'm guessing that he would prefer not to do that?"

"Yes, I don't think he would want that." Mandy paused for a moment, a little hesitant to share her suspicions with the lawyer, but decided it was good for her to know why she wasn't comfortable pushing for company ownership. "I'm not totally sure, but I think Cory has been somewhat creative with his tax deductions. He told me some of the things his accountant writes off, and while some of it might be legal, I don't think he'd want to risk that kind of an audit. And if there is anything even slightly shady, I don't want to have any kind of an ownership stake."

"That doesn't surprise me," Lindsay said. "There's a possibility he has hidden or overseas accounts as well. I'll draft up a response letting him know that if he doesn't significantly improve his offer, we'll be demanding a forensic audit and an ownership stake."

"You think he'll respond to that?" Mandy wasn't sure what to think. His initial offer had been underwhelming, insulting even.

"I do. Especially if his accounting is as creative as you suspect. His attorney knows what you are entitled to, and I've reminded him of that as well. Stay tuned, Mandy."

———————

"Connie, so nice to see you. That pink is so pretty on you." Mandy welcomed one of their regulars the next day. Connie and her friend were the first customers in for lunch, and Mandy seated them at Connie's favorite table for two, which overlooked Main Street.

"Thank you. This sweater is actually a birthday gift from my sister, Ginny, who is visiting for a few days. We always like to come here at least once when she's in town."

Mandy handed them menus, and they chatted for another minute or two before she headed back to the front desk. It was early still, not quite noon, and the restaurant was off to a slow start. Her cell phone rang, and she was surprised to see that it was Cory. Her immediate thought was that there was an issue with the kids, because why else would he be calling? They were going through their attorneys now on the divorce, and he'd been downright frosty toward her since receiving the initial divorce papers.

"Hi, Cory, is everything all right? Are the kids okay?"

Cory chuckled. "They're in school. And I'm sure you'd be the first person the school calls if there's an issue."

"Okay, good. What is it then? I'm at work."

"At work?" Cory sounded confused for a moment. "Oh, right. The restaurant. Is it busy?"

"No, not yet," she admitted.

"So you can talk for a sec?"

"Just briefly. If people come in, I'll have to go."

"I'll make this quick. My attorney spoke with yours, and she said something about a forensic audit. I don't think either one of us wants that, Mandy." His voice was charming, but there was an edge to it.

"Why not? She seemed to think it might be a good idea, to get a better understanding of the financials. She also recommended that I push for an owner stake."

Cory stayed quiet for a moment. "Is that what you want? You've never been interested in the company."

"No, but I don't want to get screwed either, Cory. I put my career on hold to support you and to stay home with the kids. My support helped you to build that company."

Cory sighed. "You're right. An audit is risky for both of us. If word gets out and there are any issues found, that could jeopardize the company and what we both receive."

"Are there issues that might be found?" Mandy asked.

"Well, that depends on interpretation. We've gotten pretty creative with a few strategies and deductions. Most of it should fly, but there's a chance some of it could unravel if they poke too much."

Mandy didn't know what to say to that. It confirmed her fears, and she stayed silent. A moment later, Cory jumped in to fill the silence.

"We'll get back to your attorney with a revised offer. I think you'll be happy with it. You just caught me off guard by sending that initial paperwork so fast. It was a knee-jerk reaction. You know I'm not like that."

Mandy nodded. Cory was normally always generous. It had seemed out of character.

"I'm still hoping we can work this out, that you'll give me another chance." Cory used his most charming voice, the one that used to make her melt. "I miss you and the kids so much."

Mandy sighed. "Cory..."

"How about dinner? Let's just start with that? And see how it goes? We can catch up, and maybe it will feel like it used to. We can take it one day at a time."

Mandy found herself feeling tempted. As mad as she was at him, she still missed him too. The house didn't feel the same without his presence.

"I could maybe make dinner work. No promises though. It's just dinner."

"Fantastic. We'll go to Straight Wharf. How's tomorrow night?"

Mandy thought for a moment. Jill was working, and Emma had the night off. If she didn't have plans, maybe she could watch the kids for a few hours. If not, she'd have to see if she could line up another babysitter.

"I'll see if I can get a sitter." The front door opened, and a party of four walked in. "Cory, I have to go. People are coming in."

"Okay, hopefully I'll see you tomorrow."

The line went dead, and Mandy exhaled. She knew in her gut that going to dinner with Cory wasn't likely to change anything. But she hadn't really spent any time with him, other than exchanging a few words when he came for the kids or dropped them off. Maybe it would feel like closure. Cory had sounded a little too excited. She knew he was thinking that they were going to get back together. Cory was used to getting whatever he wanted.

Emma arrived at Mimi's Place at a quarter to three. On the weekdays, when Mandy worked, Emma always came in an hour or so early so they could catch up a bit before Mandy rushed off to pick up the kids. Emma noticed that downtown was quieter than usual. The sky was dark and overcast, and the air was heavy and wet. It felt like rain was on the way. The cobblestone streets, usually crowded with tourists, were almost empty. It was late afternoon though, in between the lunch and dinner hours. Emma imagined that Nantucket's only movie theater was busy today. She parked behind the restaurant and went inside.

"How was it?" Emma asked when she reached the front desk.

Mandy finishing adding a name to the reservations calendar, then looked up and smiled. "It was a slow start, but we had a decent lunch rush after all. There are still two tables that are lingering, but they came in late." She hesitated before asking, "Do you have any plans tomorrow night? Any chance you might be able to watch the kids for a few hours?"

"Of course." It was the first time Mandy had asked her to babysit. "What are you up to? Something fun I hope?"

Mandy chewed her bottom lip before answering. "I'm not sure how fun it will be. I agreed to go to dinner with Cory."

Emma raised her eyebrows. "That's interesting. Are you considering giving it another try then?"

Mandy shook her head. "No. I don't think so. Intellectually, I know I probably shouldn't, but I am a little curious to see if there's anything still there. Cory is pushing hard for us to give it another try."

"He's a very good salesman. Just don't let him talk you into something you're not sure about." Emma knew Mandy was somewhat fragile when it came to Cory. She mostly seemed strong and determined to move forward with the divorce. But Emma knew it wasn't that easy. There were still a lot of emotions and history there. Sometimes people were able to move past something like this. But Emma knew she never could forgive Cory. And she suspected Mandy couldn't either.

"I won't. I don't think we'll be getting back together. It's really just dinner."

"Okay. Let me know what time you want me to come by then."

"I will. I'll have food ready that you can just heat up for the kids. And for you too of course." Warring emotions flashed across Mandy's face, and Emma could see she was unsure about the dinner.

"I think it's a good idea to go. See how you feel, and take it from there." Emma hoped the dinner would give her sister confirmation that moving forward with the divorce was the best decision.

Mandy nodded. "Thanks. I think so too. I'll see you tomorrow."

25

Cory had wanted to come by and pick Mandy up, but she insisted on meeting at the Straight Wharf, downtown near the waterfront. She didn't want to confuse the kids by having Cory come to the house and the two of them going off on a date. It was confusing enough for Mandy. Cory reluctantly agreed, and after making sure the kids were all set with Emma, she headed out.

She arrived a few minutes early, and Cory was already waiting outside, looking sharp in one of his best suits with the seafoam-green silk tie she'd given him for his birthday. Mandy stopped short as the scene looked so quintessentially Nantucket, with the ferry leaving the harbor, the salty smell of the ocean, and a stunning sunset that cast a golden glow over Cory making him look more handsome than usual. She guessed that he must have had a client meeting.

He dressed more casually otherwise, cotton dress shirts and pants usually. He smiled big when he saw her and pulled her in for a hug.

"You look beautiful," he said. His eyes met hers, and for a moment, his warmth and full attention on her made her feel a bit flustered. She had taken care in how she looked though. More than usual. Not that she wanted to dress up to impress him, but she wanted to look good. She'd curled her hair slightly, used a little more makeup than usual, and wore the black pants that made her look a bit thinner and her favorite blue-green cashmere sweater.

They were seated at a cozy table for two, and Cory immediately ordered a 1989 Château Margaux, a French Bordeaux. The Straight Wharf had one of the most extensive and expensive wine lists Mandy had ever seen, with many rare bottles that sold for several thousands of dollars. Mandy enjoyed wine, and even though Cory could afford it, it seemed a bit silly to her to spend that kind of money on a bottle of wine. But Cory enjoyed it.

Their server went off to get the wine and returned a few minutes later with the bottle of wine and a crystal decanter. He presented the bottle to Cory to confirm that it was the one he'd ordered, then opened and slowly poured it into the decanter and then a small amount into Cory's glass to taste. Cory made a production of swirling the glass, sticking his nose into it to inhale the scent of the wine, and then took a taste and closed his eyes, savoring it. He swallowed and nodded his approval. The server then poured for both of them and asked if they had any questions about the menu.

"I'm good. I think I'm to go with the rib eye, medium, and the wagyu beef starter. What about you, Mandy?"

"Slow-cooked salmon I think. And the salad to start." It was a simple salad with a homemade ranch dressing.

Mandy lifted her wine and took a sip. It was exquisite. She relaxed, and for the next few hours, it felt like happy times again. Cory made her laugh with stories about some of his clients and the young traders in the office. The food was as delicious as the wine, and she wouldn't have ordered dessert for herself, but Cory made her promise to have a bite or two of his vanilla bourbon cheesecake. And of course it was so good, she did better than that and shared it equally. They finished with coffee, and eventually Cory signaled for the check. It had been a lovely evening, and as Cory put his black card down and the server whisked it away, the happy mood shifted a bit. Sadness slipped in, joined by anger.

Cory reached over and took her hand, oblivious to her mood change. "This was a great night. It felt good, the two of us again. Don't you miss this? We can have it all again, Mandy. What do you say? Don't you want to fix things?"

Mandy sighed. "Thank you, Cory. This was a wonderful dinner and fun night. But I really don't think it would be that easy to go back. Everything has changed," she said sadly.

She saw the light dim in his eyes, and he let go of her

hand. But still, he pressed on. "I know we could make this work, Mandy. It's not too late. Why not let me move back in and we can give it a real try? It could be so good again."

Mandy was tempted. It would be so easy to do, as Cory suggested. He could move back in, and they could pretend that he'd never slipped. He swore it would never happen again. But if she did that, let him move back in, that would be telling the kids that they were back together. What if it didn't work? How long would she give him?

She shook her head. "I can't do it, Cory. I just can't. I want to, I really do, but I can't. I'm sorry."

She saw a muscle flicker in his jaw before he simply nodded and then stood. "I'm ready if you are."

The house was quiet, and Emma was reading in the living room when Mandy walked in. Emma looked up and smiled.

"How was dinner?"

Mandy knew she wasn't asking about the food. She shrugged her coat off and sank into the sofa opposite Emma.

"The food is always good at the Straight Wharf. The wine was amazing. Cory was charming, and it was really fun. Until it was over and he asked if he could move back in."

Emma inhaled sharply. "He really asked you that?"

Mandy nodded. "It's not that surprising. It's Cory. He thought he could charm his way back in. And it was tempting. The kids would love it if he moved back in. But it would be even harder the next time he moves out. And I know it would happen again."

Emma didn't say anything, but Mandy could see that she agreed.

Mandy felt her eyes well up, and she looked away for a moment and willed the tears away. She was tired of crying over Cory. "I wish I could go back to how things were, how we were back when we were more of a team and we had fun like that more often. I was blindsided by Cory cheating, but when I look back, we had been growing further apart each year. It was me and the kids and Cory and work."

"So you told him no?" Emma said gently.

"I did. I hope he knows I mean it. He had said he'd be sending a new offer to my attorney. We'll see, I guess. I hope we can work it out without having to get the lawyers too involved. That will just drag it out longer too." Mandy grabbed a tissue, dabbed her eyes, and smiled. "The Virgo in me wants this settled so I can put it behind me and move on."

Emma stood to leave and gave Mandy a hug. "It will be settled soon, I'm sure of it."

Emma's words and tone calmed her, and Mandy felt some of her tension ease. She remembered that Barbara had suggested that she make an appointment with a therapist. Mandy hadn't been keen on the idea at first, but maybe she would give her a call and make an appointment. It might help to talk things through.

26

"Tonight is Zach's first night on his own," Mandy said when Emma arrived a few minutes before three. Zach mostly worked the lunch shift, but Paul had been training him on the evenings too so that Zach could cover for him at least once a week, and Paul could have a full day off. Paul had said that Zach was eager to pick up evening shifts, so if it went well, Paul might be able to take a second night off now and then.

"Oh good. I knew he was hoping to do that soon. I didn't realize it was today," Emma said. She missed Jason and was looking forward to his return. Zach was pleasant enough, but there was an edginess about him that made him seem a little prickly at times. Unlike Jason, who always had an easy smile and loved to joke around with the waitresses.

Mandy's phone dinged with a text message, and she

glanced at it and laughed. "Brooke wants to know if we can order pizza tonight. I was planning to roast a chicken."

Emma grinned. "Pizza is much easier."

"True! Okay, I'm off. Have a good night."

Mandy headed out, and Emma settled behind the front desk and opened her laptop. She had time before the night rush began to work on marketing and social media for a while. She went into the kitchen to find out what the evening specials were and was surprised to find the kitchen deserted. It was kind of an in-between time. The evening cooks would be in at four, and the daytime assistant cook had probably just left. Maybe Zach had stepped outside for a break. She walked toward the back of the kitchen and saw Zach sitting on the back step, just outside the door, smoking. She didn't want to bother him on his break and went back to the front desk.

She checked again fifteen minutes later and was surprised to see Zach still sitting outside, with a freshly lit cigarette dangling from his lips. A wave of annoyance rose, and she forced it down. The restaurant was empty, so it wasn't like anyone was being ignored. Instead of leaving though, she walked toward the back door, and when he saw her, Zach put his cigarette out, stood, and ambled back inside.

"Hey there. Did you need something?" There was a slight edge to his voice, almost as if he was annoyed that she had interrupted his break.

"I was just curious if you had decided on the specials yet? I was going to post them on social media possibly."

"Sure. Yeah, I've got a nice Bolognese going and am going to serve it over gnocchi. And we have some fresh swordfish in, and I'm doing that grilled with a red curry sauce over cauliflower puree."

"Okay. Any chance I could get a small amount of the Bolognese? I love gnocchi, and I can take a picture."

Zach went behind the line and scooped a generous amount of gnocchi in a bowl and smothered it with the Bolognese sauce and a sprinkling of parmesan cheese. It smelled amazing.

"Thank you." Emma picked up the bowl and headed out to the front desk with it. There was still steam coming off it. She took a few pictures and posted it on social media. It looked amazing, and she eagerly took a bite, expecting it to taste like Paul's version, which he often ran as a special. But it tasted nothing like his.

It was good. Emma was just surprised that Zach's version was so different. It was heavier on the red wine, and it was a bit saltier. It was still very good though. She finished off the entire bowl, and when she brought it into the kitchen, the rest of the staff had arrived, and they were all busy getting ready for the night ahead.

Customers streamed in, and it seemed like everything was going smoothly. Emma noticed one of their waitresses, Amy, who was in her early twenties, took a dish back into the kitchen and a few minutes later came back looking upset. She brought the plate of food to the table and set it down. When she walked by, Emma called her over.

"Is everything okay, Amy?"

Amy hesitated. "It's fine now. Connie got the swordfish special and thought it was just going to be the way Paul always makes it, grilled with a dusting of crumbs on top. I did tell her it had a red curry sauce, but she didn't expect that it would be covered in the sauce. Zach wasn't happy about it."

Emma tried not to smile. She could imagine Zach being annoyed at someone ordering fish that came with curry sauce and then being surprised that the sauce was on the fish. "Did he fix it?"

Amy nodded. "He did. He had a few other orders of swordfish in the broiler and pulled one when it was ready and gave it to me. No sauce. Connie was thrilled."

"Good. How is everything else going? No other complaints?"

"Well, two people have said the Bolognese tastes different. But it's a special, so that's fine. They seemed to like it anyway."

"Yes, that's fine. Thank you." Amy scurried off to the bar to get some drinks, and Emma took a walk through the dining room. She kept an eye on the front door in case anyone else came in, but the rush had died down. She went table to table and asked everyone how their dinners were. She liked to do that whenever time permitted. The customers loved the attention, and if there were any issues or feedback, she could try to help.

Everyone seemed happy until she reached a table of two, an older couple that came in once or twice a month.

"Mr. and Mrs. Anderson. I hope you're enjoying

everything tonight?"They were creatures of habit and usually ordered the same thing—broiled halibut for her and baked scallops for him.

They exchanged glances, and then Mrs. Anderson spoke. "We never like to complain, and of course as you can see, we cleaned our plates. But it seemed a bit off tonight. My halibut was dry, and Harry's scallops were undercooked. I know a lot of people like them that way, but Harry likes them cooked through, and they've always been wonderful here. I'm sure it was just an off night."

"Oh dear, I'm sorry to hear that," Emma said. "Please always let your server know if there is an issue. We will always want to make it right. I'd like to send you an after-dinner drink or a dessert on the house."

"Oh, how nice of you. Harry, will you help me eat a brownie sundae?" Her husband nodded affirmatively.

"Would you like two or another dessert as well?" Emma offered.

"No dear, thank you. One sundae will be plenty for the two of us to share."

Emma told Stacy, the server for their table, to ring in a sundae but that she would be taking the charge off the bill. "I'll bring it over to them. Don't worry about it," she said.

Stacy had drinks ready to be picked up at the bar. She nodded appreciatively. "Thanks so much, Emma."

A few minutes later, Emma went into the kitchen to pick up the dessert. Richard was on salads and desserts tonight and was adding the whipped cream as Emma walked over.

"Is that for Stacy's table?" she asked.

He nodded, and she put the dessert on a small bar tray and added two spoons.

"What's wrong with it?" Zach snapped at Betty, an older server who he'd just handed a plate of food to.

"They ordered that curry sauce on the side," she said.

Zach grabbed the order slip and then slammed his hand down on the counter. "I'm going to have to cook a new piece. Tell them it will be a few minutes. I'll rush it along as best I can."

Betty spun around and headed toward Emma, who was about to walk out of the kitchen. As soon as they went through the door, Emma pulled her aside.

"Please apologize to your table and offer them a round of drinks on the house."

"Thanks, Emma. They'll appreciate that."

When the last of the customers left and everyone was cleaning up and getting ready to home, Emma went into the kitchen to get a slice of cheesecake to go with the cup of tea she'd just poured. She didn't do it every night that she worked, but a few times a week, she liked to indulge her sweet tooth while doing the closing paperwork.

Zach was wiping down the station and nodded when Emma walked in.

"How did the night go?" she asked him.

"Fine," he said shortly. "I think it was okay."

"Good. Thanks, Zach. See you tomorrow." Emma grabbed her slice of cheesecake and added a drizzle of raspberry sauce across the top and a squirt of whipped cream. She took her dessert and cup of tea to the bar and settled in to enjoy her treat before closing down the front register. She always enjoyed chatting with Gina at the end of the shift too. "How did your night go?" she asked as Gina filled her dishwasher with empty glasses.

"It was good, pretty steady all night."

"Any comments or complaints on anything you served?"

Gina thought for a moment. "Now that you mention it, yeah. I had an order of scallops that were undercooked, but that's an easy fix. Oh, and one of my guys got the swordfish special with the sauce on the side. He said the fish was great, but the sauce was too spicy for him. He was glad he got it on the side."

Emma nodded. "Anything else? Did you serve any Bolognese specials?"

"Yeah, a few. It went over pretty well. One of the ladies that had it though said it was very different from the last time she came in."

"Okay, thanks. It was Zach's first night on his own."

"He's just here temporarily, right? Just until Jason comes back?" Gina asked.

"Yes, I think so. Though Paul mentioned he might be open to having him stay on part-time possibly if it works out. He could use an extra sous-chef-level guy who can work lunch or dinner shifts as needed."

"Hmm. I miss Jason." Gina didn't say anything else, but

Emma sensed that she hadn't warmed up to their prickly new cook either.

A moment later, Zach came to the bar and sat a few seats away from Emma. Gina smiled warmly and set a coaster down in front of him. "Ready for your after-shift drink? What can I get you?"

"I'll have a Tanqueray and tonic, thanks." He didn't return her smile and barely glanced Emma's way. Gina quickly mixed his drink and set it down for him.

"Do you have any family left on the island?" Emma asked, trying to make friendly conversation.

Zach scowled. "No. My uncle died six months ago. So it's just me now. I'm staying in his place."

"Oh, I'm sorry to hear that."

"What other restaurants have you worked at?" Gina asked.

"I've worked a bunch of different places." He rattled off a half dozen names of local restaurants on the island, and they ranged from smaller mom-and-pop places to fine dining. Emma was shocked when he mentioned that he'd worked for a season at the Straight Wharf.

"What was that like? It's one of Mandy's favorite restaurants. She was just there the other night."

Zach made a face. "It's not mine. It wasn't a fit. I'm not really a high-end, fine dining kind of guy. Don't get me wrong, I appreciate really good food, but I'm not into the fussy stuff."

Gina was still looking at him curiously. "Did you ever work in Boston by any chance? You look so familiar, I wonder if we ever worked together?"

Zach laughed. "I recognized you immediately. I worked at Via Mollo."

Gina looked surprised. "You did? When?"

"Maybe five or six years ago. It was just for a few months."

"Oh, was it just a temporary thing then, like this?"

Zach downed the rest of his drink and set the empty glass on the bar. "Something like that. I was just there for a few months." He stood. "Have a good night."

"See you tomorrow, Zach."

He walked back toward the kitchen, and once he was gone, Emma looked at Gina. "You don't remember working with him?"

She shook her head. "No. I wonder why he left. I'm kind of curious now. I'm still in touch with some of the people there. If I hear anything interesting, I'll let you know. I didn't want to say anything negative earlier, but he kind of gives me a weird vibe. He seems very tightly wound, if you know what I mean?"

Emma nodded. "I do. He's a bit intense."

"So how did the night go?" Paul asked Zach casually when he walked into the kitchen the next day. It was a quarter to four, and the evening kitchen staff hadn't arrived yet, but Zach was there, finishing up the lunch shift. Paul had called Emma that morning to get her take on how he'd done, and she filled him in on how the night went.

"Fine. The specials were popular." Zach leaned against

the stainless steel counter and met Paul's gaze. "Did you hear otherwise?"

"Not exactly. There were no complaints, well, other than a few people said their scallops were slightly under done. I know a lot of places do them that way. I should have let you know that we don't."

"Okay, noted." Zach sounded slightly amused.

"People liked your Bolognese but several commented that it had a different taste than usual. Did you use the recipe I left for that?"

Zach shrugged. "I've been making Bolognese that way for years. Never had a complaint before."

Paul sighed. "I'm sure it was delicious. But it didn't taste the same as the last time they had it here. Consistency is important here. It's what keeps people coming back."

"Okay. No worries. Anything else?"

"One last thing. Maybe go a little lighter on the heat level if you do a curry sauce again. This is an older crowd, and they tend toward milder tastes."

"Got it. See you tomorrow then." Zach headed out the back door, and Paul watched him go.

It wasn't like he'd done a bad job. Zach was quick, and he was a good cook. Paul was glad to have him there to fill in for Jason. Now that he'd explained how important consistency was, hopefully that would be the end of it and Zach would follow the recipe more closely.

27

Mandy was nervous as she shook the hand of the therapist that Barbara had referred her to. Mandy had shrugged the suggestion off at first, but Barbara had insisted and said it would do her good to talk through her emotions with someone who was completely unbiased and a professional.

Janet Dunham seemed like a nice enough woman. She was in her early sixties and had the classic preppy Nantucket look—a simple blond chin-length bob, a string of pearls, and a soft yellow top paired with a pretty blue skirt. She led Mandy into her home office, a comfortable room with bookcases lining the walls, several tall lamps, an assortment of chairs, and two big bay windows that overlooked a grassy backyard. There was no sofa to recline on, which was how Mandy always pictured a therapist's office.

"Please have a seat and make yourself comfortable," Janet said.

Mandy tried to do that. She settled into the nearest chair, crossed her legs, and waited for Janet to begin.

"Have you been to a therapist before?" Janet asked. She sat in a padded rocking chair with a yellow legal pad in her lap.

Mandy shook her head. "No, never. This is my first time. I'm not really sure what to expect, to be honest."

Janet smiled. "There's no one right way to do therapy. It's your time to talk about whatever you want to talk about. I'm just here to listen and to help where I can. Why don't you start by telling me why you're here?"

Mandy took a deep breath. "Okay. I'm trying to process what happened with my husband and if I'm making the right decision to proceed so quickly with divorce."

"What do you want to do?"

"I want to turn back time and have Cory make different choices." She sighed. "I'm just really struggling with this and wondering how much of it is my fault."

"Your fault? Can you explain that a bit?"

"I keep wondering if something I did or didn't do or something I said may have pushed Cory into the actions he took. If I'm partly responsible."

"And if you are? Will that change anything? Should it change anything?"

"I don't know. I feel like I don't know anything anymore."

"Why don't you start from the beginning and walk me through exactly what happened," Janet suggested.

Mandy took another deep breath and then dove in. When she finished, Janet nodded.

"Please know that this isn't your fault. Cory chose to do what he did for reasons known only to him. What you have to consider is if you think he has the capacity to change his behavior in a way that you can live with."

"Do you think that's possible?" Mandy had her strong gut reaction on that but was curious what the therapist would say.

"Well, anything is possible. But Cory has already done the hardest thing, which was to open the door to being unfaithful. And he's admitted that he liked the thrill of the forbidden." Janet paused for a moment and then continued. "He might be on his best behavior if you take him back, maybe forever, maybe for a long time, maybe not long at all, but it won't be as hard for him to open that door again, and the temptation will always be there. But some people do make it work. Only you will know if you can get past it and trust him again."

Mandy nodded. "I know. And I've read that most men who cheat go on to do it again. Cory couldn't even explain why he did it, just that it fed some kind of need in him. Which is what made me wonder if I'd failed him in some way. It's very confusing."

"People are complex. Cory's reasons may have very little or nothing to do with you."

"He said that. Said it was something in him. But it still seems like our relationship must be broken in some way for him to do that." This was what Mandy kept coming back to.

"It may have nothing to do with your relationship and everything to do with his relationship with himself. Is he willing to go to counseling?"

"He said that he was, but I don't know that he was serious. I think he thought he could talk his way into me forgiving him, and things would go back to normal. But there is no more normal. Not for me anyway. My biggest struggle is with feelings of guilt about whether to try again."

"Guilt? Can you talk about that?"

"Well, I fluctuate from feeling guilty about wanting to call it quits and move right on to divorce and be done with it to feeling guilty about even considering trying to get past it—as if I'm letting people down by taking him back and allowing for the bad behavior to be forgiven. Mostly I feel like I'd be letting myself and the kids down if I do. How can I set an example for them about how someone should be treated if I condone his behavior?"

Janet stayed silent. When the silence grew long enough to feel uncomfortable, Mandy jumped in to fill the space.

"One minute, I want to try again and have our old life back as much as possible. The next minute, I almost hate him and can't stand the thought of being physical with him ever again. I actually feel repulsed at the thought of his touch. I suppose that doesn't bode well for fixing this?"

"Maybe not? Maybe your body knows what it wants or doesn't want and your mind hasn't caught up yet?"

That resonated with Mandy. She'd already set everything in motion for the divorce. Her attorney was just waiting for Cory to get back to them with the improved offer. But he hadn't done that yet, and as each day passed, Mandy wrestled with second-guessing herself. She supposed she was mostly looking for the therapist to validate her decision.

She talked to Janet for another half hour. The time went by so fast that she was surprised when the old-fashioned clock on the wall chimed that the hour was up. They agreed to meet the next week at the same time, and as Mandy walked outside and got into her car, she felt a bit lighter and was glad that she'd agreed to meet with Janet. She could see why Barbara liked her. Janet was easy to talk to and was a good listener. Most importantly, she'd helped Mandy to dig deeper into her own feelings, and when she did, she felt the tension she'd been grappling with ease just a bit. She knew in her gut that she was making the right decision.

28

"What is up with you? You're glowing. It started when you came home from New York last weekend. I've noticed it all week."

Jill looked up from her laptop to see both Emma and Izzy looking at her. Izzy was in Emma's lap as she sat across from Jill at the kitchen table. It was Friday morning, and Emma was heading into the restaurant soon for a lunch shift.

Jill smiled. She hadn't said anything yet because she wasn't convinced at first that what she and Billy had was real, but they'd been talking every day since she saw him, and it was starting to feel very real. She'd already booked a flight to head to New York the following weekend.

"I guess Billy and I are sort of dating now. It just happened this past weekend, and it's still really new."

"Good, it's about time. I like Billy and the thought of

the two of you together." Emma looked thoughtful before adding, "Maybe it's better this way, with you here. You can let it unfold more slowly, kind of ease into it?"

Jill nodded. "I hope you're right. We're not really telling anyone yet, especially the employees. We'll have to figure out the best way to handle that. For now, it's easier with me not there as much."

When Jill arrived in Manhattan the following Thursday night, Billy was at the airport to collect her. He looked as excited and as nervous as she felt, and she was relieved to see it wasn't just her feeling that way.

"I'm glad you're here," he said before pulling her in for a welcome kiss that took her breath away.

"Me too."

They went to a cozy Italian restaurant in the West Village for dinner, and it was a perfect, romantic night. The food was wonderful, but Jill didn't really care what she ate. Billy ordered her favorite wine, a rich Chianti, and they talked for hours, enjoying their pasta and wine and laughing and catching up.

"I'm so glad we did this," Billy said as they left the restaurant and walked hand in hand back to Jill's condo, which was nearby. It was a clear night, and the stars shone brightly in the sky, and Jill had never been happier. It felt so natural to finally be together. Billy spent the night, and the next morning, they went into work together. Billy went in first, and Jill stopped off at a Starbucks and had one coffee before going up to the office. They didn't want it to be obvious yet to their staff that they were together.

Jill's assistant, Jenna, let out a squeal when Jill walked in and rushed over to give her a hug. "This is a fun surprise. Billy didn't mention that you were coming in today."

Jill laughed. "I wanted it to be a surprise. It was a last-minute thing. I miss being here on Fridays. Now that things are going smoothly at the restaurant, I hope to make it back more often."

Jenna looked pleased to hear it. "Well, that's great news. I was actually just about to call you. We need to reschedule the in-person interviews for your two final candidates. The VP is going to be overseas. They want to do it next Wednesday instead."

"Okay, I'll get it done. Thanks, Jenna."

Jill walked through the office, and Billy winked when he saw her. She grinned and waved to his team. It was so good to be back in the office. She loved the energy when everyone was on the phone, talking to candidates and making deals happen. There was nothing like it. And now that she and Billy were together, it felt like they were unstoppable.

Fridays were funny days. Sometimes they were quiet, but more often than not, it was a false calm in the morning before a storm of activity in the afternoon as clients raced to get offers out to candidates before the weekend. Today was no exception, and by the end of the day, the office had several offers extended and accepted.

Which meant they had a lot to celebrate, and everyone headed out for drinks after work. And then Jill and Billy ordered takeout and went to Billy's condo, which was closest to the office and where they spent most of the rest of the weekend. It was a whirlwind and the best time ever. They were both sad when Billy dropped her at the airport Sunday night for her flight back to Nantucket.

"When will you come to Nantucket again?" she asked as he walked her in.

"I'd love to come ASAP, but do you think maybe we should wait a while on that? People in the office might start to wonder if I go too soon."

He had a good point.

"I didn't think of that. And there's probably more benefit to me being in the office with everyone anyway. So for the next few months, I'll come your way, and then we'll see. Sound good?"

He answered by pulling her close and kissing her senseless before pulling back and grinning. "Works for me. Text me when you get home."

"I will. Bye, Billy."

Jill felt like pinching herself as she settled into her seat on the plane and gazed out the small window, watching the other planes take off. Finally, she and Billy were together, and it was better than she'd imagined it could be. She just hoped it would continue and that nothing would change.

29

Mandy was on her way to Mimi's Place Monday morning a little before eleven when her attorney called.

"Hey, Lindsay, could you hold just a minute?"

"Sure."

Mandy pulled into the restaurant parking lot and killed the engine. She was early and could just take the call in her car where she wouldn't be interrupted.

"Okay, I'm all yours. Have you heard from Cory?" She felt suddenly nervous, anxious for good news.

"Yes, and he agreed to what we asked for. You'll keep the house and will have primary custody. He'll have the kids every other weekend and every Wednesday night."

Mandy nodded. "Okay, that's good."

"And he agreed to the suggested amount for child support, paid monthly." Lindsay had made the request based on their financial data. "In lieu of alimony or an ongoing percentage of the company, he has agreed to a lump sum."

Mandy held her breath, and then it came rushing out in a whoosh of relief when Lindsay told her the amount that Cory had agreed to. It was an outrageous amount of money, and Mandy was shocked that Cory had agreed to it.

"I know it seems like a lot, but Cory is smart enough to know that if we pushed and went to court, he would likely have to pay more than this. We can still do that if you prefer, but I think this is a more than fair settlement, and you can avoid additional court costs and stress if you agree."

"Okay. If I accept, what happens next?"

"We'll file with the court, requesting a divorce hearing, which can take anywhere from three to six months, and then once we have the hearing and all parties are in agreement, it will be effective ninety days after that. By this time next year, probably sooner, you'll be divorced."

Mandy felt a mix of emotions ranging from sad to happy to relieved. Ultimately she wanted to get the divorce done and move on.

"Let's move forward. Please let Cory's lawyer know that I accept his offer."

"I will, and congratulations, Mandy. With this settlement, you'll be a rich woman."

"Thank you."

She ended the call and sat there for a moment. It didn't seem real that Cory's company was worth so much and that he was giving her what seemed like such a huge amount.

The thought of the money itself didn't excite Mandy though, other than for the security it would give her and the children. She knew she was fortunate, but she would have felt far more fortunate if her marriage had stayed solid. She and Cory had been happy once. And now they were both starting over.

But at least she had Mimi's Place now too. And her sisters nearby. She'd be fine. More than fine.

———

Lunch was busier than usual, which Mandy was glad to see. It was steady all afternoon, and in between seating new people, she made the rounds, checking to see how different tables were doing and chatting with many of the regular customers. She noticed that some of their regulars were coming in more often, and they had some new repeat customers too, which was encouraging.

She also noticed that the bar had a late lunch rush and every seat was full. She went over to see if Gina needed any help.

Gina flashed her a grateful smile. "I just got buzzed that Matt's haddock is up. Would you mind grabbing it?"

"Sure thing." Mandy headed into the kitchen.

Stacy, one of the servers, was standing by the line, tapping her foot and looking impatient.

Mandy saw a plate of broiled haddock under the warming light. "Is that Gina's?" she asked.

Zach nodded. "Yep."

"Is the swordfish ready yet?" Stacy asked.

"If it was ready, you'd have it," Zach snapped. "If you hadn't returned it, I wouldn't have had to start over."

"If you had put the sauce on the side, like they asked, I wouldn't have had to return it." Stacy sounded just as frustrated.

Mandy picked up her plate of haddock and turned to leave. She'd only taken two steps before she heard a loud crash.

"There's your damn fish!" Zach yelled.

Mandy turned back and saw the plate of food that Zach had slammed onto the counter. Stacy threw a lemon garnish on it, picked it up, and ran out of the kitchen. Mandy followed and delivered the broiled haddock to Matt, who was sitting in his usual seat at the bar. She'd noticed that he liked to sit on the corner, which had a good view of the TV and also of the front desk.

"Here you go, Matt. Enjoy!" She set it down in front of him and went to leave. She would have loved to chat a bit but didn't want to interrupt his newly delivered meal. There was an art to visiting with guests, and one thing Gary had taught them was that when food arrived, you waited a bit— to give time for them to eat and enjoy and then to raise any issues once they'd had a chance to try the food.

"Thanks, Mandy. How've you been? Anything new in your world?" He smiled as he squeezed the lemon over his fish.

Since he asked, she could resist sharing her news. "I'm good. Really good actually. My husband and I agreed on divorce terms, and it will be official soon." She felt a bit lighter saying the words. It felt real now and right.

His smile grew bigger, lighting up his whole face. "Well, that is good news. Congratulations, Mandy."

"Thank you. I'll let you enjoy your lunch." She knew if there were any concerns, he'd let Gina know.

The haddock looked perfectly done to her; it was flaky and dusted with buttery crumbs. It was one of her favorites on the menu.

Mandy was still smiling as she made her way back to the front desk and answered the phone. "Mimi's Place, can I help you?" She took a reservation for that evening and wrote it on the calendar.

Gary walked up a moment later and took a peek at the reservations list for the night.

"Our reservations are up quite a bit. This is a good trend." He looked pleased.

Two older women walked by, and Mandy overheard one muttering to the other. "This place has gone downhill lately. This is the second time in two weeks that things just aren't as good. It's so disappointing."

Mandy hesitated and then went up to them. They'd just reached the door and were about to walk outside. She recognized them as the Andrews sisters, and they'd been in several times over the past month.

"I couldn't help but overhear you. I'm so sorry that you

were disappointed with your lunch today. Do you have a moment to share what the issue was?"

The two women exchanged glances and then one of them spoke. "We've been coming here for years. And we've always loved it. But the past few times we've been in, it just hasn't been the same. I always get scallops, and twice now, they've been undercooked, and I had to send them back, and then they were like rubber. There's nothing worse than rubbery scallops, except maybe undercooked ones. I'm not sure I feel safe ordering them here again."

"I'm so sorry. We do have a new lunch chef. He's just filling in for our regular chef for a few more weeks. Jason broke his ankle, but he'll be back soon."

"Jason makes excellent scallops," the woman sniffed.

"He does. Was there anything else besides the scallops?"

Her sister nodded. "I ordered the swordfish special, and it came with a very spicy sauce. I can't do spice, so this time, I ordered it with no sauce. I just like my swordfish with those buttered crumbs on top. But they forgot, and it had that awful sauce all over it. I had to send it back. Both of us had to send our food back. It wasn't relaxing," the woman said. "I know it's not your fault, dear."

"Ladies, please come in for just a moment. I want to give you a gift card for your next visit to make up for today."

"Well, that would be nice. That's very kind of you." The first woman was considerably less grumpy now, and Mandy quickly got them a gift card that would fully cover their next lunch.

She handed it to them and apologized again. "I do hope you'll forgive us and come back soon."

"Of course we will." The ladies left happy with their gift card, and Mandy went back to the front desk where Gary was taking it all in.

"We need to talk to Paul," he said.

Mandy agreed. When Paul arrived for the evening shift, Mandy asked him to step into Gary's office for a moment, and she asked Gina to keep an eye on the front desk.

Once they were all in Gary's office, Paul raised his eyebrows. "It's Zach, isn't it?"

Mandy nodded, and she and Gary filled him in.

"He's rude to the waitresses," Mandy began and told him what she'd seen that afternoon. And both she and Gary shared the customer complaints. "I know you talked to him about the importance of consistency, but he's still making the same mistakes, like undercooking the scallops."

"Okay, I'll talk to him again. But if he doesn't improve, we might have to think about finding another option."

"Hopefully he'll get it right this time," Mandy said. She hated to think of firing him so soon. Maybe he just needed a little more time to do things their way.

30

Paul went into the kitchen, dreading the conversation he needed to have with Zach. It was four now, so the other kitchen staff had arrived, and Zach was putting his coat on. Paul had just caught him before he left for the day.

"Hey, Zach, can we chat for a minute? Let's step outside."

Zach's shoulder's stiffened, and his eyes narrowed a bit. He looked worried, wary, and defensive all at once. Paul suspected he knew what was coming. He opened the back door and stepped outside. Zach followed and leaned against the metal railing, facing Paul. He stayed silent, waiting for Paul to speak.

Paul chose his words carefully. "How's everything going? Are you happy here?" he began.

The question seemed to surprise Zach. "Am I happy? Sure. It's going fine." He lifted his chin and met Paul's gaze. "I know my food is good."

Paul nodded. "Your food is good. We've mostly heard good things. Your broiled haddock is excellent. Mandy had compliments just today on that."

Zach's shoulders relaxed slightly. "What is it then?" he asked.

Paul walked him through the issues with the scallops and consistency in general. He tried to keep the annoyance out of his voice as they'd had this conversation before.

"Just be careful. If scallops are underdone, it's such an easy fix, but it's just a matter of minutes before they cross the line to overdone and rubbery. If it wasn't for Mandy overhearing the two ladies complaining to each other as they left and intervening, we might have lost those customers. And they would have told their friends."

Zach sighed. "I'm sorry about that. I'll be more careful. Is there anything else?"

Paul hesitated. It was bad enough to have to discuss food issues. Mentioning behavior was even more delicate. And in many kitchens, it was acceptable for chefs and cooks to have an antagonistic relationship with waitstaff, to snap or even yell at them. Paul had seen chefs make servers cry more than once, and it had always made him cringe. He found the behavior appalling and unacceptable. He would not allow it in his kitchen. Ever.

"Please be more respectful with your interactions with servers. I know it's allowed in other restaurants, maybe even encouraged, but it's not here. Mandy witnessed your behavior with Stacy earlier, and she explained that the error wasn't Stacy's, it was yours, so there was no reason for you to be short with her or to yell or slam things around. Even if it had been Stacy's error, it still wouldn't have mattered. People make mistakes."

Zach nodded again. "You're right. I'm sorry. I was in a mood today, and I took it out on her. It won't happen again."

He seemed genuinely contrite, and Paul relaxed a bit. He didn't want to have to replace Zach. There were still at least three weeks to go before Jason would be back. Paul had checked in with him earlier in the day, and he was doing well but couldn't come back until his doctor saw him at his six-week appointment and cleared him to return to work.

"All right, that's it then. Have a good night, Zach, and we'll see you tomorrow?"

"Thanks. See you tomorrow." Zach shuffled off to his car, and Paul watched him go. He drove a beat-up Civic. It looked like he'd sideswiped his passenger side mirror and duct-taped it back together. It looked like it was barely hanging on. Paul sighed. He hoped he wouldn't have to have a conversation like this with Zach again. Because the next time, it would end very differently.

31

Jill came in Wednesday night expecting an easy night. She'd
worked the night before as well with Emma, and Mandy
had filled both of them in on Paul's conversation with
Zach. She said he'd been on his best behavior on Tuesday,
and they were hopeful that he'd taken Paul's words to heart
and wouldn't have any further issues.

Both Emma and Paul were off tonight, and Zach was
covering the evening shift. Emma had mentioned that she
and Paul were going to go see a movie and grab some pizza.
It sounded like a date to Jill, and she was thrilled for both
of them, but Emma had assured her it was no such thing.

"We're just friends. That's all I'm capable of with anyone
right now. I'm not even thinking about dating. Paul's easy
to be with, and it's comfortable. Besides you and Mandy, I
don't really have any friends here. I've lost touch with my

friends from high school. Most of them couldn't wait to move off-island."

Jill had just nodded. "Same with me. I lost touch years ago. Mandy mentioned having some of her friends over for an appetizer party soon, on a night when we're all free. She thought it might be a good way to reconnect with some of the people we knew who are still on the island."

"Oh, that would be fun."

"Let me know if the movie is any good," Jill had said, then walked out the door to head to Mimi's Place. Emma had laughed and promised that she would.

Mandy was already gone for the day, and Gary was at the front desk when Jill had arrived. Gina was behind the bar and had restocked everything; she smiled when she saw Jill.

"I think you should have everything you need. Zach just told me the specials for tonight. He made Bolognese and lobster Fra Diavolo. You can smell the sauces when you go into the kitchen. I just went in, and my stomach is growling now."

Jill smiled. "They both sound good. I haven't had Fra Diavolo in ages. It's usually pretty spicy, right?"

Gina nodded. "It actually means Brother Devil, and the sauce is made with tomatoes, onion, garlic, red pepper flakes or Calabrian chili peppers, and other spices. It usually has quite a kick. You might want to have a taste in case anyone asks about the spice level."

"Good idea. My stomach is growling a bit at the thought of it. I love spicy dishes."

"Go ahead and try it. I can cover the bar for a few minutes. I'm not in any rush to get home."

"Thanks, Gina. I'll be quick."

Jill went into the kitchen and saw Zach behind the line, stirring one of two big pots of sauces. He looked a bit more unkempt than usual. His hair was tangled and badly in need of a cut, and his five-o'clock shadow was darker than usual. He also had deep shadows under his eyes and looked like he'd had a terrible night's sleep. But he actually smiled when he saw her, and his face brightened a bit.

"Hey, Zach. Gina just told me tonight's specials, and they sound great. Could you please give me a small taste of both?" She'd decided to sample the Bolognese too as she loved the way Paul made it and was curious if Zach's version was as good.

Zach handed her two small plates, and she went off to a quiet area by the desserts where she wouldn't be in the way. She tried the Bolognese first. It was very good and tasted just like Paul's version, which was a relief. She knew they'd had an issue with that sauce before when Zach made it his way.

She tried the lobster Fra Diavolo next, and while the lobster was delicious and cooked perfectly, she was a little concerned about the sauce. She knew it was a spicy dish, and she normally loved that and could handle a high heat level. But this was positively fiery. It was almost too hot to eat. She took a deep breath. She was tempted to say something to Zach but decided to talk to Gary instead. She knew the message might be received better from Gary than from her. And she wanted Gary's opinion first. She saved a good bite for him to try and walked out to the front desk.

Gary was writing in the reservations book and looked up when he saw her.

"Is that one of tonight's specials?" he asked.

"It's the lobster Fra Diavolo. I saved you a bite. I'd like your opinion of it."

Gary raised an eyebrow. "Okay." She handed him a fresh fork and set the plate down. He speared a chunk of lobster, pasta, and sauce and popped it in his mouth. A moment later, his eyes watered, and he reached for his glass of water and took a sip. "Wow. That heat level is off the charts." He frowned. "I think it might be a bit much for our clientele."

Jill nodded. "That's what I thought too. I know it's a popular dish, but if it goes out like this, I know we'll have a high number of returns or just unhappy customers who won't say anything but won't keep eating it either. And might not come back. I know that sounds dramatic, but Mandy told me about the two ladies earlier this week. All it takes is one bad experience for a lot of people."

Gary nodded. "I'll go talk to him. He should be able to dial the heat level back by adding more tomatoes."

"Thanks, Gary."

The night proceeded uneventfully. Gary spoke to Zach, and he said he would dilute the spice. Still, Jill worried when a young couple at the bar decided to order it. She cautioned them that it might still be very spicy.

"Oh, we don't mind spice. We love Thai food and get it at the highest spice level," the young woman assured her. So Jill took their order, and they loved it.

"This spice level is just perfect. It's so good." They raved about the dish, and Jill relaxed a bit.

The restaurant was unusually busy for a Wednesday night, and the kitchen got backed up. Jill knew that sometimes happened in the best of kitchens, and she just apologized and told customers their food would be a bit longer. She was waiting for another order of the Fra Diavolo for a young guy who was dining solo at the bar. She went into the kitchen when her buzzer went off that her food was ready.

And she was surprised at the chaos behind the line. Zach was sweating—there were beads of perspiration across his brow, and he wiped at them with the back of his hand before he reached for a sauté pan full of lobster Fra Diavolo and poured it over a waiting bowl of pasta. He slammed the bowl onto the line and hollered Jill's name. Jill was standing behind Stacy and Betty, who were also waiting for their food.

"I'm right here!" Jill said.

Zach scowled at them as Jill reached for the plate of food. She watched as Zach grabbed a nearby water bottle and took a long swig. She assumed it was water and didn't think much of it. It got hot in kitchens, especially when they got busy unexpectedly.

Jill brought the Fra Diavolo out and set it on the bar

in front of her customer. "Here you go. I apologize for the wait. Can I get you another drink? This one's on me."

"Sure, I'll take another IPA. Thank you."

Jill poured the draft beer and set it down in front of him. He'd just taken a bite of the pasta, and a funny look went across his face. Jill tensed. She knew what was coming.

"How is it?"

The man reached for his fresh beer and downed half of it in one long swallow. He pushed the plate away. "I'm sorry. I like spicy food and was excited to try this as it's a special. But that is not edible. It's like pure fire."

"I'm so sorry. I can see if he can tone it down some. Or I could get you something else?"

"If he can make that half as spicy, I'll give it another shot. But I'm not sure that's possible." He reached for his beer and took another sip, then bit into a buttered roll. Jill knew the bread would help calm the fire.

"I'll be right back."

She went into the kitchen, dreading the conversation she needed to have. Zach didn't seem in the best of moods, to put it mildly.

The kitchen was a bit quieter though. The mad rush had died down, and Zach was leaning against the counter, drinking from his water bottle.

He looked up when Jill came in holding the barely touched plate of food. His eyes darkened, and he waited for her to speak.

"Is there anything you can do to dial the spice down on

this? My customer can't eat it. And he says he loves this dish normally, so he knew it would be spicy."

"Give it to me." His words were clipped and low.

Jill handed him the plate of food, and he dumped it into a sauté pan. He poured some of the sauce off and opened a can of pureed tomatoes and dumped it in the pan, added a shake of salt, pepper, and garlic powder, and stirred the lobster around for a few minutes. He then took a spoon and dipped it into the sauce and tasted it. Then he poured it over fresh pasta and slid the plate back to Jill.

"Thanks." She looked at Zach curiously. "I thought you'd already adjusted the sauce?"

"I did. We sold a lot of it though and were low on the sauce, so I made a new batch. I guess it was spicier. My bad." He reached for his water bottle and took another swig.

"Okay, thanks, Zach. I think it's slowing down now."

Zach nodded and turned his back to her to check something on the stove.

Jill returned to the bar with the pasta and set it down. "He said the spice level should be way down. Hopefully."

The man took a small piece of lobster and pasta and tentatively took a bite and then nodded. "Much better, thank you."

The bar was still pretty busy, and Jill turned her attention to her other customers. Several of them were finishing up, and after they paid and left, the bar emptied out quickly. She'd refilled her lobster pasta man's beer, which was almost gone when she brought the food back to him.

She noticed that he seemed done eating, and while all the pasta was gone, there was still quite a bit of lobster left. Which was unusual—usually it was the other way around, and no one left much lobster.

"Was the lobster okay?" She wondered if it was still too spicy and he just hadn't said anything.

"The spice level was fine. But the lobster toughened up. The chef must have kept it on the stove while he adjusted the sauce."

"He did. I'm so sorry. I'll take it off your bill." She looked at him curiously. "Do you cook?" He'd sounded like he knew his way around a kitchen.

He nodded. "Yeah. I've been working as a sous-chef for the past five years at the Blinds. It was recently sold though and is under new management. Feels like a different place now. I'm thinking about maybe looking for something in Boston."

Jill was impressed. The Blinds was one of the best restaurants on Nantucket. Their service and food were exceptional. "Are you anxious to get off-island?" She knew a lot of Nantucket natives were. She had been. Nantucket was lovely, but it was very different from living in a big city like Boston or New York where there were so many more opportunities.

"Not really, no. I worked in Boston for a few years after graduating from culinary school, and while the experience was great, I missed Nantucket. When an opportunity opened up at the Blinds, I jumped at the chance to move home."

Jill remembered that Paul had mentioned possibly

wanting to add a sous-chef soon. She knew he'd been hoping that Zach might make sense for it. But she had her doubts about that.

"I can pass your info on to our head chef in case something opens up here if you might want to hear about it?" Maybe Mimi's Place wasn't fancy enough for him after working at the Blinds.

But his face lit up. "Could you? My name is Jared Hawthorne." He jotted his phone number down. "I'd love to work here. I've been coming to Mimi's Place for years. It's where my family always came for special occasions."

Jared's green eyes lit up as he spoke about his love for the restaurant. There was a warmth about him that was a stark contrast to Zach. She picked up the scrap of paper and stuck it in her pocket.

"I'll give this to Paul, our head chef. I can't guarantee anything, but hopefully he'll be in touch if he decides to add a new sous-chef."

Once the bar cleared out and the last customer left the restaurant, the kitchen and waitstaff gathered at the bar for their after-shift drink.

Zach ordered his usual Tanqueray and tonic and set the water bottle he'd been sipping on earlier next to his drink. As usual, he drank quickly and didn't say more than a few words to his coworkers, mostly just nodding now and then as they chattered excitedly. When he finished his drink, he left, and it wasn't until he was gone that Jill realized he'd left his water bottle on the bar.

She grabbed it and took it into the kitchen to leave it on the line for him. She knew he was in the next morning. She stumbled over a wet rag that had fallen onto the floor, and when she bent over to pick it up, some liquid splashed out of the water bottle, and she caught a whiff of a familiar scent. Jill opened the top of the bottle, and the smell grew stronger. There was a half inch of liquid left at the bottom, and it wasn't water. Gin had a distinctive smell.

Had Zach really been drinking all night? He hadn't come out to the bar at all, so if he was drinking gin, he'd brought it in. She walked by the huge trash bin at the back of the restaurant. The line cooks hadn't taken the trash out yet. They usually did that on their way out for the evening, dropping it in the dumpster in the parking lot.

Jill leaned over to get a good look at the mound of trash. She wasn't about to go digging through the trash, and she didn't have to. An empty fifth of Tanqueray was tucked along the side of the trash can, peeking out from under a cardboard egg carton. She wondered if it was an isolated incident or a regular thing. Thinking back, Zach always had his water bottle on the line. And she'd always assumed it was water. Maybe it was. She couldn't imagine he'd be day drinking too. She wasn't sure what to do other than to fill in her sisters and Paul and Gary on what she'd discovered.

32

Mandy was surprised when she went into the restaurant the next morning and Zach wasn't there yet. She checked the schedule, and he wasn't off this week until Friday and Saturday. Paul was going to do a double on Friday and had the two other guys who alternated the weekends in addition to their regular evening shifts behind the line.

By eleven thirty with no sign of Zach, Mandy was getting nervous. She called Paul to give him a heads-up, and he sounded concerned.

"If he doesn't show in the next ten minutes, text me, and I'll be on my way." Mandy hoped she wouldn't need to do that as she knew Paul was working a double the next day.

She waited ten minutes, then went into the kitchen again and breathed a sigh of relief when she saw Zach behind the line. He looked like death warmed over, but he was there. He hadn't shaved in a few days, and his hair was matted in the back. It looked like he had rolled out of bed without washing or brushing it. He had deep circles under his eyes, and she noticed that one of his hands was a little shaky as he reached for his chef's knife and started chopping celery. She guessed that he was extremely hungover. And she suspected that might not bode well for the day's service. But still, she didn't want to bother Paul unnecessarily. She just nodded at Zach and headed back to the front desk.

She texted Paul that Zach was there, and he immediately responded. Great, keep me posted if there are any issues. I can pop in early if needed.

She hoped that wouldn't be necessary.

And the day proceeded relatively calmly. The day's specials were simple—a Cajun grilled cod sandwich and a turkey club with steak fries. Easy lunch specials that were well received.

Mandy was relieved that everything seemed to be going smoothly. There were no fires that needed putting out, no customer complaints. Everyone seemed happy.

Until two thirty, when one of the servers made a mistake and ordered the wrong item. Mandy saw her go into the kitchen and a moment later heard a loud crash and screaming. She rushed into the kitchen to see Zach yelling at the poor server, who'd simply made a mistake.

"You're all a bunch of idiots!" He hollered and slammed his hand against the counter.

The server stared at him in shock. A single tear ran down her face, and Mandy felt her own fury grow.

"Betty, head out to the dining room. I'll handle this," Mandy said calmly. Betty scurried off, and Mandy looked at Zach, who was scowling. He lifted his water bottle and took a big sip. Mandy came around the line and looked at the floor by Zach's feet. The platter with the returned food lay shattered with food scattered everywhere.

Mandy met Zach's gaze, and he looked away.

"Zach, what's going on?" she asked softly.

He ran a hand through his hair. "I'm sorry. I lost my cool. I'm having a bad day. It won't happen again."

"Okay. What did Betty want?"

"She ordered the wrong special. She wanted the turkey club, not the fish sandwich."

She sensed that Zach's anger wasn't about the wrong order. It was just the straw that made him snap. "How about you make a turkey club real quick, and I'll bring it out. And then I'll send Betty in so you can apologize? Can you do that?"

He nodded. "Yeah."

She waited while Zach made the sandwich, then delivered it to the customer and sent Betty into the kitchen. She went in nervously but quickly returned smiling. Mandy felt better about that, but she was still concerned about Zach. He was like a tea kettle ready to explode at any moment. A little while later, when the rush had completely died down and about a half hour before she was due to leave, she ventured back into the kitchen. Zach was outside, sitting on the back steps and having a cigarette. He didn't turn when she entered the kitchen, and she didn't think he was aware that she was there. No one else was in the kitchen. Zach's water bottle was sitting on the line, and Mandy was curious.

She walked over and quickly unscrewed the top. The smell of Tanqueray instantly wafted up, and there was about a half inch of liquid at the bottom of the bottle. She screwed the lid back on, picked up the water bottle, brought it back to the front desk, and texted Paul.

I'll be right there.

She knew Emma was on her way in too since she was working the evening shift.

They both arrived at the same time, and Mandy filled them in with more detail.

"You really think he's drinking on the job?" Emma sounded surprised and disappointed.

Mandy nodded. "Jill told us she suspected it last night. He clearly has an issue with alcohol if he's day drinking too."

A few minutes later, Zach came out of the kitchen and walked toward the front desk. He looked surprised to see Paul there so early.

"Have you seen my water bottle? I must have set it down somewhere."

Mandy reached under the front desk and held it up. "This one?"

"Yeah, that's it. Thanks." He reached for it, but Paul grabbed it instead and unscrewed the top and sniffed the inside. They could all smell the gin.

"Zach, are you drinking on the job?" Paul asked quietly.

Zach looked away, then back at Paul. "I had a rough night last night. It was just a little hair of the dog. No big deal."

Paul nodded. "Jill said you were drinking last night too. You left your water bottle behind on the bar, and she smelled the Tanqueray."

Zach said nothing. He looked away and braced for what they all knew was coming.

"I'm sorry, Zach, but I think this has to be your last day. I can't have anyone drinking while working or being rude to staff. Or having temper tantrums in my kitchen. You're a talented cook, but you need to get help. Is there anyone you can go to for help?"

Zach sighed. "Yeah. I've been in rehab before. I know who to call if it gets bad."

How much worse did it need to get? "Zach. Please get help now. Before it gets really bad," Mandy urged him.

He was quiet for a long, awkward moment before finally nodding. "I'll think about it."

"Why don't you head out, Zach. I'll take over now," Paul said.

Zach nodded again and shuffled into the kitchen.

Mandy looked at Paul and Emma.

"Do you guys feel as terrible about this as I do?" she asked.

Emma nodded, and Paul sighed. "We didn't have a choice. It's too much of a liability to keep him if he's drinking like that and so volatile with staff. It's not fair to them or to him, really. I hope he gets the help that he needs. It sounds like this has happened before."

"That could explain why his track record is so jumpy at other restaurants," Emma said.

"It can be a stressful job. Not ideal for someone who has addiction issues. Unfortunately, it's also common." Paul smiled. "So I guess you'll be seeing more of me for the next few weeks. There's no point in hiring someone now, and I doubt we could even find anyone."

"Actually, Jill met someone at the bar who you might want to call. She got his number." Mandy fished around in the front desk drawer and pulled out the paper napkin with Jared Hawthorne's phone number scrawled on it. She handed it to Paul and repeated what Jill had told her.

"He works at the Blinds, huh? And he would be interested in working here?"

"That's what he told Jill. Give him a call."

Paul smiled. "I'll call him right now. He'll want to give two weeks' notice, I'm sure, but we can get by for two weeks."

33

Jared spoke to Paul and happily accepted the sous-chef role. The understanding was that he'd start covering lunches like Zach had done, and when Jason returned, Jared would switch to mostly nights as Paul's right-hand guy. Paul didn't have anyone in the sous-chef role. He had several cooks who were solid line cooks, but none of them had the training that Jared did or the experience at a restaurant like the Blinds.

Jared gave his two weeks' notice at the Blinds, and he was an immediate hit and a breath of fresh air at Mimi's Place after Zach. The kitchen staff and the servers loved him equally. Jared was kind and calm and approachable. He didn't mind when people made mistakes or asked questions, and his cooking was top notch. He also understood the importance of consistency, and his Bolognese tasted identical to Paul's. Jared also added his own innovative twist to the daily specials that were a huge hit. His sautéed scallops with a lobster and corn risotto sold out faster than anyone expected. And Jared cooked scallops perfectly, just the way their clientele liked them.

Paul felt very fortunate that Jared had stopped in for dinner the night that Jill was behind the bar and that she'd talked to him and gotten his number. As it turned out, Jason was not cleared to return when he met with his doctor. He wasn't fully healed and needed another three weeks.

But Jared didn't mind staying on for a few more weeks of lunch duty. He was happy to pick up shifts as needed and fill in anywhere.

Paul had heard from Zach too. He'd sent Paul a quick text message asking him to send his last check to the rehab treatment center on Cape Cod, where he'd be staying for the next month. Paul happily agreed and wished him luck with his recovery.

———————

Over the next few weeks, Emma and her sisters settled into a regular routine at the restaurant. Jill flew back to New York every other Thursday night to work Fridays in the office and spend her weekends with Billy. Billy flew to Nantucket on the alternate weekends. Emma was happy for her that things seemed to be going so well. Emma was also glad that she and Mandy had each other for support;

it was a strange time for both of them with the shocks to their marriages. Emma was moving on a little faster than Mandy because, unlike Cory, who said he wanted to save his marriage, Emma's was irretrievably broken.

It was a blessing for both sisters to have Mimi's Place to focus on. Emma regularly posted her photographs and Paul's specials on the Facebook page, and their customers expected it now and looked forward to checking out the daily posts. Mandy was busy handling an upcoming wedding, and Emma was impressed with how detail-oriented and organized her sister was. Mandy had a knack for managing events, and she really seemed to enjoy doing them. Big events like weddings stressed Emma out a little, especially dealing with anxious brides and their mothers. But Mandy effectively calmed everyone down and guided them toward making the necessary decisions.

Emma and Paul had been spending time together more and more too. He had become a good friend, and both she and Mandy found it helpful to talk to him. He assured them that going through a separation or divorce was never easy but that eventually things would get better. Sometimes, she sensed a glimmer of interest from Paul, and when she did, she usually avoided him for a few days. She didn't want to lead him on, and she wasn't looking to start anything up with anyone at the moment. The thought of dating, of starting over with someone new, was not appealing in the least. Emma didn't think she even knew how to date. She'd been with Peter since her college days and had never really been on her own. She was enjoying answering only to herself and coming and going as she liked.

She was also enjoying spending more time on her photography. When the weather was good and she wasn't working at Mimi's Place, she was usually out and about, snapping pictures. Some of her sunset pictures had turned out especially well, and Jill had suggested she hang a few of them on the dining room walls along with the other consigned artwork. She felt funny doing that at first, but Mandy insisted too, so she put her favorite photo up. It was a lighthouse in a swirl of fog as a pink sky peeked through clouds. She was pleasantly surprised when it sold two weeks later. She replaced it with a pretty shot of knockout roses along a white fence in Siasconset, and that sold quickly too.

Paul was on his way over soon. It was Thursday night, his night off, and Jill was midflight to New York. It was Emma's birthday, and Mandy had asked in front of Paul that afternoon about her plans for the evening. As soon as he heard that it was her birthday, he insisted on taking her out. He invited Mandy too, but she said that she wanted to wait for Jill to come back on Sunday and maybe they'd take Emma out then if that worked. It worked fine for Emma; she'd never been one for making much of a fuss about her own birthday. It was more fun for her to celebrate other people's birthdays since she had never liked being the center of attention.

The plan was that Paul was going to come over and

cook dinner, and then they'd go out to hear some music afterward.

At six sharp, she heard his truck pull up outside, and a moment later, he walked through the door holding a big cardboard box full of food and a bottle of wine. He set the box on the kitchen counter and bent down to say hello to Izzy, who had run right over to him. Izzy was madly in love with Paul, and whenever he came over, she ignored Emma and Jill and gave Paul all her attention.

"She is a smitten kitten when it comes to you," Emma said and laughed.

Paul grinned as he started unpacking his box and putting items on the island. "She's a smart one."

Emma watched, curious as Paul set one cooked lobster, a container of scallops, a bag of shrimp, bottles of ketchup and horseradish, a head of broccoli, garlic, two big potatoes, a lemon, and a box of Ritz crackers.

"What are we having? Can I do anything to help?"

"I thought I'd make us a seafood casserole and shrimp cocktail to start, with sautéed broccoli and roasted potatoes. You could open the wine and pour us a glass." He handed her a bottle of Bread and Butter Chardonnay, her favorite brand, and she found her opener and poured them each a glass. She watched as he worked in the kitchen and made everything look easy.

He took the lobster meat out of the shell and chopped it up, then added it to a casserole dish along with the scallops. He topped it with crushed Ritz crackers, a bit of butter, and a squeeze of lemon, then added a splash of the chardonnay and threw it in the oven, along with the sliced potatoes to roast. Once he had the broccoli in a pan on the stove, he mixed the ketchup and horseradish together for a cocktail sauce and brought it to the table, and they snacked on plump shrimp and sipped their wine.

"Peter called earlier to wish me a happy birthday," Emma said as she dunked a shrimp in the spicy cocktail sauce. "He gave me the update that Tom has been accepted to culinary school. He's really going to chase his dream of being a chef." She'd been a little surprised to hear it. Tom had a really good, well-paying job. She hadn't thought he was serious about changing careers.

But Paul seemed to approve. "Good for him. We only go around once. Might as well do what makes you happy."

"That's true. And you love it," she said.

Paul reached for his wineglass. "I do. I can't imagine doing anything else. Do you think you'll go back to teaching eventually?"

Emma shook her head. "I don't think so. I enjoyed it, but I don't really miss it. I want to see if I can do more with the photography, and I like the fast pace of the restaurant. It has a different feel when you're an owner. It matters more. I feel like we have more impact now."

"We definitely do," Paul agreed. "And it's satisfying when the things we try work out—like with the new menu."

Emma smiled. "The menu has been a hit. Turns out just about everyone loves luxurious comfort food."

"What's not to love?" Paul grinned as he checked on the casserole, pulled it out of the oven, and set it on the stove to cool. The crumb topping was golden brown, and the casserole was bubbling. It smelled amazing. He made plates for them while Emma topped off their wineglasses.

"I feel very lucky," Emma said, taking a bite. "This is delicious, Paul. Thank you."

She noticed a hint of pink rising on his cheeks.

"My pleasure. I'm glad you like it."

"You know, I was a little nervous when I heard that my grandmother left the restaurant to you too," she admitted. "I wasn't sure how it would be working together. But it's been really great. I'm so glad we're friends again."

Paul nodded in agreement. "We always gotten along great. It was always easy being with you. We like the same things, mostly."

She laughed, thinking of the one thing they didn't agree on. "Do you still like that awful hard rock music?" When they were dating, Paul always tried to get her to go with him to see some of his favorite bands like Black Sabbath, Metallica, and Iron Maiden. She went once, and that was enough. It wasn't her thing, but she knew he loved it.

"What's not to love?" He laughed.

"Ugh."

"Well, no worries. The band playing tonight at the Gaslight is more your speed. Soft rock and country."

Emma smiled at that and stood to clear their plates. But Paul wasn't done yet.

"I hope you saved room for dessert?"

"What is it?"

Paul pulled a pastry bag out of his big box along with two empty cannoli pastry shells. He piped the sweet ricotta filling into each of them, dipped the ends into a container of chocolate shavings, and handed one to Emma. Cannoli were her absolute favorite dessert. She took a nibble, savoring the sweet cream with the slight hint of anise flavor.

"I think I want a coffee. Do you want one?" She stood to make a small cup to have with the dessert.

"I'm good. I'm still finishing my wine."

When they finished eating, Emma got up and stretched. "That was so good, and I'm completely stuffed now. Do you mind if we walk into town? I need to work some of this off."

"I could use a walk too."

They finished cleaning up in the kitchen and then made their way down Main Street and to the Gaslight to hear some music. The Gaslight had live bands regularly, and this one was very good. It didn't take long before people were up dancing. Emma had no interest in dancing, but it was fun to people watch. She and Paul both ordered wine, and she ordered a glass of water too.

Emma caught Paul glancing her way a few times with a funny look on his face, and she had the sense again that he was hoping they might rekindle some kind of relationship. If she was in that frame of mind, where she was looking to date again, Paul would be a good candidate. She knew that. They were compatible. She liked spending time with him, and there had always been an attraction there. She just wasn't ready to consider a relationship with anyone. She'd told Paul that early on, and he hadn't pushed, which she appreciated. She knew there was always the risk that someone else might come along and she'd miss the opportunity to see if it could work out, but it was a risk she had to take. She just wasn't ready to date anyone. But she loved spending time with Paul as a friend. Hopefully, for now at least, that would be enough for him.

34

Mandy's first wedding at Mimi's Place went off without a hitch. Emma thought the bride and her mother were difficult, but Mandy didn't think they were unreasonable. Emma didn't care about the fuss of a big reception when she got married, but Mandy understood that it was equally important to both the bride and her mother. And Mandy's strength was in managing the finest of details.

She enjoyed every minute of planning and overseeing the reception. Paul's food was gorgeous and drew raves from everyone. Jill helped with the bar, and Emma was mostly in the kitchen, getting all the food onto the trays and off to the servers. It had been a solid team effort, and after the restaurant cleared out, she and her sisters, Paul, and a few other staff members gathered around the bar for a well-deserved after-work drink.

Paul sat next to Emma. Mandy smiled at the two of them. They were constantly together. Emma swore there was nothing there, that she wasn't ready to date and they were strictly friends. But Mandy saw the way Paul looked at her sister, and she suspected Emma was equally fond of him. She just wasn't ready to admit it yet, not even to herself.

Jill was happier than Mandy had ever seen her. Things seemed to be working out well with Billy. Mandy had been worried for her at first in case it didn't work out and things were awkward between them, but that didn't seem to be the case.

"Is Billy still coming here this weekend?" It was Saturday, but Mandy had thought Jill had mentioned that he might be coming for a visit soon.

"Not this weekend. I wanted to be here to help with the wedding and wouldn't have had time to spend with him. But the next time I go to New York, we're going to tell the office that we're together."

"Really? Are you sure about that?" Mandy thought it still seemed soon.

"It's been a few months now. We both think it's time, and I don't think it's going to be a shock to some people in the office."

"Well, good then. You can celebrate with after-work drinks."

Jill laughed. "I'm sure we will. I think they'll be happy for us. We still work well together, so nothing is changing."

Emma turned her attention to the two of them while Paul was deep in conversation with Gary and Jason.

"How are things going with your therapist? Are you still seeing her?" Emma asked.

Mandy nodded. "I really like her a lot. We meet every other week now. It's good to have someone to talk things through with."

"You can always talk to us too," Jill reminded her. "How are things progressing with the divorce? Do you still talk to Cory at all?"

Mandy bit her lip. Just thinking about it still stressed her out. "Now that we've agreed on terms, it's just a waiting game, but I should hear soon about a date for the hearing, and then it will be over a few months later."

"What about Cory?" Jill asked. "Is he still asking to come back? Even though you've agreed on a settlement amount?"

Mandy nodded. "Every time I talk to him about the kids. I think he thinks one of these times, I'll say yes if he just keeps asking. Part of me thinks he agreed to that generous lump sum because he was cocky enough to think he could win me back and avoid paying it."

Jill said nothing, but the expression on her face said everything, and Mandy laughed out loud. "I know, he's a real piece of work."

"I heard from my lawyer yesterday, and my divorce will be final next week. Seems strange," Emma said.

"Really? That's a good thing though, right?" Mandy asked. Emma didn't talk much about her divorce, and Mandy had no idea it was that close to being finalized.

"I suppose. I wasn't in any hurry to do it, but Peter was. He wants to marry Tom."

"Wow." Jill shook her head.

"Oh, Emma. It's a tough situation for you," Mandy said.

Emma sighed. "It was. I think I'm almost over it now. It will actually be a relief that it's going to be finalized. I can close that chapter of my life and move on."

Mandy nodded. "That's a good way to think about it." She wished that she was further along with her own process. She was eager to put the divorce behind her. She'd been putting all her energy into the restaurant these past few months, and it had helped to keep her mind off Cory and the impending divorce.

Mandy finished her glass of wine, said goodbye to the others, and headed home. The kids were with Cory, so the house was quiet and peaceful. She changed into her most comfy pajamas, grabbed a good book, and curled up in bed to read for a while. After a few pages, she drifted off to sleep and slept late the next morning.

She woke to the sound of the front door opening and Brooke's and Blake's voices as they ran upstairs to find her. She looked at the clock. She'd slept in, but it was still early, not quite nine. Cory didn't usually bring them home this early.

Brooke and Blake ran into her bedroom and jumped on her bed.

"I can't believe you're still in bed!" Brooke exclaimed.

"Lazybones!" Blake said and giggled.

Mandy smiled. "You're right. I slept in. I worked hard last night. What are you guys doing home so early? Did Dad have to work?"

Brooke nodded. "He said he had to go into the office. Daisy was going in with him."

Mandy felt a chill run through her. "Daisy? Was she meeting your dad at the office, you mean?"

"No, she stayed over last night too. They were up late laughing. Daisy works with Daddy."

Mandy nodded. "That's right, she does. Was Patrick there too?" Patrick and Daisy had their own house on Nantucket; maybe they were both visiting.

"Just Daisy," Brooke said.

Mandy decided to change the subject. "So what do you two want to do today? I was thinking maybe we could go for a bike ride along the trail and stop for pizza at Oath after?"

Blake jumped up. "Can we go right now?"

Mandy laughed. "No. But soon, buddy. Give me a little time to get up and get ready."

———

Later on, after a fun day riding bikes with the kids and after they'd had dinner and gone to bed, Mandy called Cory.

He answered on the first ring and sounded pleasantly surprised to hear from her.

"Hey, Mandy, what's up?"

Mandy cut right to the chase. "Are you having a 'discreet' affair with Daisy now too?"

There was a long, uncomfortable silence. Finally, Cory sighed. "The kids told you she stayed over."

"They did. What are you thinking, Cory? Daisy, of all people? Your partner's wife? What will you do if he finds out?"

"He's not going to find out. It's just a bit of fun. It's not serious for either of us."

"I don't care what it is, I really don't. If you want to be that stupid, that's your business. But I think we need to set some ground rules. I assumed it went without saying, but I don't want you to bring any of these women around the kids. For the one or two nights a week that you see them, have the focus be on them. It's not fair, and it's too con-fusing for them. They don't understand what you're doing, Cory."

"I don't understand it either. If you let me come back, it won't be an issue."

Mandy sighed in disbelief. He was like a broken record. "Cory, we've agreed on terms. The divorce is happening."

"Are you sure about that? I'm willing to do whatever it takes to make this work."

Mandy laughed bitterly. "You mean like go to counsel-ing? You said you'd do that, but whenever I suggested it, you didn't follow through."

"If I agree to go to counseling, will you change your mind?"

She sighed. "No. I think we're long past that now. We should be hearing any day about a hearing date."

There was a long moment of silence before Cory spoke. "Okay. Whatever you want to do, Mandy. I'll support it."

"I appreciate that." Mandy was certain that Cory still didn't believe the divorce would actually happen. But knowing he'd been with Daisy was the final straw.

35

Mandy heard from her lawyer the next day that they finally had a hearing date, in exactly one month. She put the date on the calendar and cleared all commitments. She wasn't sure how long it would take or how she'd feel emotionally after. But she knew she didn't want to have to worry about being anywhere other than to pick up the kids and then hunker down at home. It would still be ninety days before the divorce would be final and they could celebrate.

The day of the hearing, Mandy curled her hair and wore her favorite blue sweater and black pants. She added a string of pearls and a swipe of lipstick. She wasn't trying to impress anyone, but she felt better, more confident, if she knew she looked put together. She tucked a few soft tissues into her purse and hard candies just in case her throat got scratchy. She steeled herself to get through the court appearance.

Her attorney met her at the courthouse at nine thirty, and they went inside. A few minutes later, Cory arrived with his attorney. He was wearing his favorite suit and tie, and Mandy smiled. It was good to know he was a little rattled too. It was a difficult day for both of them.

They waited until their names were called, and then it all happened in a blur. Mandy heard her attorney speaking and then Cory's, and they went over the terms of the agreement. The judge asked both of them if they agreed or if they had any issues, and they both stated that they agreed. A moment later, the judge granted the divorce petition and said the documents would be filed, and in ninety days, they'd officially be divorced.

Cory didn't come over to chat. He rushed out of the courthouse with his attorney, and Mandy guessed he was in a hurry to get back to the office and get on with his day. He finally realized that he and Mandy were never getting back together. Mandy sighed and released the tension she'd been holding since she stepped into the courthouse. She felt a bit flat and empty. She had expected more somehow, for the proceeding to be a bigger deal, but it was a straightforward process, and now it was over. Almost over. In ninety days, she could celebrate. And maybe by then, she would feel like celebrating. Right now, she just felt numb.

"Are you okay?" Lindsay asked gently.

Mandy forced a smile. "I'm fine. Let's head out."

They walked outside, and Lindsay said she'd be in touch. "If you have any questions or concerns, don't hesitate to give me a call."

"I will. Thanks, Lindsay."

Mandy drove home and changed out of her clothes and into her softest sweats. She washed the makeup off her face, slathered on moisturizer, and gathered her hair into a ponytail. She made herself a cup of hot chamomile tea and took it upstairs into the small nook off her bedroom. That was her favorite reading spot, and she curled up on her plush oversize chair and pulled a fleece throw over her. Her eyes felt heavy as she sipped her tea and stared out the window at the ocean. The views were gorgeous from this second floor window, and it was soothing to stare at the waves crashing on the shore. It was a dark and cloudy day, and some of the waves were huge with white tips.

She felt like a piece of her had died, like her marriage was a living breathing thing, and now it was gone. She wondered how Cory felt and then hated that she thought of him still. She hoped he was miserable and full of regret, but she doubted he felt that much. Cory had always been good at compartmentalizing things, letting them go, and moving on. She wished it were that easy for her.

Her eyes grew heavier still, and she set her teacup down and pulled the throw tighter around her and slipped away, escaping into a deep sleep for several hours. She woke finally a little before two, with a grumbling stomach and to the sound of banging on her front door. That was odd. People didn't usually just stop by. Maybe it was a delivery person. She dragged herself up and slowly made her way downstairs to the front door. She peeked out the side window expecting to see the UPS driver, but it was Barbara.

She opened the door, still half asleep, and looked at her in confusion. "Hi. What are you up to?"

Barbara held up her phone. "Why aren't you answering your phone? I've been calling and calling."

Mandy yawned. She had no idea where her phone was. In her purse probably. Normally it never left her side. She kept it nearby in case something happened to the kids and someone tried to reach her. But not today.

"I'm sorry. I was napping actually. I just woke up."

Barbara looked apologetic. "And I just woke you up. I'm so sorry, Mandy. It didn't occur to me that you'd be sleeping. You've never been a napper."

"No. But there's a first time for everything. Come on in."

"Are you sure? I can just go so you can go back to sleep."

"I'm sure. I need to go get the kids in an hour or so anyway."

"Have you eaten yet?" Barbara stepped inside and held up a white bag. "I brought your favorite treat."

Mandy recognized the bag from an ice cream shop downtown. "Ice cream?" Her stomach growled thinking of it.

Barbara laughed. "Looks like I got here just in time." She handed Mandy a hot fudge brownie sundae.

"You are the true love of my life," Mandy said. "Thank you."

"I knew it might be a rough day. Let's go sit and eat."

They took their ice cream into the family room and sat on opposite ends of the sofa. Mandy spent the next hour alternating between eating ice cream and crying. Barbara hugged her when she needed it and listened as Mandy told her how she was feeling.

"It will get better," her best friend assured her. "I promise."

By the time all the ice cream was gone and Barbara had left with a final hug and instructions to call anytime, Mandy was starting to come back to life. And once she was dressed and on her way to get the kids, she felt more at peace and accepting that her marriage was really and truly over.

36

Jill was used to the twice-monthly trips to Manhattan now, and Billy was falling in love with Nantucket too. They'd talked about spending more time together there, maybe a full week vacation at some point. Both of them rarely took time off for vacation, but they agreed it was something they should do more often.

Her heart swelled when she walked into the airport and saw Billy waiting for her. He wrapped his arms around her, picked her up, and kissed her thoroughly.

"I'm so glad you're here," he said softly. The warmth in his eyes matched the way she was feeling. She kissed him again.

"Me too."

"Let's get you home. I made reservations for us at a new place, well, new to me anyway. It's a speakeasy, and it's close to your condo. Have you been to Do Not Disturb yet?"

Jill laughed with delight. "No, but the name sounds perfect. Let's go."

Billy had a car waiting for them just outside. Even though he kept his own car garaged, he rarely drove it around town. It was easier to use the car service that he kept on speed dial for moments like this. They loaded the car and then snuggled in the back seat while the driver navigated through Manhattan traffic.

Once they were back at Jill's condo, she dropped her suitcase in her room and freshened up her lipstick. Then she and Billy walked a few blocks to the speakeasy that he'd mentioned.

"Are you sure this is it?" Jill asked.

They were in the heart of the West Village, standing in front of an unassuming town house. It didn't look like there was a business there. Billy looked around and frowned, then pulled out his phone and scrolled to his text messages. He grabbed Jill's hand and led her to a side staircase that went to a lower level.

"This is it. It's a hidden entry." They went down the stairs and into one of the most beautiful restaurants. The space was cozy and seductive at the same time, with glistening mahogany floors and a flickering fireplace. Billy gave their names to the host, and they were quickly seated at a table for two. Jill sank into a cozy crushed velvet chair.

The menu was intriguing, and Jill decided to order one of their craft cocktails. She went with the Sexxy Red, which had rose vodka, elderflower, watermelon, and basil.

Billy chose the Do Not Disturb, which had bourbon, tawny port, almond, orange, and bitters.

They toasted when their drinks arrived and put their food order in. They decided to share an appetizer of tuna crispy rice. Billy ordered the smash burger and fries, and Jill went for the king salmon with roasted potatoes. Everything was delicious, and as usual, the time flew as they laughed and shared the highlights of their week.

As they were paying the bill and stood to leave, Jill was surprised to see a familiar face. Jenna from the office and a friend walked over, and Jenna looked surprised to see them.

Billy made a joke of it immediately. "Fancy seeing you here! Have you been here before? Jill lives nearby and just flew in, so we thought we'd try it."

It made sense to Jill, and Jenna nodded, but a look flashed across her face that made Jill think her assistant may have picked up on a different vibe between her and Billy. New York was such a big city, yet it wasn't unusual to run into people you knew. She was glad that they were planning to tell the office tomorrow. Jill hated keeping secrets. She and Billy were both bad at it, and she was ready for everyone to know what they were up to. She hoped they'd all be okay with it, but if they weren't, they'd cross that bridge if they had to.

They left the restaurant and slowly made their way back toward Jill's condo. She'd been too full for dessert, but now that they were walking for a bit, she had a craving for something sweet.

"Let's stop for ice cream. It's still early. I'm not ready to go in just yet. Are you?"

"I can always go for ice cream. Lead the way."

They stopped at a shop on the way to Jill's condo, and she got a big scoop of coffee ice cream with chunks of crushed toffee and swirls of hot fudge. Billy got a scoop of vanilla, and Jill teased him. "You sure you don't want something more exciting than vanilla?"

He grinned. "Why mess with a good thing? Vanilla is always good, always reliable."

They found a bench nearby and sat and ate their ice cream and people watched for a while. Even though it was after ten, there were still tons of people out and about, heading to restaurants, to night clubs, for ice cream. There was an energy in New York that Jill loved so much. At this time of night on Nantucket, it would be so quiet. The night would be over. Here, it was just beginning.

Billy reached his arm around her shoulder and pulled her close to him. She was just about done with her ice cream. His was long gone. "You happy?" he asked.

She took her last bite, then leaned over and kissed him gently. "So happy. Let's go home."

The next morning, Jill rolled over and looked at Billy, who was still sound asleep in her bed. Jill was a little nervous that today was the day they were planning to tell the office that they were an item. Billy had said he'd do most of the talking, which was fine with her. She was happy for it to be out in the open, and she really didn't think anyone was going to mind. She hoped not anyway.

She jumped in the shower, and by the time she was out, Billy was up and drinking coffee in the kitchen.

He gave her a kiss on his way into the bathroom. "My turn."

Billy had called for a car, and it was waiting downstairs for them. They reached the office a little before eight. They were the first ones there, but within minutes, the rest of the team began arriving. It was a typical Friday, busy and loud, and as usual, the day flew by.

At four, Billy came into the bullpen, the large open office where all the recruiters sat in their cubicles. He walked into the middle of the room, holding a bottle of champagne, and looked around expectantly. Everyone quickly understood that he wanted their attention. Once everyone was off the phone, Billy smiled and held up the champagne.

"We have an announcement and something to celebrate today. Jill and I wanted to let you know something. You all know we've been friends, best friends for many years?" He looked around the room as people nodded.

"Well, a few months back, we decided that maybe we wanted to be more than friends, and we started dating." He grinned. "So we wanted to let you know that we're officially an item. What do you think of that?"

There was a moment of silence and then a chorus of congratulations. Jenna caught her eye and smiled knowingly. Jill was relieved that they all seemed to be happy for them.

But Billy wasn't done yet.

"There's something else that I wanted to do, here, in front of all of you. This company that Jill and I started brought us together, and it just seems appropriate to do this here too."

Billy set the champagne down, took a few steps closer to Jill, and shocked her by getting down on one knee and pulling a small black box from his pocket. He opened it and held up a huge, shimmering, square-cut diamond ring.

"Jill, we've been friends for a long time and then business partners, and there's no one else I'd rather have as a partner in life and love. You are the love of my life. Will you marry me?"

His eyes were so full of love that Jill's initial shock quickly subsided and was replaced by a sense of peace and a rush of love. "Of course I will! I love you too, so much."

He slid the ring onto her trembling finger while the room erupted in cheers and clapping.

"Billy, I can't believe this," she whispered as he pulled her in for a kiss.

"Believe it. You're it for me, Jill. I can't believe it took us so long to figure this out. I don't want to wait any longer."

Jill smiled. She felt the exact same way. "You're crazy, but I love that about you. I can't wait to marry you, Billy."

37

"Your sister Jill is on the phone. She needs to talk to you and Mandy immediately. Says it's an emergency." Gary looked concerned as he handed the phone to Emma.

Mandy was on her way back to the reservations desk, and Emma waved her over.

"Jill's on the phone for both of us."

"Is everything okay?" Mandy looked worried.

"I don't know. Gary said it's an emergency."

Emma held the receiver so they could both hear. "Jill, is something wrong?"

Jill laughed. "No, nothing is wrong."

"What's the emergency then?"

"Well, it's not every day that your sister gets engaged."

Emma almost dropped the phone while Mandy squealed. "Engaged! Tell us everything."

Jill told them about Billy's big announcement, which was followed by the completely unexpected proposal.

"You had no idea he was going to do that?" Emma asked.

"None. We'd vaguely talked about getting married someday, but I'd thought it was a long way off."

"Are you ready for it now?" Mandy asked.

"I'm thrilled. Couldn't be happier. And I think we want to have the wedding at Mimi's Place, maybe in six months or so. Can you help me with that?"

Mandy smiled. "Of course. We'll give you an amazing wedding."

"Thanks. You're the best. I had to call you right away."

"What are you doing now?" Emma asked.

"We're heading out for after-work drinks with the whole office. Billy's buying."

"That sounds fun. Congratulations again," Emma said. She hung up the phone and looked at her sister. "Wow. That was unexpected."

"Very, but it makes sense. Those two have really been together a lot longer than most before getting engaged."

"That's true." Emma looked up as Paul walked out of the kitchen and headed her way. "Thanks again for switching shifts with me." Emma was planning to cook dinner for Paul to celebrate his birthday.

"No problem. Cory has the kids this weekend, so I'd just be sitting home alone." Mandy smiled when Paul reached them. "Happy birthday, Paul."

"Thanks." He turned to Emma. "I'll see you in about an hour."

Emma wanted to make Paul's birthday special, as he'd done for hers. She knew she wasn't anywhere near his level of skill when it came to cooking, but there was one thing she knew how to make really well. Swordfish was also Paul's favorite fish, so she picked up two center cuts from Trattel's Seafood. When Paul came over, he watched with interest while she worked. She did it the way she'd learned in the restaurant on the Cape many years ago. Richard, the cranky broiler cook who had been there forever, had a magical touch with seafood, and he'd walked her through his method.

Each piece of fish went into its own aluminum pie plate. She spread a thin layer of mayonnaise over the tops of the fish and then a dusting of seasoned breadcrumbs. The last step was to pour a quarter inch of water in the bottom of the pan to keep the fish moist. She slid the pans under the broiler and added a tinfoil packet with asparagus she'd tossed with lemon, olive oil, salt, and pepper. For a starch, she had another of Paul's favorites in a saucepan on the stove: jasmine rice cooked in coconut milk.

Paul opened the bottle of pinot noir she'd picked up earlier at Bradford's Liquors—it was a 2017 Charles Krug and a bit of a splurge, but the cashier raved about it and said it was a staff favorite. When Emma took her first sip, she had to agree. It was silky smooth and full of flavor.

When everything was done, they brought their plates outside and ate on the patio. She and Jill had picked up some pretty deck furniture. When the weather was nice, Jill mostly worked outside, and they usually ate there too.

The air was warm, and there was a slight breeze. It was a perfect Nantucket night. Paul loved the swordfish.

"I might have to try this as a special. I like the water in the pie pan trick."

When they finished, Emma cleared the plates and told Paul to stay where he was. She returned with the bottle of wine and a plate of dark chocolate–covered strawberries, which she also knew Paul loved. He wasn't much of a cake person.

She handed him a big gift bag too, with a bright red bow.

"What's this?" He looked surprised and pleased as he took the bag and peeked inside. He couldn't see anything though, because it was stuffed with colored tissue paper.

"Open it and see." Emma topped off their glasses with a bit more wine and settled in her chair to watch him open his first gift. She hoped he liked it. She'd tried to think of something she knew he needed and wanted, but she worried a little that he might think her gift was too practical, not as exciting as a fancy sweater or something.

She knew she'd made the right decision though when he opened the box to discover the razor-sharp chef's knife. It was a professional grade, and she remembered he'd complained the last time she was at his place that his knives were pitiful and he really should get new ones.

"Em, this is awesome. Thank you."

"I'm glad you like it. There's something else in there... keep going."

He reached in and pulled out a box that held two sauté pans, both a pretty shade of blue-green.

"These look nice too."

"Have you heard of them? They're called GreenPans, and I saw them on Instagram. Someone was raving about how awesome they are, and they're nonstick too, so easy to clean."

Paul smiled. "I love them, thank you."

He stood and pulled her into his arms for a thank-you hug. And then surprised her by lightly touching his lips to hers ever so briefly for a kiss.

"Now don't freak out. I just wanted to thank you properly. Well, that's not entirely true. I think you know I want more than that. But I know you're not ready."

But Emma had been thinking about her friendship with Paul a lot lately, and after speaking with Jill earlier, she realized that maybe she didn't need to wait any longer. Maybe she and Paul were sort of already there, just not officially dating.

So she surprised him by leaning in and kissing him back.

"Maybe it's been long enough," she said.

38

The following Thursday, Jill worked the bar as she wasn't going to New York that weekend. Billy was coming to Nantucket, and Mandy was having them over for dinner Saturday night. Emma was coming too, after working the lunch shift.

Gina was working the front desk when Jill arrived. She smiled when she saw her. "If you get slammed at the bar, I am happy to jump in if you need help."

Jill appreciated the offer. Thursday nights sometimes were busy at the bar. "Thanks. I'll holler if I need a hand."

She went in the kitchen, and both Paul and Jared were behind the line. Paul said a quick hello, then disappeared into the walk-in refrigerator.

"What do we have for specials tonight, Jared?"

"We're doing a roasted striped bass with a red pepper

and goat cheese risotto. And we have oysters Rockefeller for an appetizer special. Oh, and a braised veal shank— osso buco."

Jill nodded. "That must be what I smell. I love osso buco."

Jared grinned. "Well, you have to try it. So you can tell the customers what it's like, right?" He made a small plate with the braised veal, whipped potatoes, and a bit of the risotto.

"Yes, for the customers. Thanks, Jared."

He handed her the plate of food, and Jill took a bite of the veal. She knew that osso buco braised for hours until the meat fell off the bone. It was so tender and flavorful. She tried the potatoes next, and they were light and fluffy and loaded with butter and cream. The risotto was rich and creamy and delicious.

She looked at Jared. "I am seriously impressed. This is all so good. Did you make the veal?"

Paul heard the question as he stepped out of the walk-in carrying a case of chicken breasts. He glanced at Jill's plate.

"Jared made all that. His potatoes are better than mine."

Jared flushed, and they all laughed. "I'm sure they are not," he said.

"It's fine. I'm tired of making whipped potatoes anyway," Paul teased. "Seriously though, Jared's food is awesome. And Jason is back to full schedule and doing great. We have a really solid team."

"We really do," Jill agreed. Both Jared and Jason were

great to work with. She didn't work the lunch shifts, but both Mandy and Emma had sung Jason's praises, and they were all so grateful that Jared had stopped in the bar that night and that he wanted to work with them. His cooking was on a similar level to Paul's, and they hadn't had that kind of consistency in a long time, according to what Gary told them.

Word was getting around too, that the food at Mimi's Place was better than ever. Mandy said that reservations continued to be up, and overall sales were up too. Which was a huge relief.

Jill finished her plate quickly and headed back to the bar to get ready for the night ahead.

It was a busy night. Her bar filled up early and stayed steady. She was surprised to see a familiar face come in a little past seven. Cory and one of his colleagues sat at the bar in two seats that had just opened up. Cory had never struck her as an eat-at-the-bar kind of guy. She knew the restaurant had a wait though, and she knew he didn't like to wait either.

He smiled big when he saw Jill. "Congrats, Jill. I heard about the engagement."

Jill was surprised that Mandy had told him about her engagement. She didn't realize they talked that much.

"Brooke told me. She's excited to be a flower girl eventually," he said.

Jill smiled. That made more sense. She knew her niece was excited about the wedding. It would be her first, and she and Blake were going to be in it, as flower girl and ring bearer.

"What brings you in tonight?" she asked, setting cardboard coasters in front of Cory and his colleague.

"We closed a new client today. Ross's biggest client to date, so I thought a celebration was in order."

Jill glanced at Ross, who she guessed was around thirty. He looked the part of a finance guy; he was tall and blond, with a square jaw and blue eyes. "Congratulations!"

"Thanks. It's pretty exciting," he said.

"I promised him a steak dinner if we closed this client, and I love the steak here. I didn't expect that there'd be a wait for a table on a Thursday night," Cory said.

Jill smiled. "Thursdays have been busy. We have a new sous-chef now. He came from the Blinds, and he's good." She told them about the specials, and Cory was impressed.

"The Blinds is as good as the Straight Wharf. I'm tempted to get that osso buco." He glanced at Ross. "What are you thinking?"

"You mentioned steak, and I'm going to stay with that. The New York strip sounds pretty good."

"Can't go wrong with that. I'll do the veal. Ross, you like red wine?"

Ross nodded affirmatively.

"Jill, we'll take that magnum of Opus One, please." Opus One was their most expensive wine, and a magnum held two bottles. She put their order in and went off to the wine cellar to get their wine and a decanter.

Jill decanted their wine and set the crystal decanter between them. "Did you want to wait a bit before pouring, to open it up?" Normally, Jill would offer a taste of any wine she opened, but not for an older or expensive wine that was going to be decanted. Usually, they'd let the wine sit for at least an hour to open up. But she suspected that Cory probably didn't want to wait.

"Go ahead and pour," he said. "I'm sure it will still be delicious."

She did as instructed, pouring him a small taste first. He made a big production of tasting it, swirling the glass and sticking his nose deep into it before taking a sip. Mandy had told her that he did that and it always embarrassed her. He was a bit over the top about it.

"Excellent. You can pour."

Jill bit back a chuckle, filled both their glasses, and then went to attend to a new arrival at the bar.

Cory and Ross made a good dent in their wine before their food even arrived. By the time they finished the appetizer, she noticed that Cory's voice was getting louder and more animated as he and Ross talked. She heard bits and pieces of the conversation, and the gist of it was how wonderful Cory was and how well his year was going. They talked and laughed and drank all through their meal, and the wine was almost gone by the time they finished dessert—cheesecake for Ross and an ice cream puff for Cory.

The chocolate cake was Emma and her grandmother's

favorite dessert, but the ice cream puff had always been Jill's favorite dessert at Mimi's Place. The pastry puff was made at a local bakery and delivered fresh each day. It was filled with a scoop of vanilla ice cream and smothered in hot fudge. She wanted to introduce it to Billy the next time they ate at the restaurant. She knew he'd love it.

Cory was signing his charge slip when an older blond-haired, blue-eyed man walked in and made a beeline for Cory. He did not look happy. But Cory smiled when he saw him. "Hey, Patrick! I didn't know you were still on the island. I thought you were flying back to Boston earlier."

"I was. I was on my way to the airport when something was brought to my attention, and I confirmed it with Daisy before coming here." He paused for a moment, and Jill watched with fascination, noticing how the expression on Cory's face changed to apprehension mixed with guilt.

"Is it true you've been having an affair with my wife?"

Cory took a sip of his wine and looked away. Finally, he spoke. "Well, I wouldn't exactly call it an affair. That implies something more serious. It was just a bit of fun. It didn't mean anything," he assured his partner.

Patrick reached back and slammed his fist into Cory's face. He didn't see it coming and looked up in surprise, with blood running from his nose and onto his silk tie. Ross looked on in horror. Patrick turned his attention to him.

"Ross, I can give you a ride home." He glanced back at Cory. "You disgust me. You'll be hearing from my attorney soon." Patrick turned and walked away.

Ross hesitated, and Cory waved for him to follow. "Go ahead. It's probably best if I get a cab home anyway. I'm sorry you had to see that."

Once he left, Cory swallowed his last sip of wine, wiped his bloody nose with his napkin, and pulled out his phone. Jill watched as he pulled up the Uber app and ordered a ride. He handed Jill the credit card slip. She glanced at it and wasn't surprised that he'd left a huge tip. Cory had always been a generous tipper.

"Thanks, Cory. You've really made a mess of things, huh?"

"Yeah." He smiled slightly and slurred his words a little. She was glad he'd ordered a ride. "That's what I'm good at. It wouldn't have happened if Mandy had agreed to take me back."

Jill didn't know what to say to that so she said nothing and grabbed a wet rag to wipe down the counter. Once Cory left, she'd spray the area with cleaner.

Cory pulled his jacket on and stood, swaying just a bit. "It'll be fine. It will work itself out. Patrick will get over it." Cory sounded like he was trying to convince himself. He was so used to getting away with things. But Jill didn't think he'd be able to talk his way out of this. Of all the people to have an affair with, he chose his partner's wife. She knew Mandy would just shake her head at his stupidity.

The bar was empty after Cory left. Jill was glad that the altercation hadn't happened earlier when she had a full bar. The restaurant cleared out soon after, and everyone gathered at the bar for their shift drink. Jill noticed that Jared settled into the seat next to Gina. She seemed oblivious to the fact that Jared kept stealing glances at her. Jill thought it was cute. She knew Gina was single, and she thought Jared probably was too. She knew the other younger servers thought he was extremely good looking, with his dark hair and green eyes with the longest lashes Jill had ever seen. Why did men always get the long lashes?

She got everyone their after-shift drink and then took her own glass of chardonnay and sat on the other side of Gina.

"So what was all that commotion about earlier? Did someone really punch Mandy's soon-to-be ex-husband?"

Jill nodded. "He did, and he completely deserved it."

39

Jill called Mandy the next morning and filled her in on Cory's visit to the bar and what had transpired. Mandy was horrified but also agreed with Jill that Cory deserved it. She felt bad for Patrick and didn't understand how Cory could do something like that to one of his closest friends and his business partner.

"Oh, and Patrick told Cory he'd be hearing from his attorney. What do you suppose that means?"

"I'm not sure. Unless maybe he wants to split up the company. I don't think I'd blame him. I wouldn't be able to work with Cory after learning what he did."

"Is Cory with Daisy? Will she stay with the company, do you think?" Jill asked.

"I really don't know. I guess it depends on if Patrick still wants to stay with her and if they both want to work on things and work together. I can't imagine. Cory said it wasn't serious with Daisy, and I could see both of them just having fun and not considering how their actions would impact others. You know she's never been one of my favorite people," Mandy said.

Jill laughed. "Kind of sounds like they deserve each other. You know, you might want to call your attorney and see if this could affect your settlement if they split up the company."

That hadn't crossed Mandy's mind, and now that Jill mentioned it, she immediately worried that it could have an impact.

"Good idea. I'll give her a call. Oh, can you come over Sunday night? I'd like to have you and Emma over to meet some of my friends. We do this now and then. Everyone brings an appetizer and a bottle of wine. I have plenty of wine though, so don't worry about that."

"Sounds fun. I'm going to New York this weekend, but I'll take an early flight back. And I'll bring wine. You can never have too much wine."

Mandy laughed. "That's true. Thanks for the heads-up on Cory. I'll give my attorney a call today."

As soon as they hung up, Mandy called Lindsay and filled her in. "If Cory and Patrick split up the company, will that affect my settlement?"

Lindsay assured her that it would not. "If you had done a percentage of the company or alimony payments, it may have had an effect as Cory's overall income could change.

But since you are doing an upfront lump sum that is based on where the company is now financially, you're fine."

Mandy breathed a sigh of relief. "Good, because I don't want to have to go back to court again or delay this in any way."

"Less than ninety days now, Mandy. It won't be much longer, and then it will be official."

"Thanks, Lindsay. One less thing to worry about."

———

Mandy fed the kids early Sunday night and settled them in Brooke's bedroom with a movie a little before seven. They'd spent the day at the beach, and most of that time, the kids were in the ocean swimming, so they were tired. They usually went to bed by eight, but this was a Disney movie they were both excited to see, so she hoped they'd enjoy it and be asleep by the time it was over. Brooke's bed was a trundle, and she pulled out the bottom mattress and set it up for Blake. Once they were all tucked in and the movie was on, Mandy headed downstairs. She was starting to feel hungry too.

She'd made chicken salad sliders for her appetizers. Her sisters and her kids loved her chicken salad. She gave it a twist by adding a squirt of lemon, honey, and mustard to the mayonnaise as well as a handful of slivered almonds for some crunch. She opened a bottle of Daou cabernet and poured herself a glass.

Everyone arrived within a few minutes of each other, and the food all looked so good. Mandy introduced her sisters to Kate and Kristen Hodges, who were twins.

Jill recognized them. "It has been a long time. I think your mother was at our grand opening."

"She was," Kate said. "Kristen and I were both in Boston that weekend for a girls' getaway. We went shopping in the Back Bay and ate our way through the North End."

"It was so fun," Kristen agreed. "We were sorry to miss the event though. I hear Mimi's Place is doing great."

"It is, now that we have Jason back for lunches and Jared as our new sous-chef," Mandy said proudly.

"We need to get in there soon," Kate said.

Barbara handed Mandy a casserole dish with her hot artichoke and spinach dip. Mandy set it on the kitchen island and figured they could all just help themselves. She knew her sisters knew Barbara already, but they hadn't met her other guest, who arrived last.

"Jill and Emma, this is Angela. She's not from Nantucket, but she lives here year round now. I met her through Kate and Kristen. Angela also runs a cleaning company and cleans for us and also for Cory's company."

Jill looked intrigued. "Do you do all the cleaning yourself? I hear that commercial cleaning is a huge growth area."

Mandy laughed. "This is the sister who's a recruiter. She's always fascinated with people's jobs."

Jill smiled. "It's true, I am."

Angela didn't mind the questions though. "I don't clean as much as I'd like actually. The company is really busy, and I've hired a lot of cleaners to help. I do whatever is left over."

"She actually likes to clean," Kate said.

"Well, that works out great for us." Mandy couldn't imagine enjoying cleaning, but she knew Angela found it relaxing, and she was the best cleaner Mandy had ever hired. Even when Angela didn't do the cleaning herself, her workers did just as good a job. Mandy wasn't surprised that business was booming for Angela.

Everyone had brought something delicious, and they all helped themselves to dips and sandwiches, stuffed meatballs, cheese and crackers, and for dessert, Kristen had brought brownies.

Mandy poured wine for everyone, and they took their wine and plates of food onto the back deck and settled on the several sofas and comfy chairs that were grouped in a semicircle facing the ocean. It was an unusually warm night with just a slight breeze. The water was calm, and the setting sun made the sky turn rose pink. In the distance, the last ferry of the night headed out of the harbor.

They all chatted easily. Mandy wasn't surprised that Emma seemed to hit it off with Kristen, who was an artist and was interested in Emma's photography. Jill was intrigued by the book that Kate was writing. Kate wrote mystery novels, and Jill loved mysteries.

It was a fun night, and the time flew as they ate and chatted and had a bit more wine.

"Oh, I heard from my attorney, and she said it shouldn't change anything if Cory and Patrick go their separate ways," Mandy said to Jill. She'd meant to update her earlier.

"Does everyone know about his latest shenanigans?" Barbara asked her.

Mandy thought for a moment. She'd told her friends about the divorce and Cory's cheating early on. But she hadn't had a chance to update them on his affair with Daisy and Patrick belting Cory at the bar. She filled them in, and everyone agreed that Cory deserved to be embarrassed by Patrick.

"He wasn't like this when we were first married," Mandy said. "Success changed him. The Cory I fell in love with wasn't like this."

"No, he wasn't," Barbara agreed. "I know you're not ready yet, but I have no doubt you'll find someone better. As my mother always says, 'everything happens for a reason.'"

Mandy just smiled and looked around the room, happy to be with her best friends and her family. She wasn't ready to think about dating yet, but she felt optimistic that she would be one day soon.

She held up her wineglass. "Cheers to that."

40

When her divorce decree finally came through, Mandy met Jill and Emma at the Club Car for Friday night drinks a little after six. It was Cory's weekend with the children, so she didn't have to rush home, and she was excited to be out with her sisters. It was a rare night that they all were off and they had something to celebrate. She stopped to admire the flower boxes below the windows of the Club Car before stepping inside. It was a charming building, with its weathered wooden shingles, and it did look like a train car. It was one of her favorite places on the island to go for a relaxing drink.

Once they were settled at the bar and had their cocktails of choice, chardonnay for Mandy and Emma and a dill pickle martini for Jill, Jill proposed a toast.

"Happy divorce day, Mandy!"

"Congratulations," Emma added.

"Thanks so much." It had been a bittersweet day. They'd signed the final paperwork earlier that morning. Mandy was relieved that it was over but also felt a trace of lingering sadness that the marriage had failed. Her lawyer, Lindsay, had been incredible. As she'd assured her, the settlement that Mandy had agreed to hadn't changed, even after Cory and Patrick decided to split the company. As far as the day-to-day went, it didn't change things much as Patrick kept the Boston office and Cory the Nantucket one, and each kept his respective employees.

She and Cory had settled into a fairly amicable relationship. They both wanted what was best for the kids, and that meant getting along as well as possible. Mandy limited their communication to specifics about the kids, pickup, and drop-off coordination. And it had taken a while, but Cory finally seemed to realize that it was truly over.

"How are you feeling about it?" Emma asked gently.

"I'm good now. I had a mini meltdown earlier after I talked to my lawyer. It just hit me that it was really over. But I snapped out of it and realized it's a good thing. It just took me a while to get there."

"That's understandable," Jill said.

"I have some news too." Emma leaned in and smiled. "Paul and I are moving in together."

"That's awesome news! Your wedding will be next," Jill said.

Mandy smiled. The planning for Jill's wedding was

done, and it was going to be impressive. She was flying the whole company in and putting them up at the Wauwinet, a gorgeous waterfront hotel that reminded Mandy of *The Great Gatsby*, with its sweeping grounds and croquet lawns. Emma made a face. "Um, no. Neither one of us wants to get married anytime soon." But then she added, "Okay, that's not completely true. Paul said he'd marry me anytime I'm ready. But he's been divorced for years. I told him I'm in no hurry, and I might never want to do that. And he said as long as we're living together, that's fine by him."

"He adores you," Mandy said.

"He is a keeper," Emma agreed.

They ordered appetizers to share and, after a while, another round of cocktails. The Club Car was busy as usual, and they saw a number of familiar faces and chatted with people they knew as they came up to the bar to order drinks.

"Who is that guy who just walked in, end of the bar? He looks familiar. I think he comes into Mimi's Place now and then," Emma said.

Mandy followed her gaze and nodded. "That's Matthew Flynn. He comes in for lunch sometimes. He's a nice guy. He lost his wife to cancer a few years ago, and his kids are in college. He runs a boat business, sightseeing and deep-sea fishing."

Jill looked at her carefully. "You know quite a bit about him. He sounds like a good candidate for you when you're ready to start dating."

Mandy laughed at the idea. "I chat with all the customers

when they come in. He's often by himself and sits at the bar, so we've gotten to talking a bit. I don't think he's interested in dating anyone, and I know for certain that I'm not ready yet."

"He's coming this way," Emma said.

Mandy smiled and caught Matt's eye as he approached them. She noticed, not for the first time, that he was a handsome man. She liked his sandy blond hair and his warm blue eyes. He had been coming into Mimi's Place more often lately, at least twice a week. She always enjoyed chatting with him. He loved the food at Mimi's Place. His eyes lit up as he reached them, and he smiled.

"Hello, ladies. I don't think I've ever seen the three of you in one place. Usually it's one of you at a time, right?"

Mandy nodded. "Yes, this is a rare night off for us. Matt, I'm not sure if you've been introduced to my sisters. These are Jill and Emma."

He shook both of their hands. "Nice to officially meet you." He glanced at the three of them. "Is it a special occasion? Someone's birthday maybe?" He seemed to pick up on the sense of celebration.

Jill grinned. "Yes, we're celebrating that Mandy's divorce is final today."

Matt's eyes grew wide, and he seemed to choose his words carefully. "That is a milestone. Congratulations." He waved the bartender over. "Their next round is on me."

"You got it." The bartender went off to make their drinks.

"Thank you. You didn't have to do that," Mandy said.

"It's my pleasure. I won't keep you ladies though. Continue your celebration. I see my brother just came in, so I'm off to meet him. Have a great night."

As soon as he was out of earshot, Jill leaned in and spoke softly. "He's clearly interested in you, Mandy. Just an FYI... keep it in mind."

Mandy laughed. "Okay, I'll keep it in mind." A few minutes later, she brought up another topic that they needed to discuss. She thought they were all on the same page but wanted to make sure. "Our year is up soon. Do you know what you want to do about Mimi's Place? Do you want to keep it or sell it? Emma, do you know what Paul wants to do?"

Emma nodded. "We discussed it when we decided to move in together. We both want to keep Mimi's Place. If you want to sell, we'll find a way to buy you out, and I'll move into his place. If you both want to keep it too, then we'll probably get a bigger place together."

"I don't want to sell," Mandy said. "Mimi's Place has saved my sanity this past year. I've wanted something else to focus on for so long, and I really love it there. I want to try to expand our wedding business."

"I love Mimi's Place too, and I'd like to keep it but stay involved as more of a silent partner, like Grams was. My place is in Manhattan with Billy, though I really have loved being here this past year. And we both want to try to make sure we get back here more often, maybe for a few weeks every summer as well as occasional weekends."

Mandy smiled. "I think we could work that out. I think we need to toast to Grams. She knew what she was doing when she left us Mimi's Place—especially with that year-long condition. She always loved Paul, and I know she'd be thrilled that he and Emma are together again. And we all needed to spend more time together. It went by so fast."

"It really did. Her diary was an inspiration," Emma added. Mandy had given the diary back to Emma and Jill, and they'd both read it.

"And Matt is in the same business that Grampy was," Jill said. "Maybe it's a sign."

Mandy laughed. "Stop matchmaking. Let's raise our glasses to Grams."

"To Grams and to Mimi's Place," Emma said.

"Cheers!" Jill clinked her glass against the others.

"And to helping our dreams come true," Mandy added.

ACKNOWLEDGMENTS

A very special thanks to my early readers, Cindy Tahse, Jane Barbagallo, Taylor Hall, and Amy Petrowich. I appreciate you all so much! And thank you to Dominique Raccah, Deb Werksman, and Jessica Thelander for believing in this book and for helping it to reach more readers. Thank you all for your insight and suggestions on how to make the story better.

ABOUT THE AUTHOR

Pamela Kelley is a *USA Today* and *Wall Street Journal* bestselling author of women's fiction, family sagas, and suspense. Readers often describe her books as feel-good reads with people you'd want as friends.

She lives in a historic seaside town near Cape Cod and just south of Boston. She has always been an avid reader of women's fiction, romance, mysteries, thrillers, and cookbooks. There's also a good chance you might get hungry when you read her books as she is a foodie and occasionally shares a recipe or two.